PENGUIN BOOKS

HOLY PICTURES

Clare Boylan has been in journalism since leaving school, working for radio and television as well as for newspapers and magazines. *Holy Pictures* is her first novel although she is well established as a short-story writer. Her stories have appeared in magazines in England, America, Denmark, Australia, Sweden, South Africa and Norway, and in anthologies such as *Winters Tales*. A collection of these stories entitled *A Nail on the Head* was published in 1983. Clare Boylan lives in Wicklow with her journalist husband and three cats.

CLARE BOYLAN

HOLY PICTURES

PENGUIN BOOKS

Penguin Books Ltd, Harmondsworth, Middlesex, England
Penguin Books, 40 West 23rd Street, New York, New York 10010, U.S.A.
Penguin Books Australia Ltd, Ringwood, Victoria, Australia
Penguin Books Canada Ltd, 2801 John Street, Markham, Ontario, Canada L3R 1B4
Penguin Books (N.Z.) Ltd, 182–190 Wairau Road, Auckland 10, New Zealand

First published in the United States of America by Summit Books 1983
First published in Great Britain by Hamish Hamilton 1983
Published in Penguin Books 1984
Reprinted 1984

Printed and bound in Great Britain by
Cox & Wyman Ltd, Reading

Set in Linotron Aldus by
Rowland Phototypesetting Ltd,
Bury St Edmunds, Suffolk

FOR MY HUSBAND

CHAPTER I

The children were walking. Doll, as usual, was pushing a pram. Nan carried a paper bag from which came the sound of bells. Mary was struggling with a hen.

They set out on a dark afternoon four days before Christmas. They had to go a long way. It was five miles to the mountains which were heaped around the city like old velvet cushions, softening the roofline of ordinary red-brick houses in Terenure and Rathfarnham, and could even be seen from the hilly parts of the city centre. At the feet of the mountains burrowed dark corridors of trees and linked shadows which twisted upward into forests.

'Wait for me!' Mary called. Her words were white pillows in the air and she stopped to look at them. She kept getting left behind. She had to run to catch up. Her boots made her clatter like a horse. The path had the sheen of the ears of black cats and this was called black ice. She bent down and picked at this skin of the pavement to see if it was really black. It was too thin to be lifted. Ahead of her, the big girls glided like nuns.

'Come on along, me old segocia,' Doll sang out teasingly. She offered a hand to the younger child but Mary could not take it. Her arms were busy with her bundle. Nan tucked a hand into Mary's armpit and the three of them hurried across the road, pushing the fourth child, whose red face bulged serenely out of a mass of tatty frills.

'Where are we going?' Mary said.

'A picnic.'

'A *picnic*? Why? It's going to snow.'

It was very cold. Their coats were thin. A church bell rang out the hour of three and Nan hurried the smaller child along, scarcely able to remember why they had left their homes on a black afternoon in December to separate themselves from the friendly villages and venture up hilly tracks where there were only settlers and tinkers and madmen.

The sky hung in loose grey folds. It made the red-brick terraces as bright as fairisle patterns on a cardigan. The streets all looked the same: Hallinan's Mansions, Cardinal Square, Victory Terrace. Here was the main road with a first glimpse of the shops and the start of the village: Kelly's, the tongs wave shop, where the smell of ladies' hair burning drifted out to mingle with the fleshy scent of sponge cakes from the cake shop next door. This was called The Cake Box and, in its window, meringues and cream horns were displayed on pedestal stands with doyleys made of silver paper. Next came Wyzniaks, the hardware shop. The owner, who spoke no English, was known as Mr Fishneck and customers had to demonstrate what they wanted by mime while he played a guessing game and dashed back and forth between the tin baths and buckets, pulling open drawers and sacks, cowering from a continuous rain of blows which came out of the handles of mops that hung from the ceiling like the bodies of criminals.

When they got to the village Mary forgot about the cold. 'Oh!' she cried. The shops were beautiful. Each window had a frame of coloured paper chains and pieces of cotton wool stuck on like snow.

The ordinary things, the tins of Clipper Peas and packets of Gold Flake, the boxes of Liverpool Virus and stacked bottles of Cockles, had been pushed out of sight. There were chocolates and tins of biscuits, bottles of coloured scents. There was the feeling which always came with Christmas, that the adult world had come to its senses and done away with all that was dull. 'Oh, Nan,' Mary sighed suddenly. Nan knew what she was thinking. They no longer had a right to Christmas. They were not the same as other families. She squeezed her bundle for comfort but it convulsed with anger and made a noise. Her shoulders shivered. She began to cry. She made no sound but a tear dribbled down the side of her face. 'If you cry,' Nan said, 'the tear will freeze on your face like the diamond in Mrs Mumtaz's nose.' She managed to draw back the tears that were in her eyes but there was still one, wobbling diamond-bright, on the end of her nose. Doll rooted in the end of the pram and came out with an old piece of pink blanket that was used for wiping smears from the baby's face.

'Don't cry,' she said. 'We'll have a look in the Argus Palace.'

The Argus Palace was not like any other sweet shop. The wood was painted a villainous shade of beetroot-red which had no gloss and toppled off in curls to show streaks of rotting wood underneath. From dusty boards on the inside the sweets rose in chaotic mounds, clamouring at the glass in their angry shades; magenta gobstoppers, purple nancy balls, bull's-eyes, marshmallow pillows, liquorice straps, collapsing chocolate creams. Molten jellies sucked on the windows like thirsty fishes. Every so often, viewed from outside, a human hand could be seen clawing its way through the pile of injured confection to retrieve a fistful of a particular species. They were sold, not in proper paper bags, but in cones rolled from sheets of newspaper. It was known as the secondhand sweet shop. Every child was forbidden to give it custom. Every child believed that it offered better value than the Tartan Sweet Shop, with its neatly segregated sweets in hygienic glass jars.

They found themselves powerless to pass by the Argus Palace with its swirling breath of dust and chocolates, its faint grip of nausea and its damaged confectionery which knew it was there to be eaten.

The children admired a pile of marshmallow pillows, pink and white, sagging beneath the weight of an enormous slab of everlasting toffee which acted as a plinth for a giant-size chocolate Santa. He was chocolate-brown all over. He was like a great fat laughing nigger.

They watched this for a time in silence and then, by silent agreement, moved on past the cinema and the church, beyond the park with its tall wintry trees shuddering over their hoard of slimy leaves. They passed the old folks' home with its morgue where Nan and Dandy used to go and look at the faces of the dead and guess which ones had gone to heaven.

The last of the shops was Deegan's Drapery. It observed the season by revealing a pink flowered nightgown in the window. On top of this was arranged a card which bore in red the legend, *For Her!* Then came the houses; mean cottages crammed with poor Catholics, big thin city houses yawning colourless gardens. All the gardens in the suburbs were neglected. Now and then an odd-job man was given a shilling to mow the lawn and pull out a snarl of weeds, but there were no window boxes, no velvety borders, no shining shrubs of holly. Inside, it was different. Because the afternoon was dark some of the rooms were lit and the glow of lamp or firelight showed Christmas trees shivering with tinsel. In dark and airless drawing rooms, where children were never allowed and even ornaments were imprisoned behind glass, nature had taken over. Green trees bloomed with fairies, ribbons, candles.

To make the journey go faster, the children counted Christmas trees. 'Twelve, thirteen, fourteen . . .'

'Nan,' Mary said, 'I'm hungry.'

'Don't look at me,' Nan teased. 'You've got the dinner. You've got enough to feed a horse.'

'A horse?' Mary's voice went thin. She clutched her bundle so tightly that it emitted an offended cackle.

'Hold on,' Doll said more kindly. 'There's mountains of food in the bag – lovely food – cold ox heart and bread pudding and ginger snaps. We can't have it yet, though. It's for the picnic.'

'What's in the other bag?' Mary demanded of Nan.

'A surprise,' Nan said.

They did not stop when they came to the next village. They had to reach their destination before dark. The baby would be hungry for the contents of the glass feeder which was warming his woolly feet. They urged their legs up the steep hill that spanned the river.

Because it was Saturday a row of boys' buttocks jutted up from the bridge, their spattered legs flailing black boots. Years ago a young woman had killed her landlady with a hammer in one of the small houses on the river and dragged her body to the water. The bulging corpse, sailing under the bridge, was witnessed by a solitary boy. More recently, and not to be spoken of, the river fled away with another human discard. Two boys were there to see. Since then the bridge was jammed with boys afraid to miss a gruesome thing, should it happen.

After that the houses began to thin out. The children walked between fields luminous with frost. A frozen mist had descended and the air swirled like boiling water. Spectral sheep and cows offered up laments. The hill cottages lay like lumps of fallen coke.

A man stood outside one of these cottages, hacking a patch of icy soil with a fork. He wore a thin jacket with a vest underneath and greenish baggy trousers. He had a tweed cap. When the children came into view he stopped work and raised his cap to scratch his head. They were nice children; the thin one pushing the pram had a face as round and pale as a bar of soap and the smaller one with the sleepy eyes and the yellow hair was a pretty article.

They disappeared into a patch of mist and then came out again, silvery in a spot of moonlight, and the man with the fork frowned because the two that came out first were now women. You could tell by their softness. They passed so close that their breath clouded his face and he thought he could smell the scent of women. After they had passed, his feet remained where they were, one planted in the soil, and the other resting on the fork, but the upper part of his body twisted round to follow them. They stamped on, their reddened noses pointed toward the forest and he could see then, to his disappointment, that they were only children after all. As the girls grew more distant he was relieved of his thought. They ceased to be women or children. They were only sticks, blackened on the horizon.

CHAPTER 2

In spite of her chest Nan had been picked to play the fairy in the school concert the summer she was fourteen. She sang, 'We are the spirits of the glen, fairy ladies, fairy men.' She frowned into a glaring blue sky.

Mary trailed behind carrying her schoolbag. It was the biggest honour, being chosen for the fairy. No one knew why it had fallen on Nan, except that it had been promised her by Mother Ignatius years ago when Nan was going to be a saint. She had not been particularly well-behaved in the past year. She had fallen into a connivance with Dandy Tallon and she had developed a chest. The fairy was never allowed to have a bust. She wore a party dress and did a dance. Parents were invited.

'You'll need a new party frock,' Mary fretted. It worried her, the way Nan was going.

'A party frock and long white stockings!' she attempted to impress the vital order on mother when she got home. Mother was only partially listening.

'There is a creature with green teeth and a face like an oatcake,' she complained, 'sitting in the dining-room. She has been there all day long. She insists on waiting for your father.'

Father was a charitable man. It was a nuisance for everyone. He had a weakness for poor buggers down on their luck. The house was frequently filled with tramps and alcoholics and other unappetizing types. Nellie refused to have anything to do with them. She would not lower herself to serve those beneath her station. She was in the back garden beating a rug which had been thrown over the clothes-line. Father was at the factory. It was left to mother, and mother never really knew how to respond to anyone except the neighbours.

'Take her up a cup of tea, Nan,' mother said. 'Not a pot – a cup.' She put a hand into the deep flowery pocket of her dress and pulled out her cigarettes and a box of matches. She frowned. It was the effort of being harsh, which did not come to her easily. She sat at the kitchen table in a chair that was usually Nellie's.

Nan brought the cup of tea into the dining-room which was reserved for grown-ups and visitors. A woman sat by the window doing her knitting. She had swarthy skin with little holes and when she grinned her big teeth were the slimy yellow of the insides of banana skins. 'Ah, the little girl,' she said. 'You're the spit of your da. Hospitable too.'

'Father's out,' Nan said. 'We don't know when he'll be back.'

'I don't mind waiting,' the woman said. 'He'd be hurt if I didn't wait. I'll wait all night, if necessary.' To indicate her preparedness, she pointed to a large buckled bag which was fat as though equipped with a week's clothing.

Nan put the cup on the table and ran back to her mother. 'She means to stay. She's revolting. I don't want her here,' she said.

'When you're my age,' her mother said. 'You'll put up with a lot of things you don't like. Now go and see if you can get Nellie in to make us some tea. And see what's wrong with the cat.'

The cat crouched on the window sill making a gagging noise, its head sunk into its bony shoulders. Mary watched from the inside of the window, her nose propped on the ledge.

'There's a magpie. Bertie's afraid,' she said.

'Nellie! Mother wants you,' Nan called from the doorway. Nellie swiped the magpie irritably with her carpet beater on the way in and the bird hop-scotched over the cracks in the baked mud of the lawn. She came and stood in the kitchen, scowling at everyone.

'What are you seeking?' mother said. 'A boy to beat? Mr Cantwell will be wanting his tea.'

'He wants his tea in a mug, collecting human refuse and sending it home for me to wait on,' Nellie said.

'Mr Cantwell has paid for this house. It is his right to use it as he pleases,' mother said uncertainly. Nellie put her hands on her hips. 'Rubbige!' Mother looked lost. 'Do not give impudence when talking to your betters,' she pleaded. Nellie, normally agreeable and placid, could be most difficult to deal with when it came to social status. 'Me betters is them that knows their equals.' She flounced into the scullery where she lit the gas under a big black frying pan and began tearing at a brown paper bag. A pile of kippers slithered into the pan and the smell ruined the summer air. 'Nan Cantwell – do a few cuts of brown bread and throw some cups and saucers on the table for me betters,' she called out. She remained to orchestrate her hellish panful.

Nan brought a tray to the dining-room. She stood and stared at the woman who looked like a horse and wore a blouse made of lace and muslin cut low at the front. The visitor put her head to one side and smiled coyly. She extended a chicken-claw hand to Nan. 'We weren't introduced,' she said. 'Etta Gorman.' Nan went forward to take the hand. 'I'm Nan,' she said. She was engulfed in a strong, powdery smell of lilacs, less acceptable than the smell of kippers. She retreated and began setting the table. The woman avidly counted the place-settings with her eyes. 'Do you children eat with your parents?' she probed. 'No, we eat with Nellie in the kitchen,' Nan said. 'Ah,' the woman said. 'Ah.' She was expressing a double relief. Counting the cups, she saw that there was a place set for her. She had also learned that she would have father to herself, undisturbed by children. She didn't count mother.

Nellie was in a bad mood. Father arrived late. He kept them all waiting for their tea. When Nellie complained that there was a person waiting in the dining-room all day who would not state her business but expected to be waited upon hammer and tongs, he did not bother to slap her buttocks and tell her she was a jealous girl. He seemed paralysed.

He gazed at her helplessly. 'What?' he said. 'What?' It made Nellie go pink with offence.

'A woman with green teeth,' mother said quietly.

'Etta Gorman,' Nan said.

At this father's face lit up with a genial smile. 'Ah, Etta. Poor Etta,' he said. 'Poor bugger's down on her luck.' He shrugged off his overcoat and flung it at Nellie. He bounded out to greet his hideous guest. Mother, who had stood up when father came into the kitchen, sank back into her chair. He had not said hello to her. She spread her skirt over her knees and frowned down at her hands. 'Nellie,' she said. 'You may bring up the tea now, such as it is.'

'Ma'am,' Nellie swore. She went into the scullery where she banged the oven door several times and then brought out the kippers which had dried into a tormented curve like the prisoners of Indian braves staked out under the boiling sun.

In the summer the kitchen table was placed in front of the window and in winter it was pulled to the other side of the room so it would be close to the fire. When Nellie came back from the dining-room she began dragging at it bad-humouredly. Although it was summer she said she was that aggravated she needed toast. Mary began tearing up the day's newspaper and folding the strips into twists. She squatted over the grate and piled in the papers. Over this she arranged a lattice of small sticks which were kept with the coal in a box made of wood and brass.

Nan and Nellie moved the table. They brought out bread and jam and a long fork for toasting. Nellie took the seat nearest the grate and thrust her feet toward the flaky fire. She took a thick slice of bread and impaled it on the fork. She lit a cigarette and then leaned toward the fire, expertly managing her cup and her cigarette and the fork of toast. One side of her face went red from the fire and it took on the squashed appearance of a boxer who has received a blow. She looked more ferocious than ever but the children relaxed and spooned jam into their mouths because they knew she was appeased. 'Well,' she said, raising a boiled eye and shaking the toast to disperse the smoke. 'We might as well get used to her. She's here to stay. He's after telling me to put a hot jar in the bed in the Indian room.'

The Indian room was the spare room, filled with locked trunks and mementoes of father's years in the army when he served in India in the cavalry.

'She's horrible,' Nan said. 'She smiles all the time and her teeth are covered in green slime.'

'I'll have my nightmares,' Mary threatened.

Nellie handed the blackened toast to Nan. 'Don't youse be foolish,' she warned. 'She's not the first and she's not the worst.'

Nan put a lump of melting butter on the toast and spread it with a rasping noise. They were silent, thinking of the weeks to come with mother and Nellie in a bad humour and the awful Etta Gorman grinning at them over her knitting.

Nellie said the Indian room had become a depository for tramps and termagants. Some of them rested there for months on end, only coming down to the dining-room at meal-times. Mother was easy-going but she hated having to entertain the neighbours in the company of these reeking misfortunates. Father had endless patience with them. He gave them his whiskey, used them in his health experiments and found them employment. None of the family could understand why he was so fond of them. At home he sought a very high standard of organization and hygiene.

Lately he was becoming more and more odd. He stayed out till all hours and did not come home to his meals. He developed a dislike of public places. He began to talk in his sleep.

The children found the worst tramps diverting. They liked the things that came out of ragged pockets: sweets, small coins, twists of tobacco. The men always made a fuss of them. Unfortunate women were never any fun. They were rarely even poor. Nan thought that Nellie was wrong. This one was the worst.

'She had a lace blouse on open down to there.' Nan poked the centre of her rib cage. 'Her chest was half bare. You could see them.'

'Her diddies,' Mary filled in for Nellie's benefit. Nellie's small blue eyes focussed on Nan with interest.

'Why would a woman down on her luck be showing off her chest like that?' Nan mused.

Nellie pulled the fork from the fire and inspected a slice of bread, unevenly scarred. She threw it in Mary's direction, but she was watching Nan.

'Sex,' she said.

'Sex,' Mary said, liking the word.

Nan made a face. She did not know enough about sex to contribute an argument but she could not believe that it had anything to do with the old and decaying Etta Gorman.

'Well, you needn't make a grimace, Nan Cantwell,' Nellie said. 'I've had me eye on all the holy Josies that do hang about this house and let me tell you there's nothing the matter with them that wouldn't be cured by a rub of the relic. They may be a wet-lookin' lot but the half of them has their drawers on fire for your father.'

Mary tittered.

'He's an attractive oul' divil in his way,' Nellie ruminated.

The absurd idea brought fresh squeaks from the children.

Nellie looked severe. 'Sex,' she said, 'is a very peculiar artist. It is the fanged serpent.'

'A *green* fanged serpent,' Mary shrieked. The children were now in an uncontrollable state of hilarity.

'Woe be to the man or woman about whom sex drapes its treacherous coils. It is not the purgative of the young and beautiful. It falls like a monkey on the backs of the damned. It drops out of hell like a bomb from a Seplin.' She threw an arch glance at the convulsed faces. 'I speak,' she said, 'as one that knows.'

They buried their laughing mouths in cupped hands. Avid eyes crept up on the maid as they searched her big plain face for a link with her past.

'I was a shy young thing.' It was how she always began. She pushed out her lower lip into a rueful rubbery ball. 'I would fly like a startled deer from the embraces of men. Men took to me like bees to the bonnet.'

They were entranced. They loved to hear stories of Nellie's perilous past, gazing into her face which was like a cake of uncooked soda bread. She had a wide, drooping mouth, roughly coloured in with purple lipstick, and little badly matched blue eyes. Now and then, when she spoke, she pulled her fingers back through her hair and the thick, oily black curls sprang apart in alarm. There was a little 'fzz' noise where the cigarette touched her perm and an interesting smell. When she talked to the children, Nellie made no concession to their age. She liked their company as they liked hers because they did not involve the troublesome issue of station. They were neither above her station nor below it and at the same time they were not her equals.

There was speculation over whether her reports of her younger days were exact. She was not a beauty. She had, as evidence, three children, and, as Mrs Guilfoyle had pointed out to their mother, there was no mench of a husband.

'Bat Carney,' she recalled. 'A big hairy beast. Hands like cuts of meat. I was only fourteen, serving me time with Mrs Nugent in Rathfarnham. Me heart'd go through me like a dose of salts when I'd hear the knock on the door and Mrs N. calling down from her bed: "Onswer the door to the fish min, Nillie"' – in mincing tones Nellie approximated the accent of the woman who was above her station. 'I'd be near to fainting when I'd see them hands latched around a haddock. No sooner would the fish be in the larder than he'd have me in his clutches. Many's the time the big ox got me trapped in the laundry room and flung himself on my untried body. I would struggle as his mouth came down on mine, but it was not an even match.

'"Nellie," he'd say to me, "Darling Nellie"' – she paused and frowned at the children. She pursed her lips and manoeuvred them around her teeth. 'Me and me big mouth,' she said at last. 'This is no talk for the likes of youse.'

The children squirmed delightedly.

'"Nellie," he'd say, "put your hand in me pocket. I've got something for you. I've a lovely stick of rock in me pocket."' Nellie flung back her head and squealed with laughter. She beat her big thighs with the palms of her hands; and the children shrieked with laughter too, although they were disappointed that Bat Carney had said such an ordinary thing.

'Oh Sacred, I'm killed,' Nellie sighed happily. She wiped tears of mirth from her eyes and stood up. 'I could use another cuppa.' She picked up the teapot and headed for the kitchen. Mary watched her behind wobbling in the blue, spotted dress, as if it too was shaking with glee at the incomprehensible joke.

There was a rattle of water in the tin kettle and then a sigh. Nellie's moods altered quickly. 'I wish,' she cried out with vehemence, 'I wish in vain, I wish I was, a maid again.' She was singing. She was their maid. She always had been. Mary fervently hoped she always would be.

Nellie said she would go when the sun went down. She liked to give herself orders. There was a small square of sun on the wall, like a badly cut frame, and the contents of this were as follows: an impression of the leaves of a thin shrub frenziedly dancing about in the garden, the outline of a jam jar carelessly placed upon the table, and, over these, the shadow of a wandering tail of smoke. They watched it narrowing and it was like a clock. When it closed Nellie would leap up in anger and demand to know where the time had gone on her and then in a mixture of anxiety and reluctance she would hurry away to her children.

'Culchies were the worst. Artie Cullen. Got me up to his lodgings after the pictures and threw me on the bed. Before I had time to say kiss-me-ass for a hap'orth he was tearing at me wellington boots.'

'Why?' Nan demanded.

Nellie was off again, hooting with joy. 'He said if his landlady found me muddy boots on the bed he'd be out on his ear.'

The kitchen door was flung open and the father burst in, his face as red as the torn remnants of the kippers he held aloft on a plate. 'What is the meaning of this?' he quizzed through clenched teeth.

He strode stiffly across the room and thrust the plate under Nellie's nose, which twitched. Her peaceful gaze fell on the mess of bones and shredded flesh. 'They're kippers, sir,' she said. 'As to their meaning, I am sure I do not know.'

'Insolent swine! Is that what I pay you for? To make a monkey of me in front of my guests?'

'I was not informed, sir, that company was expected.'

'Ha!' He grinned with triumph. 'So it's good enough for me, coming home after ten hours of hell at the factory?'

'There's nourishment in kippers,' Nellie argued.

'Filthy,' said father. 'I couldn't eat them. No one could.' It was true that the fishes bore the marks of failed attempts at dining.

'Gone off, have they?' Nellie was interested now. 'Now that's queer. Kippers is famed for longevity.'

'I wouldn't give them to the cat,' said father with contempt.

'The cat wouldn't turn up his nose,' Nellie said. 'Here, Bertie!'

The cat made a wary appearance in the door of the scullery. 'Come on, puss,' father said through gritted teeth. The animal's muzzle jerked at the air. He could smell the fish. Father charged. 'Come on, you cur! Enjoy yourself. I break my backside so you can have kippers for tea.' He dived suddenly, holding the plate at an angle as if it was meant to slice off the animal's head. The cat let out a yelp of terror and darted under Mary's chair.

There was a moment when they were all frozen into a tableau, father crouched with his reeking plateful, the children, stiff with anxiety, the cat, under the chair with its ears down, attempting to make itself invisible, and Nellie, studying with interest the extraordinary look of disbelief that shrank the points of father's eyes – and then father's voice, shrill with offence: 'The cat's a coward!'

The animal slid off on its belly and lurked behind the coal scuttle. This damning evidence so attracted father that he forgot about the kippers. He set down the plate and advanced on the cat, entreating it in a voice gentle with menace: 'Come on, boy! Good fellow!' From behind the coal scuttle there came a hopeful growl. 'Good Bertie!' Father's shadow swam up the wall behind the coal box. The cat showed a face flattened with fear and he spat.

'Leave him, you!' He turned, surprised, to see Nan standing at the table, her face defiant, her hands bunched into fists.

'Pardon?'

'Leave him alone, you bully. Bertie's nervous. You're frightening him.'

'He's afraid of birds,' Mary witnessed. 'And grass!'

He looked about him in a puzzled fashion, dislocated by the treachery that surrounded him.

'Afraid of birds?' he repeated faintly.

He made a sudden bound across the room toward Nan. She ducked, thinking he was going to strike her. Instead, he reached into his pocket and pulled out a coin. He threw it at her and she trapped it by clapping her hands. It was a little threepenny piece, embossed with thistle. Nan closed a cautious fist around the coin and studied her father's face. He was looking pleased. 'That'll sort him out, the skulking swine,' he said. 'You're to go to the butcher's shop on Monday and buy me a cow's pluck.'

'Why?'

'Because I have said it.'

She frowned. Father laughed. He reached out a hand to ruffle her hair but she ducked again. She kept up her brazen expression. 'You're a right bugger,' he said with admiration.

When he was gone, Mary pulled the shivering cat from behind the coal container and fashioned him into a shape that she could hold. She kept a wistful eye on the sliver of sunlight, like an arrow slot in a tower, that rationed Nellie's time.

Nellie had to smoke a Woodbine. The children waited patiently until she looked up and said in resigned fashion: 'Do you know what I'm going to tell you. I worked for a woman once and she had a partiality for a cheese called Gorgonzola. Gorgonzola. Gentry, she was. Well, this cheese does be left lying until it's gone green merulious mouldy, riddled with worms. The gentry do pick the worms out on their forks and they do eat them.'

The patch of sun had narrowed into a quivering golden thread on the wall when Nellie's passionate concern with unusual information exerted itself and the children sat immobile, haunted and enchanted, while she told them about Hammer, never seen by day, who roamed the streets at night, danced to the moon and swallied live spiders; about Shyster, who sold old clothes and hens from a creaking pram and who was rumoured to abduct young children and sell them into slavery.

These stories she repeated every night, half-truths about the harmless eccentrics of the city, but tonight she added a new tale and the children did not like it, for the great pleasure of Nellie's stories was that they involved no threat to themselves. 'There is a darkie watching this house. I'll say no more,' she said.

'A black man?' Mary said, astonished. There were no black men in the city, only the niggers in the shows in the Gaiety and in *Uncle Tom's Cabin*.

'It's a woman,' Nellie said, astounding the children beyond all imagining. 'Indian, I'd say.'

The sun was gone. Nellie stood up heavily, swearing at the time. Although it was meant to be part of her duty she did not bother with the dishes. They were left to the children, who did not mind. She plodded into the scullery and came out wearing a man's raincoat and a sou'wester. It was always bad weather in the outside world as far as she was concerned. She paid no further attention to the children. She never said goodbye. Goodbyes were an extravagance if you saw a person every day.

'Jersiful Maysus!' She began to sail across the red-tiled floor in an amazing fashion, yelping in angry fright. She had stood on the plate of kippers. She regained her balance, wrestling with the back of a kitchen chair, and stamped her feet angrily to clean the soles. 'Oul' bastard,' she grumbled. 'He done it on spite.' She pulled down her hat and slammed out the door. The tail of a kipper flapped gaily from the sole of one galosh.

CHAPTER 3

Etta Gorman remained for the weekend. She accompanied them to Mass on Sunday and sucked on her teeth for sustenance while the priest read out a Temporal letter. It concerned women in sport. The congregation wore the stupefied and respectful look of civilians witnessing a king. Father's face went pink. His eyes were a furious blue. It was the signal for a rampage.

They walked home behind him cautiously, mother with Miss Gorman, Nan beside Mary, but he never said a word, not until he had installed them in the living-room and used his wrought energies to crank up the gramophone. 'Terrible times,' he sighed. 'Rousing stuff.' He put on his record. The women sat about like figures from the wax museum. They still had their hats on and hands like mice in tight grey fabric gloves.

'Rousing stuff!' he challenged.

It was an impression of the Ave Maria sung by a woman. He always put it on when there were people. He played it at great volume so that the woolly pink clouds of praise poured from her mouth in a terrified scream as if provoked at knife point. Throughout the recital he would watch them shrewdly for signs of appreciation until mother cried out for her head and the children darted from the room squeaking into their hands. Today no one laughed. Mother and the children were entranced. Etta Gorman hid her teeth under lips grimly sealed.

Halfway through the ordeal there was a surprising turn of events. He lowered the volume. It disturbed them all. They looked up in surprise. The anguished victim of the gramophone needle was revealed to be a very young soprano with a voice that was frail and pure, like a scarf of chiffon blowing in the wind. They leaned into the sound and risked its emotion. They maintained this alert immobility until the last fluttering note was possessed by the drizzle of the record machine.

The grown-ups had sherry. The children went to the kitchen and put chickens in the oven and roasted up parsnips and potatoes. When the meal was being eaten, father made a speech. Man, he said, was a beast, but a noble beast. Woman was not a beast by nature but a creature of refined passion. When she left her sheltered pasture and pursued the paths of man, she too became a beast, but, being deficient of muscle and courage, she was a flabby beast. For months afterwards the children entertained one another with taunts of 'flabby beast'.

They set off after lunch, neglecting shop windows and the lure of children shouting from lanes. Mary did not complain about the punishment to her feet as they plodded to Ranelagh and then Ballsbridge where the prettiness of Herbert Park was curtailed by a spiky green railing. Both were accustomed to this route, which they followed each year to the Spring Show at the Royal Dublin Society pavilions for free samples of cheese and boot polish.

They knew nothing of sport except that it had to do with men. The absence of boys in the family sheltered them from the world of muddy boots and sticks and clubs and racquets. Girls at school lumbered after one another in the yard playing tag but there was nothing organized. Occasionally photographs in the newspapers showed lady golfers, posed uselessly with their clubs, like the Queen with her little spade when she was planting a tree. Nan had seen the slender arms of lady tennis players dragged into the air by their racquets when she passed the outside of the park. On those occasions she thought that the thin wrists and hands were too delicate for the solid wood frame and handle, that the raised hands had a supplicant look, like Dives, the rich man when he went to hell and would fain have licked the sores of beggars. It excited her to think that these ladies were sinners. She had never lingered to watch a tennis match before. She hadn't the curiosity. It was waiting to be aroused by the terrible letter.

The letter of the bishops had been read out by Father Mirrelson. 'It is the belief of Cardinal la Fontaine that women taking up tennis, swimming, golfing and other masculine sports has led to them wearing less and less clothes and the bishops of the whole diocese have passed the following resolution: "Invading paganism is reaching appalling excess in regard to Christian modesty. We see women and girls becoming addict to sports which are utterly incompatible with the dignity and honour of women. This excessive fondness for sports exposes women to moral dangers, to habits of conduct wholly at variance with the mission of women in family and society.'''

Sitting with their parents in church, dressed up and charged with zeal, both children had thought how fortunate they were to be Catholics, to have an opportunity to shun the paganism of women's sports, unlike Minnie Willard and Doll Cotter, who were Protestants and doomed to hell. It occurred to them also that there was no mention of a penalty attached to the *viewing* of these activities.

They went into the park. People lay on the grass with hats over their noses. The children ran through beds of portly tulips. They came to the courts, which were modestly guarded by ranks of grown-ups in Sunday clothes. A hidden activity emitted muted poppings and the watchers clapped their hands now and then with a polite noise like dry leaves tumbled by the wind. The children crept between legs and squeezed themselves to the front.

What luck! There were ladies on the court. They wore white dresses that flapped about their legs. Their faces were pink as they chased after a grey furred ball. One hit the ball with her racquet. The other copied her. They were just beginning. When the ball sailed through the air they had to leap from the ground to send it back. Once it caught in a green net which divided the ladies and one had to stoop to fish it out, but after that trouble she merely returned it to her partner.

The children crouched tensely on the edge of the grass. They were afraid of missing something – dreaded a moment when the other would turn with glittering eyes to say: 'Did you see *that*!'

There was, it seemed, as the afternoon simmered on, nothing to see. Now and again came a gasp from the onlookers. It might have been the heat. It was very hot. The sun got in their eyes and made a fuzzy halo round the dancing hair of the players. Into the air they rose, their dresses too white for definition, white blots against a sizzling sky. They no longer leaped and ran. They glided. They *flew*. White birds dipping and swooping, weightless as the sparrows of the air, stately as the lilies of the field.

The children stayed all afternoon. The sun beat on their arms and noses and drew up weals of red but in their hearts there grew a small nut of coldness with the knowledge that these sprites on the court were not miserable sinners at all. It was a mistake.

They were invulnerable even to the venial sins which thickened the air like germs and were breathed in through the nose to nibble at the white icing of the soul.

The sun struck at their senses.

The players seemed to move in slow motion. Their task was a devout suspension of the ball. So graceful was their play that they appeared to be moving in time to music. The music was in Mary's head where it had stayed since the morning. 'Ave Maria,' sang the lady with a voice like a scarf in the wind. The players soared. 'Why, they're angels,' Mary thought sleepily as they floated through the air, their white hems billowing over ankles as frail and velvety pink as the stalks of new mushrooms.

CHAPTER 4

At school the girls wore a uniform of loose green tunics and green felt hats with a grey ribbon. They formed part of an untidy foliage in the gravel yard at the first charmless clank of the chapel bell. Mary ran off with the despised juniors. Nan belonged with the big girls. Dazed with adolescence they yelled at one another. Voices wheeled giddily while their sensible boots munched the gravel drive.

'Primmy's run away from home. Father caught her with a fella.'

'Lizzie Callaghan's got an apple pie in her schoolbag.'

'I learned a terrible bad word. It's called arse. It means your backside.'

In linked twos and threes they mounted the granite steps and were swallowed into a stew-coloured gloom. A nun, shadowed in the corridor, quelled their sex with a praise.

'Thou O Lord shalt open my lips.'

'And my tongue shall announce Thy praise,' they grumbled in subdued chorus.

'Incline unto my aid, O Lord.'

'O God, make haste to help me.' The children's boots sounded like bags of chestnuts being emptied on to the wooden floor.

Mother Mary Ignatius had a newspaper under one arm and she carried a box of pins. She was used to the ways of girls growing up. She had been dealing with them for fifty years and she thought they were the same as they had always been except that now in 1925 some of them smelt old and worldly. They had taken to wearing Bourjois scent from Woolworth's.

As she delivered the prayer her eye weeded the crocodile for signs of neglect. Now and again she reached out and pulled at an unwashed ear or scoured a pink cheek with her thumb for traces of rouge. She knew a lot but because she was old and tired easily she restricted herself to what was useful. She reminded the girls to wash their necks *and ears*, to wear stockings that were whole and to behave modestly.

She stopped the prayer and sighed. 'You girls, come here,' she beckoned. At the back of the chaste forest of green serge, Mother Ignatius had spotted eight women's thighs. Two plain bouncing girls with legs like tree trunks stepped forward and two pretty, shapely ones. 'Now,' said the nun, 'why did you do a wicked thing like this?'

'I don't know,' the children said; and they did not.

It had been Dandy Tallon's idea. Just outside the school gates she had hitched up her gymslip so that the tops of her stockings showed, with knotted garters, and her thighs, up to where they disappeared into a billow of brown interlock. A man on a bicycle whistled. The stout Tallon twins, Bluebell and Daisy, and Nan who was their friend, were impressed by this success. They followed suit.

'She can't kill us, she can't kill us, she can't kill us,' they chorused in delighted fear as they hurried into school.

'I will tell you,' Mother Ignatius said softly as if she had some important confidence to impart. 'Your legs are nothing to be proud of. Now, see how you like going around for the rest of the day like this!' She fell painfully to her knees and began pinning sheets of newspaper around the abbreviated hems. When she came to Nan she looked up and shook her head. 'What has become of my good girl?' she said sadly.

'I don't know,' Nan said.

The procession divided through wooden doors that were open along the corridor. The nun waited until the four bad ladies had rustled into their classroom. She resumed the prayer. New noises drifted out to mingle with her choir, chants and whispers, the clatter of wooden desk lids, as the school day began.

Nan's class was taught by Sister Immaculata, a tall nun well suited to her name. She was so clean, so transparently pale, that she appeared to have been washed inside as well as out. She liked to tell stories of child martyrs, murdered for their faith by Jews, Communists, pagans or Protestants, in any case disposed of before they began to display signs of coarseness. Her stories dripped with blood. She had a hunger for blood and seemed, herself, to possess none.

The rest of the class was seated when Nan came in with the Tallon sisters, crackling with newsprint.

The nun dismissed the Tallon girls and told them to sit at the back of the class. Their father was a Protestant. She focussed on Nan until her long nose seemed to blanch yet fainter. 'You,' she hissed, 'are the bane of my life.' She paced to avoid the sight of the errant girl. 'Jesus was not murdered by Jews alone,' she said cunningly. '*You* drove the thorns into His precious skull and through the cells of His sacred brain until blood gushed over His brow . . .' She paused, pulling her pale lips together like a flawless darn in a piece of linen. There was not time. Not today. The priest was coming. She dismissed Nan with a contemptuous wave. Nan went to sit at the back of the class with Dandy Tallon. 'Take no notice,' Dandy whispered. 'Think of her sitting on the lav.'

The nun's face had got a very peculiar look. Her head twisted to avoid the starred sea of innocent gazes. Blessed was the fruit of Mary's womb. Mary was the Immaculate Conception, conceived without sin. It had to do with down below. The nuns said they would know in good time.

Time had already eroded the smooth surface of their skins and bolstered the fronts of their gymslips. The thirty-seven children of thirteen years, or fourteen, whose blank morning eyes followed the agitated gaze of the nun at the blackboard, were all undoubtedly structured around ambitious wombs.

'Girls,' Sister Immaculata said. 'We are growing up.' The nuns always gave the big girls a lecture about their bodies the day the priest came, before exposing the holy minister to their gathering ripeness. It was gifty.

'In the next few years certain changes will occur in your bodies. These are not a matter for idle chatter, curiosity or display. They are the por-ten-tous man-if-es-tations of your impending duties as wives and mothers.' Her hand shot out and the little moons of her clipped nails glowed like haloes over her saintly fingers. 'Alice Devlin, what is a portent?'

The child that stood up was hopelessly overgrown. She knew it was her fault. She shrugged to diminish her manifestations and an unhappy tide flooded her face. To apologize for her size, her voice had shrunk away to nothing. 'It's to do with motherhood,' she breathed. Alice's face sank to apoplectic plum while the children struggled to control their delight.

'A por-tent is an o-men. An o-men. Do not wriggle, Alice, you are making a display of yourself. Alice, you are a stupid girl. What are you?'

'A stupid girl,' Alice answered, bright with relief.

'The rest of you who titter so vulgarly are not merely stupid, but also ignorant. Father Feeney will put the laugh on the other side of your faces.'

This caused some of the bolder ones to laugh out loud, provoking each other with dancing eyes, for the priest who came each year to examine them on the contents of the Penny Catechism was a feeble threat. He was a desiccated old man, older than one's father, fifty or more.

The nuns did not like the older girls. They preferred the little ones who were superstitious and easily subdued. In the infant class there was a sticky seat where disobedient children were compelled to sit and told they were stuck fast until given permission to leave; and there was a picture of a green devil in the corner. Isolated in its sneering company for half an hour, the most defiant child could be brought to heel. A wooden stick threatened punishment for impudence and in a tall cupboard the pink and white powdered cubes of Hadji Bey's Turkish Delight were kept as prizes for excellence, causing confusion to the children who never knew if the thing they had done was right or wrong. The small children did not form mutinous gangs. They took no notice of each other. They were absorbed in the anxiety of keeping in step with the hazardous shifts of mood and expectation of anyone older.

It was the big ones that had to be watched. They were given to notions of individuality. They were drawn to the outside world. They were putty in the hands of the devil.

Sister Immaculata thrust her beautiful hands into her sleeves and strode along the aisles that divided the rows of desks. She challenged the girls with her gaze. She endured the thrust of their bodies against shapeless tunics, and other proliferations of womanhood, oily hair and spotted chins.

'You will ask yourselves, "Why am I different than when I was a little girl?"' The children lowered their heads and raised sly, interested eyes. The nun swept a glance of pale contempt over them. 'The answer is: "It is none of your business." In regard to those parts of your bodies which are not actively engaged in saying your prayers and learning your lessons, you need remember only three things – cleanliness, concealment, mortification. Does anyone wish to ask a question?'

Brigid Killian put up a hand.

'Weak minds are the devil's playthings,' said the nun mysteriously.

The child's wavering hand was stuck in the air. The nun looked away irritably. The rest of the class began to snigger.

'If there is anything you wish to know,' the nun said with finality, 'turn to Mary.'

Mary was on a shelf on the wall. The artless little figure of God's mother peered out behind an explosion of blowzy pink roses in a blue glass vase. Our Lady had a dress of white and blue which came to her feet. She wore a belt of darker blue which was called a girdle, and caused Nan to smile, thinking of father's corset factory. Although you could not see behind the flowers, her bare feet were standing on a snake's head. There was a litter of petals on the shelf and the flowers in the vase were yawning and elderly.

The children were encouraged to bring flowers from their gardens for the holy statues. The small ones arrived in procession with straggling fistfuls cultivated in their own patch, which they had watched and bent over. There was a glut of tributes. There was competition. Those unhappy offerers, whose flawed wallflowers the nun flung scornfully in the wastebasket, wept silently at their desks for hours.

The older children no longer cared. They had transferred their worship to Lillian Gish and women in the real world.

The nun, halfway down one of the four aisles and facing the back of the class where she could keep an eye on idlers and laggards, sensed a fresh gust of confusion.

Children simpered, scowled, dug each other in the ribs. Our Lady lost their small attention. The nun whirled irritably. She found herself looking at a young fellow, red-headed and grinning in the open doorway. He wore a priest's habit. She frowned at him in puzzlement. She had been looking forward to the parched masculinity of Father Feeney. This was a boy, impudent-looking. 'Father Feeney's banjaxed his back,' the boy grinned. 'I'm here to deal with the young ladies' – he threw them a mischievous look – 'Father

Percy!' He stretched out a hand and smiled.

The nun clasped her own two hands in doubt and then swept forward bravely and allowed three of her snowy fingers to be pulverized in the young man's grasp. 'Good morning, Father.'

To cover her confusion she turned crossly to the class. 'Where are your manners, girls? Has the cat got your tongue? Say good morning to Father.'

'Morning, Father.'

'Good day to you, ladies,' said the priest. And he winked at them. The children could not believe their luck. They squirmed in startled delight and their mouths hung open so as not to miss a crumb of his performance. Sister Immaculata poked them with glacial glances. The priest's face grew serious. The children, moulded by his influence, became holy. 'God,' he said gently, 'is your father. That is the most important thing. Learn that and use it with every law and every lesson. He is your father. Your father loves you.' The children thought about their fathers, furious, untouchable. Fathers made rules, mistrusted fun, got the best meat. God was their father. It was how they had always pictured him. 'Now,' said Father Percy, 'for the sticky business.' He smiled at them, restoring merriment. 'I'm going to make it hard for you lot.' He rubbed his hands together and then parted them to bring a wandering finger in a circle around the rapt faces. 'You!' he said. A plum-coloured face jerked in fright. Sister Immaculata muttered a savage aspiration.

His finger had landed on Alice Devlin. The child stood up. Her bosom heaved in despair and rose to meet her abject chin. 'Who made the world?' said Father Percy. Alice glanced imploringly at Sister Immaculata and the nun impaled her with a look so threatening that the child lost her voice completely. Her mouth opened and closed like a fish.

'Speak up, child,' the priest said kindly.

Alice squirmed and thrust her head forward.

'. . . od,' she squeaked pitifully.

'Who did you say?' the young man jested. 'Sweeney Todd?'

'God,' the girl wailed.

'Ah,' said the priest. 'And a very nice job He made.' For Alice was pretty; extremely so, when she writhed and blushed.

'Sit down, you foolish child,' Sister Immaculata commanded. She shot an angry look at the priest. He did not notice. He was enjoying himself.

'Now,' he grinned, looking about for another pretty victim. 'Did God make anything else?' He picked out Dandy Tallon. Dandy stood up cautiously. There was a faint rustling noise from the newspapers that parcelled her legs. He looked with enjoyment on the tall girl with green eyes and vivid hair. 'The ten commandments?' she said hopefully.

'Is that all?'

'Yes, Father.'

The nun's tongue clicked in disgust. 'Her father's a Protestant,' she told the priest.

'Ah, yes,' Father Percy said. 'God made those too.' He turned to her and bowed. She looked down into her lap as if a frog had suddenly appeared there. The children stared as a tide of pink lapped its way up around her ears, engulfed her jaws, her nose, her forehead, deepening to crimson, darker and darker until her eyes watered with the pressure. It was as if all the blood of the martyrs had erupted from her bone-white soul.

'God,' he said, 'made the world.'

He called on Nan. 'Where was the first Mass celebrated?' Nan was painfully aware of her shape. She bound her bosom with bandages each morning but it always seemed to show. She kept her head down, hoping he would choose someone less amply built. It was as if he had deliberately picked on all the most immodestly contoured girls in the class.

'What is your name?' he persisted.

She stood up. 'Nan Cantwell, Father.'

'Come here, Nan Cantwell.'

She stayed where she was. It was the worst thing in the world that could have happened.

'Here.'

She eased her way out of the seat. Her paper pinnings rattled. She had to walk all the way to the top of the class under the agonized eye of Sister Immaculata. The priest smiled in amusement. 'What is this? Have you been practising mortification?' She thought she saw the nun nod very faintly. 'Yes, Father.' 'Let's have no more of this nonsense. Take out those pins at once. All of you girls seem ashamed of your bodies. Your bodies are God's work. Are you ashamed of God's work?' 'No, Father.' She bent to remove the pins. Sheets of newspaper swam to the floor. She attempted to lower her gymslip but succeeded in performing a rude gyration. Our Lady looked on mournfully. The priest chuckled. The nun moaned. 'Now,' he prompted, 'where was the first Mass celebrated?'

Her limbs felt huge and sweating under the gaze of the holy man. She could feel the nun's eye burning into her backside that was barely covered by the green frill of her gymslip. Her mind was able to contain nothing but embarrassment. 'In the Ark of the Covenant,' she blurted out.

The nun could stand it no longer. 'Enough of this,' she cried. 'Enough of this.' 'Yes, yes,' Father Percy agreed mildly. 'Enough of that. Does anyone know any Irish jig?' Before she could be stopped, Alice Devlin was on her feet. It was the thing in which she excelled. She lost all her shyness when she was on the stage, a row of medals slapping her splendid chest. Alice heeled and toed up the aisle. The priest applauded loudly. The children clapped. The nun crept to the door and crouched there in an abject manner like an animal that needs to be given exit, and there she waited for it to be all over, while Alice thundered up and down the classroom floor, her bosom bouncing, her cheeks brilliant and her skirts flying over her well-muscled thighs while the priest whistled a lively tune and eyed her with solid temporal enjoyment.

'Never. Never. *Never* in my born days did I dream to witness such a dis-gusting exhibition of grossness, lewdness and unmitigated stu-pidity!'

The priest had been got rid of. The nun stalked the classroom furiously, cracking at stary ears and knuckles with her ruler, squashing their exuberance with her awesome resentment. The duller ones had been made to snivel. The boldest ones were impressed by sarcasm or physical pain.

She glided back to her desk and subsided into the seat. Her colourless eyes swam back and forth, looking for signs of the thing that had to be wiped clean in souls before they could be given back to God. In-dividuality. She had imposed a sufficient level of fright. The knowing girls had been restored to the mute uniformity of childhood.

'You are to sit in silence for the rest of the day and pray for your conversion,' she said. 'Please leave the lids of your desks in a raised position. You are offensive to my sight.'

Only the frailest of creaks accompanied the lifting of the lids. The children reached into their desks for history books and books of English essays which were the least dull of the contents and stayed meekly gazing on a single page.

After being good for an hour, Alice Devlin felt the devil leaking from her body. Slithering, hot; a smell of molten iron. The pain made her feel sick, grinding core-deep, she was a circus lady sawn in half. Her head swam and she gripped the edge of the desk in fear. She made a low noise, like a cow.

The nun looked up from her holy office. The noise came again, a woman's noise, resigned. 'Alice Devlin,' she called out. 'Go at once and ask Mother Ignatius for a rag.' She stayed where she was, bewildered, trembling with pain and nausea. 'Alice Devlin! Do not play the fool. You know what I mean!' Her blue eyes bolted, struggling with the throbbing pain and the need to decipher the mystery of the rag. She turned to Mary.

Nettie Mulvey grew bored and drank the ink from the white vitreous well sunk into a hole in the surface of the desk. Francie Small watched until the last liquid berry of indigo splashed on to the crooked teeth of her companion and then she said thoughtfully: 'You're a goner.'

The sunny mane of Dandy Tallon's hair, badly tamed by a black velvet ribbon tied low at the back of her neck, tickled Nan's cheek. They sat close together. They liked each other's feel, which was safe. They breathed infamies about the men they knew, fathers. Nan told Dandy her pa had brought home Etta Gorman who had upset the house at breakfast by wanting porridge. Nobody ate breakfast except father. There was no porridge. 'There is no wholesome food in this house,' father had said. He had finished his bacon and eggs and was denuding a rind of rasher very thoughtfully, nibbling expertly as if playing the mouth organ. 'A spoonful of oatmeal though,' Etta had argued. 'I did not intend avarice.' And father's eyes had grown wistful with self-pity. 'Do you know' – he leaned across the table –

'that the eggs I am given for my breakfast do not come from the hen. They are purchased in the shops.'

Fathers. Dandy's father was a big beast of a man, Ned Tallon. He beat the girls on their bare backsides and threatened worse violence when Primmy, who was seventeen and had a job in Harold's Cross in the rosary beads factory, tried to go out with a boy. Last night there were ructions. Spying at the drawing-room window father had seen the ghostly shadow of a man's hat suspended in a pool of light from the lamp-post. It dipped protectively over the golden frizz of his eldest daughter's hair. He had bounded out to punch the invisible face beneath the hat and dragged in his daughter to lock her in her room. There, while the rest of the family wept and pleaded, he deliberated on her punishment. He would cut off her hair. He would break her bloody face so that no cur would look at her again. Primmy did not wait to hear out her father's threats. She opened the wardrobe door and took out the suitcase that had been packed for weeks. She unlatched it soundlessly and stuffed nightdress and underwear on the top, and a photograph of their mother. Mother was a pretty little red-headed woman with a damaged heart. She came from the country and loved open spaces and wild flowers.

All her daughters had been given the names of wild flowers – Primrose, Dandelion, Bluebell, Daisy. She hated the way the family was locked into the house. She had given Primmy her savings of ten pounds in case she needed to get away. With this and her suitcase, Primmy clambered out of the bedroom window and down the drainpipe. No one knew where she had gone. Probably on the boat to England. But she had got away.

Nan knew now what had prompted the Tallons to rebel against the nuns that day although she still couldn't tell why she had done the same. Dandy's green eyes burned painfully under her long, golden lashes. Nan burrowed a hand into her friend's grey wool shirt sleeve. 'Maybe her boyfriend was waiting for her,' she said. 'Maybe they'll get married.'

Dandy's face soured with anger. 'Maybe you think that's all she needs, another oul' scourge to scald the heart out of her. You mind your own business.'

Lizzie Callaghan had been praying for her conversion for hours and hours. It had not occurred. The thing that held her mind and swelled out until it was like a great, empty balloon occupying the whole of her was the content of her schoolbag. She had made it the night before and then could not bear to leave it behind her so she took it to school. She was gnawed by desire. She bent cautiously and unfastened the buckles. She lifted out the white enamelled dish and sat gazing at an outsize, seeping apple pie. Her fingers dove irresistibly and pulled out a piece and put it in her mouth. She chewed rapturously.

In the yard outside the break had commenced with a clanging of the bell. Children looked hopefully around the lids of their desks but Sister Immaculata allowed them the briefest glance of disgust and resumed the reading of her Office. They could hear the ragged screams of children playing in the concrete square; a cry for a teacher: 'Miss! Miss! Winnie Higgins was swinging Maisie Taylor by the leg and she dropped her an' I think her leg is broke!'

The girls in the class became more alert. Signals were transmitted. They focussed on the stolid Lizzie Callaghan who had an apple pie. Those who were closest to her pinched her and pulled her hair and made signals to her that she had to share it. She shook them off for a while but then good-naturedly nodded her agreement.

Clods of apple pie were dug out and passed around by hand. Fingers darted out to receive the drooping pastry with its tantalizing grey, acid mash. They stuffed their fists into their mouths to suck the juicy crumbs. What made it gifty was their belief that the nun could not see them. The power of the nuns were awesome but it did not extend to the outside world and the apple pie had been transported in from the world. They giggled silently. They munched. Daisy Tallon allowed herself a soft, satisfied belch. The nun remained anchored to her desk, fluttering helplessly like a black plague mast.

CHAPTER 5

Father suspended the cow's pluck from the clothes-line by means of a metal curtain hook and a pair of elastic trouser braces. It was a trick he had learnt in India. He tested the arrangement to make sure it was secure and the spongy entrails danced and spat blood on the grass. The children jumped out of the way.

This was in the evening. The thing that had bubbled bright pink when Nan unwrapped it from the butcher's paper now glistened blackly, socking the air with its blind thrust. 'Used to hang a piece of meat from a pole.' He prodded the offal with a stick to keep it in motion. 'Drew the tigers. Swine came from miles around. Eight females in one night. You had to get your shot in pronto before they tore each other to pieces.'

It was to give Bertie a lesson in courage. The prize was on his territory. When cats came from miles around to compete for it, he would be compelled to fight them off.

He was goading the lights with a twig. He had to blood the air, he said. It made Nan think of the bowel of Blessed Oliver Plunkett which was cut out of his living body by pagans and burnt before his eyes.

Mary did not like the thing swinging like a big, loose fist. When they ceased to notice her she turned away and watched a lighted window in the house. She could see her mother's back and she bound her heart to the familiarity of its yielding shape. She pictured herself as an orphan and tears filled her eyes. She was moved to think of herself deprived of her mother's lovely black hair, wreathed in a mist of yellow tobacco smoke.

Mother's head jerked uneasily and Mary wondered what had upset her. Another head appeared at the window, blocking her view. Etta Gorman. The women had to keep each other company because they declined to watch the raising of the cow's innards.

Miss Gorman rubbed at the glass with a piece of knitting and Mary had a startling view of her dark, pitted skin and her long teeth clenched in a smile. Greenish teeth, green mouldy like Gorgonzola from which the gentry did pick out the worms and did eat them. A chanting voice deep inside her: 'Green lady, green lady, come down to your tea . . .' A fragment of a ghostly rhyme from her earliest years. She had forgotten it but its hollow footsteps still echoed. She raced along the garden path and pounded on the back door.

The noise started at two in the morning. A low moan rose in spiral to a gnashing wail. NnnyarrrwoorrrGAARH! Mary was first awake, sitting up rigid in the bed, her blankets pulled to her chin, shaking horribly, waiting for the banshee. She wakened Nan who tried to pull back her share of the blanket, then sat up rapidly, absorbing the cacophony. There was an urgent slapping of feet on the lino stairs from the Indian room and Etta Gorman's panic-stricken cry: 'Wake! Wake! There's a murder being done!'

'It's the cats,' Nan said delightedly and they leaped out of bed and ran to the landing. Father was already there, crouched at the window, a magician's cunning touching the corners of his mouth. He peered as though it were vital to avoid being spotted and motioned to the children to keep down. 'Buggers are in business,' he hissed with satisfaction.

The children squatted at the window and beheld a most wonderful sight. A dozen or so stringy cats, luminous in moonlight, sailed upward at the clothes-line in slow-motion ballet. Tortoiseshells rose, sooties fell, white cats hung suspended from the prize and dropped flailing like souls to damnation, and a marvellous round yellow tom launched bravely at the sky, like a cow jumping over the moon. They sailed, they clawed, they squabbled, they sang. Howls of rage and pain and terror enlivened the night. There was a ring of despair to their discord. One could tell that they wailed more in fear of their performance than in jealousy of their competitors.

'They're tearing the tripes out of each other,' father supplied a commentary.

'This is Satan's business,' said Etta Gorman, her big yellow toes with their horned nails planted righteously on the cold floor.

'Bertie will live to thank me,' father said, and mother who had crept sleepily from her bed and was clutching a woollen shawl over her nightdress said quietly, 'Do you suppose he will?'

Mary maintained a tense silence, her lips and nose flattened on the glass, which was wet from her breath. At last she breathed a sigh of relief. 'Good Bertie,' she whispered so quietly that no one heard. She sneaked around the flannelled legs.

The bolts of the back door shuffled. She felt the sweetness of the summer night, scented bravely as if their garden was a proper one filled with flowers. The soles of her feet gripped the cool, mealy surface of the path.

She scampered along the wall, past the gutter, and her toe kicked the metal strainer where the teapot was emptied. It rocked and laughed like a sea animal – 'goilk, goilk, goilk'. Her head shot fearfully to the window but the ghostly lozenges pinned to the glass had not shifted their focus and she stilled the little tinny noise with her foot, realizing how small it was against the fearful laments of the cats.

When she got to the coal shed she bent to the hole where part of a rotten plank had been ripped away. 'Bertie!' she breathed. 'Bertie!' She opened the door an inch or two and tried to peer into the blackness. A dull tide of slack and dust rose against the retaining plank which was wedged across the entrance. Old sacking was stored at the back of the shed. She thought she detected some abject shape pinned against the wall but it did not seem to contain life. 'Bertie?' The shape emitted a croak of fright. A portion of it moved and Mary found herself fixed in the beam of two eyes pale and popping with terror so that they perched on the cat's nose like boiled goosegogs.

She clambered over the rubble and black dust oozed between her toes. Gently she unrooted the cat from the sack. His body was dull with fate. She held him tightly and hurried back to the house. On the way up the stairs she held the back of his neck to stop him from squealing. The gathering on the landing was rigid with appreciation, like people in a box at the opera, and father was instructing the women: 'The black one! The black one! See!' Mary held her breath and squeezed past them. She let the cat go at the bedroom door and he leaped on to the untidy bed, spattering the counterpane with frivolous black blots from his toes. He tunnelled beneath the blankets playfully and Mary burrowed down beside him and pulled the furry head to her chin. They fell instantly to sleep, coiled into snores and purrs, and stretched in the blankness of their dreams, leaving the good sheets like a miner's shift.

* * *

The morning had a drawn quality, tense and lemony, as if the sky had not slept. The contest ended at dawn with subdued snarls of envy when the tubey remnants of the offal were dragged off by the ginger tom. The spur having vanished, the rest of the cats forgot about it and sprang away indifferently.

Father was disappointed. He thought there should be winners and losers and an invalided section for him to treat. And there was no sign of Bertie.

'Get up! Get up! The sun is scorching your eyeballs!' He burst into the children's bedroom with his usual greeting and flung back the bedclothes to annoy them. They lay huddled together, doughy with sleep, dusted with coal, and in between them skulked the cat.

'God's truth!' father swore. 'You are all against me.' He pulled out the animal. 'I shall burn the blasted thing. I shall get myself a proper beast – a dog. Dogs have a sense of loyalty.' He went out swinging the cat by its scruff and Mary bounded over Nan's body and ran after him pleading. Nan got out of bed sleepily and went down to make the breakfast.

When they got to the kitchen there was a diversion which made them forget about the cat. Etta Gorman was in her overcoat. She had her bags packed. She was off. She could take a hint, she intimated. They need not beg her to stay.

The children exchanged secret smiles but father stared, dumbfounded. 'Mags!' he wailed at the ceiling.

'You need not trouble after me,' Miss Gorman held up her horsey head. 'I shall fare better in the poorhouse.'

Mother hurried down to the kitchen. She was still wrapped in her shawl. She peered at them wearily. She was not properly awake after her disturbed night.

'Miss Gorman is leaving,' father accused. 'She says you did not make her welcome.'

Mother shrugged apologetically.

'Mrs Cantwell was decent to me,' Etta Gorman said. 'You were the one who plotted to make the dumb animals torment me. I can assimilate a hint.'

'No, no,' father protested. 'Our cat, you see, is a coward . . .'

'So you called in neighbouring cats to do the dirty work!'

'You misunderstand,' mother said, but her eyes glistened with merriment.

'Tell her, Mags,' father said.

Etta Gorman left. She did not wait for breakfast, having already found the hospitality unsatisfactory. She was not, she was thankful to say, obligated for any charity already partaken as she had knitted a pair of stockings for the little girl, her Mammy having dropped a heavy hint that they were wanted for the school concert. Nan accepted the brown paper parcel and stowed it away on the mantelpiece behind the Toby jug. She gave her mother a look of amazed gratitude. Mother had remembered the concert after all. Perhaps she was proud of her.

The incident had an upsetting effect on father. He would not eat his egg. He told mother he would eat no more eggs from unknown sources. 'Buggers in the shops are all bad hats,' he tipped her. Mother peered at his plate. 'I'll poach you a fresh one,' she offered but he snatched his breakfast away and said she was out to hang him. He wanted a hen – a Rhode Island Red – he banged the table with the palm of his hand three times for emphasis – laying in the garden by morning.

Mother flinched. She normally stayed in bed until breakfast was over. It meant she only had to see him at tea-time when he was expansive with opinions he had tried out on people at the factory.

There was a terrible neatness about him at this early hour, his wavy blond hair stamped flat with his comb, his white shirt radiant against the navy suit, so that, when he was made mad with rage by a provocative egg or the wrong shade of toast or some unwise statement coming over the wireless, his anger remained captive in his disciplined frame. He became coloured with red, a concentrated red cube like Symington's soup. He looked, Nan thought, like a Rhode Island Red.

'A hen?' Mother fidgeted with the end of her plait. She had left her bag in the bedroom. She was longing for a cigarette to go with her cup of tea but she did not wish to appear to be thinking of herself while father was suffering. 'A hen? At a good address in the suburbs? Hens are very dirty creatures.'

'That's right, argue with me! Put me off my blasted cup of tea,' he pushed his saucer away with violence so that the cup fell over and tea flooded the table. 'There are homes – I could name you homes – where the head of the house is obeyed without question.'

'Dear, don't upset yourself.' Mother watched with trepidation the advancing finger of tea.

'Don't upset myself?' He scoffed at this piece of wit. 'I work like a black night and day to keep a houseful of women in idle luxury. A houseful of women! You gave me no son. On top of this I support a half-witted skivvy. And what is my thanks? My guests are made unwelcome. I am given poisonous food which plays hell with my stomach. And this . . .' he swept a hand roughly across the desolation of the breakfast table upsetting a small condiment pot – 'this chaos!'

Mother had the tips of her fingers pressed to her forehead.

'I'm off up to the bathroom before I lose my temper,' he scowled. 'Mags, give the child a half a crown.'

Mother's alarmed eye peered through her fingers. 'What for?'

'What for? What for?' His gaze was wild.

'Nan, get my bag.' Mother's hand darted out and touched Nan urgently on the shoulder.

'Yes, mother,' Nan said, but she did not move. She watched her parents anxiously. With an irritated growl in his throat, father left the room and went to the bathroom. He spent a long time at the mirror every morning. He had already dressed and shaved but he liked to leave ten minutes for a final inspection and he gargled with an antiseptic and patted on cologne. When he was safely out of the room Nan went upstairs for her mother's bag. On her way down again she could hear her father in the bathroom. He was whistling.

Mother received her handbag as if it was a lost child. She smiled. Her fingers burrowed into its depth and she brought out her purse and her cigarettes. She dipped into the little leather change purse and removed a silver coin. She put it on the table. She did not know what else to do. She took a cigarette from the packet. She watched it a while and then her mouth inclined toward it as if for a kiss. Her lips clamped on its tweedy end. She lit it and shook the match vigorously as if it was a dangerous blaze. She took the cigarette from her mouth and frowned at it. 'Someday, he will go too far,' she said. There was no indignation, only a helpless regret, as if someone very dear might travel a long distance and be out of reach.

He came back wearing a smart overcoat and a smooth beige hat. He faced them in his glossy pink and beige splendour. Mother and the children were never at their best at this early hour. They made a disconsolate circle around the ruins of the breakfast. 'Get a move on, you idle bloody lot,' he said cheerfully. 'Sun is scorching your eyeballs.' He turned to go out when his eye was arrested by the glint of mother's coin, silvery under the saucer like a waiter's tip. He connected it to Nan with an imperious finger.

'Is that there to tempt the servants or are you going to pick it up?' She took the coin reluctantly. 'And make sure you get a good one.'

It was Mary who found the courage to speak. 'A good *which* one, pa?' she wheedled.

'A hen,' he told Mary. 'A good laying hen,' he emphasized to Nan and to mother he instructed: 'She's to buy a hen from Nellie's Jew.'

Mary's eyes grew round with excitement and her mouth fell open. 'Shyster?' she breathed.

Nan's eyes flickered sharply from Mary to her father in startled query.

'I have said it!' father barked.

CHAPTER 6

Wertzsberger, wine merchant; Buchalter, baker; Weinronk, baker. The Jews lived in a network of narrow streets around South Circular Road which was known as Little Israel. It was a foreign territory, connected to the ordinary city only by the pavements beneath and the sky overhead.

'Wertzsberger.' Nan mouthed the strange-sounding names as she dawdled along Clanbrassil Street. She stopped to watch her green-tunicked reflection in a window piled with bread that was brown and shiny as conkers. She felt that a part of her had escaped. 'Weinronk.' She was on her way to see Shyster, the Jew.

His real name was Schweitzer. No one knew his first name. He wheeled a creaking pram filled with old clothes and terrible noises. Corner boys chased him but the small children were respectful because the bigger ones said that the pram was filled with devils. At night the children were haunted by a memory of the muffled squawk and cackle of spirits.

There were about five thousand Jews living in Dublin.

They had come without money, without professions, without English. They found things to sell. All of them were tallymen or *vickla*. Shyster sold secondhand clothes and another thing, a most useful commodity. It was his combination of trades that made him a legend and attracted Nellie to add him to her store of 'God's demented'.

He wheeled his pram through the streets where children were put to sit on the step because there was no space in overcrowded rooms. He beckoned to the littlest ones: 'Come and see my babies. Babies for the oven. Babies for the dinner table.' Bristling with dread and interest the children pushed one another forward. Shyster lifted away layers of sweat-smelling wool, lifeless cotton. He had a delicate wrist movement. He might have sold lace or linen. The infants pressed forward, reassured by familiar smells in the clothing. Inside, the demons rattled.

The bottom layer was a gentleman's tweed overcoat. It bubbled with hidden activity. Shyster smiled at the children. He whipped away the greenish tweed. Bundles of rusty life, raisin-eyed, razor-beaked, flew up into the stricken faces. Screaming and bumping into each other, clawing the air for mothers who were nowhere to be seen, the children raced away. The small sirens of their voices could still be heard when they had vanished from sight.

It was different when he wheeled his pram into town where there were grown-ups, paying customers. There he would employ his best English for a phrase learnt by heart. 'Hens, two and sixpence. Used clothing, no infection.'

'But sometimes . . .' Nellie's eye bore into her wonderfully frightened audience. 'A squawk was heard from under the pickins' that was like no hen ever heard by mortal ears. It was the cry of a young child.'

There was an ordinary explanation. Shyster kept the hens beneath the clothes to stop them from flying away.

Nan was fourteen. She wasn't afraid. At any rate – she felt in her pocket the half-crown and forced herself to walk on – she was more afraid of father than of Nellie's Jew. She pulled herself away from the tempting shops and turned into a maze of smaller streets. Little red-brick houses, like toy houses, had front doors on the street. They all looked the same. Nan did not know where to go. 'Excuse me,' she said to a young woman sitting in a dark hall with the front door left open. She was about twenty-five with dark, half-sleeping eyes. She came forward slowly. 'You tell your mama I sell her a nice quilt, only a shilly a week,' she said urgently. Nan ran away.

Soon she got used to these overtures. People tried to sell her boots, shawls – even money. At last one of them told her that Shyster lived on Abel Street. You could recognize the house by its yellow door. This fact alone shocked her. The rich painted their front doors in white. Ordinary people used dark green or black or a wood stain. No one used yellow, like a tinker's caravan.

When she found the house she was surprised by the beauty of the door. It was the bright yellow of a buttercup. The letter box gleamed like gold. She lifted the flap and let it go with a small sound. Someone raised the flap from the inside by poking at it with a finger. The door was drawn slowly back.

All she had seen through the slit of the letter box were two brown eyes, warily considering. Now, in the widening gap of the door, she was introduced to a fantastic sight, the dining-room where a large table was spread with a snowy cloth. Eight candles as translucent as Sister Immaculata's fingers stretched from a stand of gleaming silver and there was wine on the table and sparkling glasses. It was fit for a palace.

The door had been opened by a wild-looking man whose long nose ploughed a raging black beard. There was so much to see that she could not take it all in at once. It was not until the man spoke very softly – 'come in, child' – and beckoned with fingers so delicate that they might have sold lace or linen, that she realized and stepped back, unnerved.

'Shyster!'

Behind him a plump girl of twelve or thirteen, with pink in her cheeks and brown ringlets, laughed delightedly.

'Poor Ivor,' she said. 'You must not tease him.'

'Ivor?'

'My brother,' the girl said. 'Ivor Schweitzer!' She took Nan's hand and drew her into the mysterious splendour.

It was the first time she had been inside a Jewish house. She expected to feel some faint sense of danger for she had been warned by the nuns that one's faith could be threatened by keeping company with people of misguided persuasions. Apart from the beautiful dining table, the house was disappointingly ordinary. The furniture was shabby and badly matched. The squares of carpet did not reach the edges of the stone floor.

A woman came from the kitchen, followed by a girl of perhaps fifteen. They both had the dark, curling hair and pink plump faces of the younger girl. The woman looked large and firm as a gentleman's armchair in her green velvet dress.

'Good girl, Gicki!' she beamed on Nan's companion. 'You have brought the little goyim.' She smiled at Nan. 'You like rice pudding?'

'Yes.'

'Good child. You know what is to do?' Her English was not fluent.

Nan hesitated. 'No.'

It caused them to laugh. They threw back their heads and showed the solidness of their teeth. This made Nan nervous. She turned to

Shyster but he looked angry and left them. The women glanced at one another guiltily and stemmed their mirth with rounded hands.

Nan took her hand from her pocket and held out the half-crown. 'I've come to buy a hen,' she said.

The three who looked so alike were taken by a fresh seizure of laughter until the oldest one, wiping tears from her eyes, said, 'Hush, my darlings, we shall be eating the cold food in the darkness. The Shiksa wants a hen.'

The girl who had greeted Nan explained: 'It is the Sabbath.'

'I don't know very much . . .' Nan said doubtfully. The girls began to giggle again but their mother stopped them. 'We have to be very quiet,' she said.

'Because of the Sabbath,' Nan said.

'No. Because of our brother, Sam.'

'Is he ill?'

'Oh, no! He is learning to be a surgeon.' They led Nan into the tiny kitchen and shut the door so that they could talk.

'I am Gickla,' the youngest said.

'I'm Nan.'

'I'm Becca,' said the elder sister.

'We not work on Sabbath,' their mother explained.

'All food is prepared yesterday. The little Shiksa comes to light our fire and our stove and our candles.'

'Today she did not come,' said Becca.

'So you have come instead,' Gickla explained.

Nan found it hard to concentrate. Her attention was pulled by the glamour of the tiny room. Every available space between stove and window and table and sink and cooker was taken up with pictures of film stars cut out from magazines. Some of them were brown and grease-spattered but they smiled with radiant happiness and uniqueness in their furs and jewels and shiny top hats.

'You like them?' Gickla noticed Nan's rapt stare. 'We are mad about the movies.'

'You all go? Together?' Nan was envious.

'No.' The mother looked regretful. 'Papa passed away. The boys are religious. There is only us ladies.'

Nan's heart struggled with excitement and envy while she lit the jets on the stove and then the oven and the coal fire and finally set a dewy bud of flame on each of the five white candles.

'Is that all?' she said then.

'Sit down. Sit down,' said Mrs Schweitzer. 'You want some rice pudding. Gickla, get the child some rice pudding.'

Nan sat at the kitchen table and Gickla brought the pudding in a large tin dish and Becca set out a small pudding bowl and a spoon. There were raisins in the pudding, and pieces of cherry. Nan spooned it slowly into her mouth and felt the pieces of fruit between her teeth, while the two girls fixed her with their moist brown eyes and told her about all the men and women who had become famous on the screen and the films they had seen, which were quite unlike the matinées, where true love triumphed and the audience wept.

It was a grown-up world, but an adult world quite different to any Nan had ever glimpsed. She could not picture it. She wanted them to go slowly, to point out the people in the photographs, to break down the words, like Sister Immaculata. When her head was whirling with a glittering, dancing swarm of these beautiful grown-up people, they began to tell her about the Four Horsemen.

This was a wonderful thing at the Scala Cinema, a moving picture with sound. The voices of Rudolph Valentino and Alice Terry did not actually speak out of the screen. It was a man who came out beforehand. He was draped in heavy robes. He stood in front of the curtains and delivered, in sepulchral tones, a prologue about death and pestilence. The film, which was called *The Four Horsemen of the Apocalypse*, was about this sort of thing.

When the audience had been whipped up into a stew of fear the picture began. They sat back, thinking they could relax, that the ordeal was over. Worse was to come.

Loudspeakers had been set up at the back of the cinema giving off startling noises to simulate the sound of firing cannons. The audience, feeling itself under fire from all quarters, panicked. There were riots in the cinema. Many people fainted and had to be carried away. The film was a huge success. Men and women queued for three and a half hours before it was due to commence.

By the time Gickla finished speaking Nan realized that she had barely eaten a spoonful of the delicious pudding. She was too excited to swallow. She went to the cinema every Saturday with the Tallons but it was always the Thomas Street Picture House, which they called The Tommo, or the Phoenix Picture House on Ellis Quay, known as The Feno. It was twopence into the Tommo. The Feno was the cheapest. On Saturdays it was a penny and this was known as the penny rush. It was rough. A man kept the queue in order with a whip.

They did not show proper films at the matinées, but cartoons and serials. The children's serials were not really thrilling. It was difficult to work up a proper sense of fear over the girl tied to the railway track for she was always freed in time for the following week's episode.

Nan had never been to a real film in one of the adult cinemas. 'How much is it to get in?' she demanded.

'A *shilling*,' Becca taunted.

'Mama took us both on Becca's birthday,' said Gickla.

A shilling. Nan and Mary got twopence for the tram fare to school. When there was time they walked, but when school was over they were so hungry they had to spend their money on an eccles cake at a bakery in the city. Father was generous when in a good mood, but he handed out sweets or brought home ice-cream; he rarely gave money, and he disapproved violently of the cinema, calling it licentious filth, which the children associated in their minds with dirty hair. It was true that the matinée queues rang out with the taint of unwashed bodies.

She never had as much as a shilling at once. Today she had half a crown in her pocket but that was for the hen. The hen! She had almost forgotten father's hen.

She took the money from her pocket and put it on the table. The dimpled faces looked amused. It was as if they had never known anything but material comfort. Rich, sweet, greasy smells, rising from the stove, reinforced this impression. 'My father sent me,' Nan said. 'I have to buy a hen.'

Mrs Schweitzer arched a thick black eyebrow. 'Ivor not sell his hens on the Sabbath,' she said.

'I'm sorry,' Nan said. 'I forgot.' She put the money back in her pocket.

The woman watched the vanishing coin in alarm. 'Perhaps,' she said slowly, 'if you leave money on table and pick a hen yourself, it not amount to the same thing.'

'Come,' Gickla said sharply. She fetched a metal bowl and filled it with yellow meal and Nan followed her to the yard. The concrete path had a net roof to keep cats away. The ground had a sandy covering of grain out of which a few hens picked fastidious feet. There were dozens of hens dozing like fat cabbages and a couple that lurched toward the children, squinting dangerously and giving abuse. Gickla threw a fistful of grain into the air and the birds jostled and squawked and dropped foolish faces.

'There!' Gickla set down the bowl and wiped her hands. 'I cannot sell you a hen but I can make it easy for you to choose.'

'They all look the same,' Nan said.

'Don't be silly. Use your eyes. See how they fight for the food. That one is a fool. She pecks at her sister's eyes instead of the grain. This one just eats and gets fat and lays brown eggs. Choose for yourself. I only advise.'

But Nan's attention had been caught by a thin bird that neither dozed nor quarrelled but watched from a sad, glassy eye.

'Gickla?' A thought had struck her. 'You and your sister wear nice dresses but Shyster – Ivor – is dressed in rags.'

Gickla frowned and threw another handful of seeds to the birds. 'We dress to suit our purpose.'

'I don't understand.'

She offered Nan a sideways smile, like the photographs of the women in films. 'You think, perhaps he should wear a three-piece suit with a silk handkerchief and a gold fob watch to sell old clothes to the poor. He dresses for his business.'

'I'm sorry.'

Gickla laughed. 'You are always sorry. We are merely poor. Mama makes our dresses from the best cast-offs. All our money goes to make Sam a surgeon. Becca and me went barefoot until we were twelve but now that men notice us we must wear nice dresses so that we will have husbands.'

She put her hands on her hips and stuck out her plump chest. 'See! Already there are grown-up men calling to see me.' She laughed. 'Mama always sells them something.'

Nan looked away. She watched the thin, isolated bird. It flinched when some big bossy bird jutted its neck in an ill-tempered manner.

'I'll take that one,' she pointed. 'What's its name?'

Gickla looked at her with amusement. 'Betty.' She waded through the angry feathery mass. Birds rose around her ankles, barking in fright. She picked up the little docile hen firmly, holding its wings to its breast. 'Have you brought a scarf?'

'A scarf?'

'You have to wrap her up to carry her home.'

'I'll hold her under my arm.' She held out a tentative hand. 'Here, Betty.' The bird pecked feebly at her fingers.

'Do as you like,' said Gickla. 'If you hold her under your arm, she will do her business in your pocket.'

She borrowed Gickla's woollen headsquare and it occurred to her as the dark child tied the angry bird up like Dick Whittington's bundle that perhaps Gickla was using it as an excuse to see her again. Gickla was more clever than she was. She held her bundle tightly as she said goodbye to the women. She could feel the hen's feet stamping exploratively through the cloth. Every so often it emitted an impatient grunt. 'You wash my scarf if that hen does her business,' Gickla admonished.

'You get your mama to take you to the Scala,' Becca smiled. 'You tell your mama I sell her a most beautiful model coat in navy repp, only a shilling a week.'

Nan watched the closed bedroom door that belonged to the brothers, where Sam studied to be a surgeon and Shyster sulked because the women laughed and sold hens on the Sabbath.

''Goodbye,' she said regretfully.

'Come back soon!' A trio of plump hands waved.

'Oh, I will.'

She ran then, clutching the warm, struggling bird, holding it with care in case it should lay an egg.

It began to rain. By the time she reached Portobello Bridge Nan's gymslip was soaked through and the drenched hen shrank in the scarf like a piece of stewed meat. Nan heard the church bell ring out seven times. She was late.

For a while the warm rain came down in lumps like the drops of sanctifying grace that fell from the Holy Ghost and then it stopped and the mildewed mountains and the toy villages, the stout-coloured river and the grey people were lit up pink by a violent blood-orange sun.

There was a brief illusion of silence after the blankety hissing of the rain and then the streets spat out sharp noises. Tram tracks glistened like eels as they writhed out from under the rattling cars. The tyres of bicycles sucked the wet cobbles. Iron wheels of horse-drawn goods vans made the noise of a boy running a stick along a railing. 'He can't kill me, he can't kill me, he can't kill me,' tapped out the sedate hooves of a little pony with bald patches. She ducked her head and ran, ignoring the sulky 'parp' of a Cluly's horn as its wet sporty driver sped past at fifteen miles an hour, splashing her with mud.

When she got home Mary was sitting on the front step, her lank plaits plastered to her cheeks from rain, her face green with fright.

'They're all gone out and I can't get in,' she shrilled accusingly. 'I've been sitting here for hours and hours and I'm afraid Hammer'll come and get me.'

'Where's everyone gone?' Nan said.

'Father never came home and Nellie's gone home. Mother's at her sodality.' She wiped her nose with her sleeve.

'Never mind,' Nan said. 'Look what I've got.' She pulled back a corner of the scarf to show the hen which grunted unhappily.

Mary's face brightened. 'You went to see Shyster?'

'Oh, it was nothing much. He wasn't very interesting. Let's go and fry ourselves up some rashers and bread and black pudding.'

'And tomatoes. Oh, *let's*.'

When they had washed up after their tea and had changed their clothes and dried the hen in a towel, they went to find a suitable house for the bird. They decided on the coal-house. Bertie, being a coward, would not bother it. They pulled out the pile of sacking from the back and spread it over the coal dust.

'There should be straw,' Mary said.

'I suppose so. And grain for her to eat.'

'Last Christmas's crib is still in the Indian room. There's some straw in that,' Mary said. She stood up, wiping coal dust from her hands on the front of her dress in a business-like manner.

'I'll get some scraps and a dish of water,' Nan said. 'I'll try some stale bread and rasher skins. Oh, I wish we had asked mother to buy porridge for Etta Gorman.'

Mary hurried to the house and climbed the stairs. She went to her parents' bedroom and reached into one of father's army boots. The key of the Indian room was kept hidden in his boots. It was a secret. She peered out the window at the dusty violet evening in case her mother or father should be returning, but there was no one. She crept to the return landing and let herself into the room. As always, she held her breath when she went in.

The Indian room was a foreign city, deserted. There were pieces of brass and strange lumps of carved furniture, a sly little stone goddess, with twisted legs. Men in splendid uniforms gazed dully out of beige photographs and a grinning sword was anchored to the wall. The floor was occupied by a single bed, a wardrobe and a big leather trunk filled with father's mementoes. Over the trunk was flung the withered skin of a tiger.

The crib was not to be seen. She looked under the bed but there was only an immaculate flowery china bowl.

The wardrobe revealed father's uniform from the horse regiment and a pair of riding boots. She thought it must be in the trunk. She pulled away the tiger skin and dust rose in a musty snarl. She unfastened the straps from their stout metal buckles. She pushed. The trunk was locked. She stood for a moment, dreaming, then went back to the wardrobe. She took out the boots. The legs were very long. Her arm went in all the way before she could reach the toe. The cold ring of a little iron key skidded into her grasp.

Before opening the trunk she examined her conscience. She was soon to make her first confession and she was militant against sin. There was nothing in the 'thou shalt nots' about opening things that were locked. She ground the key against its spring and pushed up the creaking lid. She looked in. A lot of queer things started happening. She felt as if she was a musical instrument, being played. Her free hand plucked at her gymslip and there was a pricking feeling in her armpit.

Her teeth bit deep into her lower lip. She was looking at a framed photograph of smiling teeth in a dark brown face, a girl.

There was a bunch of dried flowers, some women's clothing, bright and shapeless, an embroidered shawl. On top of these things was a small bunch of old letters, addressed in weak green ink and one letter separate, its ink still bright as mint cordial. Her hand shook when she lifted out the letter. 'Thou shalt not,' said a voice in her head. She supported the lid of the trunk with an aching shoulder and used two hands for the letter. A smell of perfumed dust, like the scent of Benediction, climbed into her nose.

There was no address, but a date in the spring. 'Mr Cantwell,' said the looped green words, 'at long last I have found you. Soon I come. Make ready, for you belong to me. Your obedient, Mumtaz.'

Mary put the letter back in its envelope. She let down the lid of the trunk and fastened the straps. She ground the little key in its lock and returned it to the black riding boot. She locked the door of the Indian room and brought that key back to its secret boot. Slowly she walked down the darkening stairway and went outside to where Nan was feeding the hen.

'You've been crying,' Nan said. 'Crybaby. You're afraid of the dark.'

Mary's wet face was blank and Nan felt sorry. 'There,' she said, pulling her limp school hankie from her blazer pocket. 'Dry your eyes and I'll tell you the most interesting thing you've ever heard.'

She told her about the Four Horsemen, the figure in robes who warned of plague and pestilence, the firing cannons, the fainting women, all of which could be witnessed at the Scala for a shilling.

'A shilling,' Mary said.

Nan turned her attention to the hen who had spread her wings on the dirty sacking to finish drying them. She pecked cautiously at a piece of brown bread. 'Perhaps Betty has laid an egg by now.' She climbed in over the make-shift bedding, and lifted the hen. There was nothing.

'*Betty?*' Mary said.

'Betty. That's her name.'

'You can't call her Betty. Hens in books are always called Betty. She's our hen. She's special. She's beautiful. Besides, Betty is too like Bertie. Neither would know which was being called.'

'Betty's her name,' Nan maintained stubbornly.

'I shall call her Elizabeth,' Mary said fiercely. 'After the young queen.'

CHAPTER 7

Mary began collecting hair. It was in a pillow-case. There was a bristling ball about the size of a coconut. It looked like a coconut except that it moved. It *crept*. Mary grew so used to it that she took to showing it off without explanation. 'Look!' She would hold open the mouth of the pillow-case. At first all the person could see in the clothy white light was a loose-looking coconut. Then the thing expanded, showing different shades and textures. If one looked long enough there appeared to be heads and bodies, waving eyes and furry legs, like a huddle of spiders. People rarely made any comment but one or two of them gave her a halfpenny.

The collection was for Nan, although she had not told her so. It was a means of making money. The night Nan told her about *The Four Horsemen of the Apocalypse* she saw that there was a way to rouse the older girl from her languor, to bring her back from her lonely distance. For the first time in ages she had seen Nan's face light up with excitement and warmth at the thought of the plagues and the cannons.

There were not many opportunities for children to make money. She wasted a penny lighting a candle to St Jude, the patron saint of hopeless cases. She polished the hall for Mrs Lehane, but was only given a Fry's Cream Bar. One day she read in the paper an astonishing thing. There was a company willing to hand out money for the hair that came away on people's clothes.

Ladies' hair combings made up into plaits, coils, curls, 2 shillings per ounce, the advertisement read. *Transformations from 50/-. Certified Hair Specialist, 106, Upper Leeson Street.*

At first the collection was meant for her hair alone. She hadn't a lot. Her hair was thin. She was a thin person. She clenched her lips together as she tugged the brush through her hair. She picked the colourless wisps from the bristles. Her scalp went pink as ham. There was hardly anything in her bag.

'You'll go bald,' Nan said. She was sitting on the edge of the bed, her petticoat down around her hips, tying bands of cotton across her breasts. She frowned and tossed back her own hair which was thicker than Mary's and coloured like a cake. It was smooth on the top but the ends curled around her face and fell over her grey eyes, making them look sleepy. She would have nothing to do with Mary's collection. She was annoyed because her sister would not tell her what it was for. In the end she went and told Nellie and it was only partly from spite. She really did begin to believe that Mary would end up with a pristine pink head like a rosebud.

Nellie came and stood in the doorway, her arms folded over her apron. She watched Mary's ruthless brushing with a critical look. 'When your hair falls out you'll be treated for worrims,' she said quietly. Mary frowned at Nellie's reflection, blocking out the background in the wardrobe mirror, her apron navy with white dots like the sky at night, her face large and plain as the moon. She put the brush down. Her hair stood out around her head in wavering spikes. The pink colour crept down from her scalp and descended over her face like scarf. Hard little tears like pips squeezed out of her eyes.

'There now,' Nellie said kindly. 'You can have some of my hair. Me brush is like a gorilla's armpit.' It was true. She went off and returned with a brush foaming with black hair. The ratty black snarl came away like a hairnet and swam down to the depths of the pillow-case to cling to the wisps of blonde. After that Mary was hungry for everyone's hair. She kept offering to brush Nan's hair when she was getting ready for school. Once, she was brave enough to stand behind father as he raked his spruce blond hair to a glassy sheen before going off to work, but he spotted her and bellowed 'muck off, you swine!' brandishing his comb as if it was a cut-throat.

She brought her pillow-case to school and queued behind girls in the lavatory. Those with ringlets and tongs-waved styles raked tiers of frizzy hair from their ornate heads. Mary shadowed them. She stripped their combs. Her collection was growing. At home she emptied it on to the kitchen weighing scales. It didn't weigh anything.

For a time she forgot about it. Father brought Mrs Graham home to stay. She was a poor bugger. She had been locked out of her lodgings by her landlady. Her son was a black-hearted villain who would not give her a cup of tea. For once, everyone sympathized. She was old, with diluted blue eyes and a little bit of silver hair fluffed up on top of her head like potato on a shepherd's pie. She kept saying sorry.

She could not shake hands because of her case. It was an old cardboard suitcase tied with string and she held it against her body with both arms. Nellie took her to the Indian room and brought her a cup of tea to compensate for the negligence of her son. She could not drink it. She could not let her suitcase go. 'Sit on it, ma'am,' Nellie suggested, and she did, perched on the case which had been placed on the bed, her feet swinging with pleasure as she sipped the strong tea. She was so happy with this arrangement that she asked if her meals could be brought to her room. After a day or two, Nellie began to tire. Everyone grew uneasy about the old lady sitting on her luggage.

There was speculation about the content of the case. It was discussed in the kitchen and in the dining-room. Clearly it was stuffed with money or valuables. Even father became indignant. He said she wasn't pulling her weight. He decided to have a word with her. Mrs Graham smiled at him with her bewildered pink gums. Father pointed at the case. 'I'm afraid you'll have to come clean with us, if you are to remain a guest under my roof,' he said. 'Why don't you mind your own blithering business?' Mrs Graham wondered. He came downstairs again, complaining of the smell. There was a smell. Nellie had spoken of it. Nobody could place it but it was getting worse. Father no longer referred to her as a poor bugger down on her luck. She was 'that woman'. 'That woman will have to go,' he grumbled. 'Turning my house into a cesspit.'

The only one who did not mind the smell was Mary. She was impressed by the suitcase filled with money. There were stories of children who had moved the hearts of rich old misers and been left fortunes in their wills. She began bringing up Mrs Graham's tray. She would have been glad to keep her company but the visitor sat on her case and waited until she was gone before attending to her meal.

One day when Mary came up with a cup of tea the suitcase was open and Mrs Graham was bending over it, examining her secret.

Mary fled down the stairs again, spilling the tea, shouting out that she had seen what was in the case. Father and mother emerged from the drawing-room and Nellie ran from the kitchen. Nan came in from the front garden with the cat under her arm. 'There's no money! There isn't any money!' Mary cried out in excitement. 'No money?' Father was bewildered. He felt betrayed. 'Well, that woman!' Nellie exclaimed, and she flounced back into her kitchen, annoyed at having wasted her time. 'She's just a loony,' Nan said sulkily. They all went away. Mary was left standing on the stairs with no one to tell.

A day or two later father was seen crossly ushering Mrs Graham out the door. She held on to her case in fright and told them sorry, goodbye, consider the lilies of the field. They waved, their fingers stiff with failed hospitality.

Only Mary followed her to the gate, reluctant to let her go, hoping at the final moment to find the proper word to convey her understanding of the importance of that suitcase, which was crammed to collapse with holy pictures.

Nellie tracked down the smell. There was a pile of meat on top of the wardrobe, chops, chicken, slices of beef, green putrified. For the two weeks she had enjoyed their hospitality, she had been scraping the meat from her dinner plate on to this lofty hiding place. It cheered everyone up. They felt vindicated. 'The woman should be locked up for her own good,' father said, and Nellie agreed, suggesting that she had lost her marbles. Mary thought it was a long time since she had seen them all in such good humour, Nan's wild laugh restored, mother wiping tears of mirth from her eyes, and she wondered why it was that they failed to realize that Mrs Graham had only hidden her meat out of politeness. She couldn't eat it because she hadn't any teeth.

Every day Nan visited the shed to see if Elizabeth had laid an egg. Elizabeth did not lay but she grew domesticated due to Nan's frequent visits. She became discontented with her sooty refuge and spent most of her time in the house, walking between people's legs, running from the swipe of Nellie's dishcloth, leaving black arrows all over the clean floor. On fine days she sat on the front step and arched her neck whenever someone came in or out, hoping to be patted on the head.

For the two weeks of Mrs Graham's stay, Elizabeth was on trial. The children grew fond of her. Mary gave her a present of an old cloth duck, to make her feel broody. Nan stole an egg from the larder and placed it beside her in a nest of straw to remind her what she was meant to do. Elizabeth kicked the egg about in a feckless manner. Father was growing impatient. He suggested remedies. The bird should be dosed with black molasses or boiled in a pot.

He brewed up some tarry stew and attempted to push spoonfuls at her stubborn beak. The following morning he went out to see if she was alive or dead. She seemed well enough. He picked her up. There was a cloth duck underneath her and a brown egg. He was very pleased. He brought in the egg and had it boiled for his breakfast. He insisted everyone gather around to admire it. Mother had to be got out of bed. Nan and Mary immediately recognized the egg that had been left there some days earlier. Father dug out spoonfuls of the egg to demonstrate its superior texture. It had a superb flavour.

After that Nan brought an egg out every day when she went to feed the hen and in the morning Mary was sent to fetch it for father's breakfast.

The Martindale girls next door threw a party on a Friday afternoon after school. They were restless. They wanted boys to dance with. Gladys, who was seventeen, had a gramophone. To her surprise, Nan received an invitation. She had never had anything to do with them before. They were country girls. They played leap-frog in the lane and threw out piles of Bessie Bunters, nearly new. Girls who had brothers were allowed to come empty-handed. All others had to bring food. Mary was not invited. 'No kids allowed,' said Dilys, who was fifteen.

Nan made a Queen of Puddings. She left it on the kitchen table, covered with a cloth, while she went to get dressed. She took her blue taffeta dress from the back of the wardrobe. It was chilly with unuse. She had not worn it since her confirmation. When she did up the little buttons at the back, the dress bit into her armpits. She shivered. She was disturbed by the shape of her body under the childish frock. Her legs had grown too long. She did not recognize herself. She ran downstairs.

On her way out through the scullery she dipped her fingers into a stone jar and rubbed flour over her face to take away the shine. She let herself out by the back door. She meant to slip out into the lane and enter Martindale's by the back so as not to be noticed. It was her first party with boys. She did not want to bother father, but when she came out into the bright sunlight, feeling strange in her stiff party dress, he was there at the end of the lawn, making a bonfire of some letters.

He scowled at her through the ribbons of smoke. 'Where do you think you're off to?'

'Gladys Martindale asked me to tea.' She held out her dish, still covered with a cloth. 'I've made a cake.'

'There are fellows in there!' he pointed. 'Young swine! I can hear them.'

'Some of the girls have brought their brothers,' she said calmly.

'There is music,' he accused.

'Gladys has been given a present of a gramophone. She has invited us all to hear it.' It was amazing the ease with which she could lie this year. It was like being able to speak a foreign language. It took so little out of her that father could see straight away that she was telling the truth. He had run out of argument. 'Why have you not brought your sister?' he said wearily. 'She didn't want to come,' Nan said. 'She's in the drawing-room. She's reading.'

He let her go. She unlatched the back gate. 'Here!' he called out angrily. 'What's the matter with you?'

She turned, nonplussed. 'Nothing.'

'Look at you. You're like a ghost.'

'I'm fine.'

'Don't argue with me, you're . . .' he could not put his finger on it: the bleached face, the woman's figure defying the confines of the pretty little dress; her listless insolence. He had never expected her to grow up. It offended him. He liked her small and robust. 'You're peaky!'

'I'll be all right,' she promised.

'No, no.' He shook his head sadly. It was up to him. He could not trust anyone else. 'I shall get your mother to boil you a sheep's head.'

It was Gladys who opened the door, her face red with excitement, black jet beads dancing on her chest. The room behind her was dark. The curtains had been pulled. The milky glass bowl that covered the light bulb was covered in red crepe. There was a lot of noise, the scuffing of feet on the bare boards where the carpet had been pulled up, a recording of Jack Payne's London Dance Band, tortured under the needle of the gramophone. 'Come in, you sly little sparrowfart,' Gladys greeted. Nan did not know what to say. She was confused by the music. She held out the Queen of Puddings. 'I brought you this.' Gladys made a face. She stuck her fingers in her ears. 'I can't hear you,' she shrieked. 'The noise! 'Tis cat melodeon!' She smiled and ran back into the dark red room, startling a boy who was attempting to smoke a cigarette. She seized this boy and arranged him into a dancing partner.

Her eyes grew accustomed to the strange light. She could see that the dividing doors had been opened between the dining-room and the drawing-room. The big dining table had been pushed back against the wall and all the food was laid out on this. A cluster of boys hung around it gaping or cramming their mouths. In the other room there was dancing. A half dozen of the best-looking boys were shoving chosen girls about the floor with gormless expression. The girls were coy under the boys' mesmerized looks. Nan could not take her eyes off them. There were others in the background, a row of girls standing at the wall and some couples squirming on a sofa. In the weak red light Nan recognized no one she knew. She decided to put the pudding on the table with the other girls' offerings. She hoped there might be a sandwich with no crust or a nice little cake, but the table had a destroyed appearance. It had been arranged by the girls to appetizing effect; cold corned beef and pickles, cooked sausages, coconut biscuits, jellies, tinned fruit salads and some unsuccessful cakes, but the boys, in their hunger, had managed to introduce the various substances to one another so that cream trailed over the meat and specks of jelly slid into the mangled cake. It made her shudder. She took the cloth off her dish and put the pudding, with its nicely browned crust of meringue, in a safe place.

'Hiya, dreamboat!' She was disturbed by a voice. It was a coarse-looking boy; curls sprang round his lardy face. 'Not you, shipwreck!' he snorted when their glance connected. All the boys laughed. Some of them rolled their eyes at her in an inviting manner. She frowned at them, scratching her armpit where her dress was too tight. A spoon, already smeared with food, came down and crashed into her meringue. She watched as its owner rooted through the delicate layers of bread pudding and jam and shovelled mounds to his face. She was upset by the army of boys' hands, clawing through the food, indiscriminately ferrying sweet and savoury things to their open, laughing mouths.

She moved away and pushed a path through the dancers. She went to stand at the wall with the wallflowers. Already she was bored. It wasn't like the parties she was used to, where all the girls shrieked with laughter and danced with one another and then sat down to a nice tea. Everyone else appeared to be having a good time. Even the other girls, standing at the wall like dunces, spoke in excited whispers and had brilliant expressions on their painted faces as if they expected something to happen. Something did. ''Tis cat!' the girl beside her said crossly. ''Tis cat melodeon.' She turned to look at Dilys Martindale, whose mouth had been lipsticked into a red ribbon of bliss on her thin face. Behind the happy mouth, her teeth were gritted bad-temperedly. Nan studied this with interest. 'Look at all them boyos stuck into the grub,' Dilys complained. 'While we're sprayed up agin the wall like dogs' doings.'

'What are you going to do?' Nan wondered.

'I'm going to start the games.'

'Games? Oh, good.'

Dilys stepped out into the centre of the floor. She clapped her hands several times, loud enough to get on everyone's nerves. She went over to the record player and lifted the needle. Jack Payne died drowningly.

'Spin the bottle!' Dilys's untutored voice squawked. 'All form a circle in the centre of the floor for spin the bottle.'

To Nan's amazement, the guests obeyed. The dancers fell into languid huddles on the floor. Even the boys at the table dropped sods of food and ran for a place in the circle. Nan squeezed a space for herself. Only the couples on the sofa remained where they were.

'What sort of game is this?' Nan whispered to Dilys. 'How do you play?'

'What sort of an eejit are you?' Dilys retorted smartly. 'Keep your eyes open, infant. You might learn more than you bargained for.'

Dilys had placed an empty lemonade bottle in the centre of the circle. She reached out a wicked finger and gave the bottle a poke at its back. It began to spin, setting up a clatter on the wood floor, spurting red dregs from its bottom. Everyone watched intently. It slowed to a rattling stagger. There was tension. The girls contacted one another with their elbows and made little squeals of excitement. Nan studied their avid faces. She was relieved to see, on the other side of the circle, the homely faces of Bluebell and Daisy Tallon. They did not look as overwrought as the other guests. The bottle had stopped. It was pointing at a wild-looking girl called Mamie Farrell who went pink and threw her hands over her face. Nan guessed she was going to get a prize. Mamie took away her hands. Her huge blue eyes studied the boys in the group and her rabbit's teeth rested on a moist, smiling lower lip. The boys watched with devotion. 'Joseph O'Brien,' she simpered and a large, leering boy cheered himself and leaped out of the circle. He went out of the room with Mamie Farrell. That was all there was to it. She shrugged her perplexity at the Tallon twins. They made wry faces.

Before Dilys began to propel the bottle again Nan wriggled out of her place and moved to a space between her friends. 'Where's Dandy?' she hissed to Bluebell.

'She's all right,' Daisy said shortly.

'Why isn't she here?'

'She is here.'

Nan looked across. She was not in the circle. If she was, all the boys would have been going wild about her. The only ones not in the circle were the fools on the sofa. Her head spun around in alarm. The girls on the sofa had big oafs on top of them but she could see one of Dandy's red party shoes dangling from a foot. She glared back at Bluebell in accusation.

'Leave her be,' Bluebell warned.

'No, I won't,' Nan said. 'You may not care about Dandy, but I do. I'm not going to leave her to some big sweaty gorilla.'

Bluebell's large hand detained her painfully.

'We all care about Dandy,' she said. 'Leave her be, I said. It's little enough chance she gets, with father.'

Nan returned uneasy attention to the game. The bottle twirled. The group stared. Nan tried to concentrate. When the bottle stopped it faced a good-looking boy with oily black curls and pink cheeks. 'Andy Murray!' a girl whispered approvingly. His high colour and vain mouth reminded Nan of father. She did not like him. He was looking at the girls as if they were his property. They did not seem to mind. 'Her,' he said. Nan realized people were looking at her.

'Pardon?' To her shame, she went red.

'He's picked you,' a girl said. 'You have to go outside with him.'

'Why?'

There was a rattle of laughter. 'It's a surprise,' said the sly voice of Dilys. 'You're going to get a nice surprise.'

She stood up to get away from them. She walked to the door. Andy Murray came after her with a swagger. She passed Mamie Farrell coming back into the room. She had a flushed and sodden appearance. She looked like Nellie after she had spent the day poking sheets and towels with the handle of a broom in a steaming tub of grey water.

When she was in the hall she was amazed to see that it was still bright daylight. Sun poured in through the fanlight over the door. She blinked at this bright stream and had a daring thought. She would leave now. Tomorrow, she could collect the pudding dish.

She was wondering about manners, if it was all right to go without saying goodbye, when she was dragged back into the hall and all the light vanished, leaving her senses clogged with a smell of wool. She was caught up roughly against Andy Murray's wool suit. He appeared to be trying to push her into a cupboard. She struggled. He held her tightly and pitched her into the alcove against coats and boots and cardboard boxes. He began to kiss her. For a moment Nan was surprised, then she realized that she had known all along, had merely resisted. It was a strange, wet rubbery feel. Steaming breath chugged into her face. She could feel the skin of his cheek, soft yet hairy, like a pig's cheek. Her mother's kisses were like clouds. The experience filled her with panic. It was outside the range of her imagination. It was as if an insect or a small animal had got into her mouth.

She bit.

The boy reeled back. He grabbed his mouth and glared at her angrily. 'Bitch,' he said.

'Just don't do that again.' Nan threatened.

'What did I do?' he said.

'I know about that. That's French kissing. It's a mortal sin.'

'There's no harm,' he said. 'Here!' To her dismay she saw that he had not been put off. He pulled her to his body and held her roughly. In the shadowy light he could not see her unfriendly expression. She could see him quite clearly. She saw the hairs in his nose as his face descended. She saw the expression on his face, the open mouth, the greedy eyes. He looked like the boys she had seen at the table, cramming their mouths with food. She jabbed his shin with her patent shoes. He leaped back and yelped with pain. She wanted to say something terrible to him to help recover her damaged pride but he whined at her in a puzzled way and she thought: 'He doesn't understand any more than I do.'

She went back to the party. Several people looked at her with interest when she came into the room on her own. She did not rejoin the circle. She went to the window and pulled back an edge of the meat-coloured brocade curtain. She watched the remains of the day that was locked outside.

The street was almost empty. It was tea-time. 'It's the real world out there,' she thought. 'That's where I belong.' And she wondered why people in houses made different worlds for themselves. She had often heard her mother's friends agreeing among themselves that it was good to have your own front door that you could shut behind you. Whatever their lives were like behind those doors, they didn't have to face the world. Behind her she heard a scream of joy as the bottle lurched to a stop and elected another winner to the coat cupboard. She did not turn to see who it was. She preferred looking at the pink sky and thinking that it was their particular piece of sky and that in other parts of the world it was blue or navy dotted with white or the grey of an army blanket.

Some boys ran along the pavement, chasing a wheel with a stick. A scrappy little dog jumped at their elbows in a frenzy of delight. All the boys yelled with an elderly instinct for terrifying the pursued. Their screams ran behind them in a ragged stream. Watching them Nan saw that she did not belong out there any more. She had outgrown that world. A woman came out of one of the houses and clung to her gate calling for Ellen and Bess. It was Mrs Two-eggs summoning her evasive twins. Her real name was Mrs Halloran but each evening she would stand at the gate and cry to her hiding children, 'Come in to your tea and two eggs!', so that all the neighbours would know she did not give them bread and jam for their tea.

Behind her, the band struck up scratchily, 'My Blue Heaven'. The game had been abandoned. Couples were shuffling round the floor.

A girl in a flowery smock came down the street, pushing a pram. It was dirty Doll Cotter. Nan waited until she came into sight of the house. She knocked on the window and waved. The girl looked up, pushing pale, limp hair from her eyes. She saw Nan and she smiled. She looked puzzled for a moment, hearing music, seeing the peculiar red light from the room. She realized it was a party. She walked on. Nan could see her head bent over the pram, her hands gripping the handle so hard that the little white bones of her knuckles poked up like the ivory handles of knives.

'I should go after her,' Nan thought, but inertia dragged her down. It bound her like chains.

For as long as Nan could remember, Doll had always been wheeling a pram. Doll was the eldest of the nine Cotter children. Her hands seemed welded to the ancient pram, battle-scarred and held together with pieces of twine. Only the contents were seen to change; enormous pop-eyed babies, sometimes with tufts of yellow hair, sometimes black, a masculine glare or a coquettish blink of female lashes from under knitted bonnets. Once there were two infants, identical, crammed in at either end of the pram, a year-long marathon of threshing and wailing and hands like little wet crabs snapping out from the blankets, trying to pull the features from one another's faces. They probably meant no harm, but they had stolen Doll from her time. She had long forgotten, as had everyone else, that she was sixteen. To the grown-ups she was a woman, a little mother. To children who passed her in class, who knew more sums and more dances than she, she was a dunce.

This was one reason why she was never invited to parties. There was another reason. Minnie Willard and her gang lay in wait behind walls and bushes for Doll and when she passed they would chant, 'Dirty Doll, dirty Doll,' for Doll, like Minnie, was a Protestant.

Protestants were not supposed to have big families.

'I shall go after her,' Nan willed herself. As if to encourage her, a rough hand pulled at her arm. She turned, but it was only Dilys Martindale who had found herself a boy to dance with and was filled with generosity.

'Have ye not got yourself a boyo, ye poor herring,' she sympathized. 'Here, which one do ye fancy? Any one ye like. I'll fix it for ye.'

'I don't like any of them,' Nan said.

Dilys glared at her crossly. Her smiling red mouth had got smudged so that it wavered like a smear of jam. 'You're pig ignorant, that's all you are,' she said. 'An ignoramus!' She flounced off, dragging the boy who had been working up the courage to ask Nan for a dance.

Suddenly Nan wanted, more than anything else in the world, to be home having tea with Nellie and Mary. She could leave now, no one would care. Guiltily she remembered Dandy. She was still on the sofa although when Nan looked all she could see was a mangled scrap of her red dress trailing over some cushions and, waving in the air in alarm, a red party shoe.

Dandy would never forgive her. She would probably refuse to speak to her for days for leaving her in the clutches of the hairy monster. She would make it up to her. She would bring her home to tea. Dandy liked listening to Nellie's stories. Nellie would not be pleased at having an uninvited guest, but her moods were easier to cope with than Dandy's.

The record has been changed. There was an orchestra playing 'When You Are in Love'. The dancers moved slowly, their faces stricken with emotion. 'Excuse me, excuse me, please.' Nan held her two hands in front of herself and tried to make a path to the sofa. She was invisible. Each twirling couple gave way to a fresh barrier.

The childish faces bathed in red light, the strenuously raised arms, reminded her of the Infant of Prague over his red votive lamp, his face anxious because the little ball he held up was the world. She stood on the outside and the dancers moved like a merry-go-round. Excluded by the pivoting feet and dazed by the strange light and the painful music she had a vivid memory. It was the tune, the drizzling sound that accompanied it. She remembered a day when she was four or five and she had been taken into town by her father. It was raining. There was an old man in the street with a barrel organ and the same sad waltz came out of it. A shuddering monkey hopped at its side holding out a tin cup for money. Father gave her a coin to put in the cup but she had never seen a monkey in her life and she thought it was a man, burnt to a crisp. She approached it with the coin and the monkey came forward on its chain to examine her and she had to look straight into its miserable, grinning jaws. She began to scream. 'I want my Mamiandadi! I want my Mamiandadi!' Father had pulled her back roughly. 'You are not to say Mammy and Daddy,' he commanded. 'You are picking up common phrases from the children in the street. You are to address your parents as Mother and Father. Your father is here,' he added for comfort. 'It is all right. I am your father.'

But she was not comforted. She had not been seeking her father. It was her mother she wanted. It was her mother who taught her to say 'God bless Mamiandadi' when she went to bed, and it was how she saw her mother, the Mamiandadi, with her beautiful long hair and her large, handsome, reassuring body. She was in bed for weeks with the door shut and when she came downstairs again she was a different lady. She was thin and weak and from time to time she remarked dispiritedly: 'He was a boy. I almost gave your father a son.' From then she was mother.

For years Nan did not forgive her father for taking away the Mamiandadi but then she had forgotten about it completely. Now, remembering, different thoughts occurred to her. She was amazed to think that father had taken her out to the city on her own and that it had then slipped from her mind. She remembered most vividly of all the face of the monkey as her father pulled her away, shaking his tin cup desperately as she ran off, still clutching in her fist the coin.

The music came to an end. The dancers congealed into limp shapes. Nan was able to pick her way to the sofa easily enough. The dancers smelled of more mature company, scented, heated and powdered smells. She laughed when she reached the sofa. Poor Dandy, smothered under the shiny Sunday suit of some grasping lout. 'Never fear, pal, help is here,' she smiled and wasted no further time, reaching out and roughly seizing the hefty shoulder of the boy. His face came up full of amazed rage. 'What the blazes?' Nan took no notice. She spoke to the sleepy, smoky eyes of her friend. 'Your da's waiting for you at the front door.' 'My da? Oh, God!' Dandy pushed the dazed boy aside and stood up, desperately brushing the creases from her skirt. She had failed, in her alarm, to notice Nan's wink.

She bolted out the door. Nan hurried after her. 'It's all right,' she caught up with her in the hall. 'He isn't really there.' She caught her friend's hand. It was trembling. 'It was just a joke.'

'A joke?' Dandy's look was blank but her eyes blazed dangerously.

'Sorry,' Nan said. 'I didn't mean to give you a fright. It was all I could think of to rescue you from that sack of hammers.' In spite of Dandy's annoyance she started to giggle. She pushed her fingers against her lips and glanced apologetically at her friend. Dandy looked different. Her normally pale skin was tinged with pink. She looked aloof and beautiful. She had developed a way of standing so that her red dress seemed to flower from her body like petals. She could not imagine when it had happened. When she took her fingers from her mouth, her own face had grown thoughtful. It was a relief when Dandy put an arm around her and gave her a smile. She could smile too then. 'Seriously, though, what do you think of him?' Dandy grinned. '*Seriously,*' Nan laughed. 'I think he's a. . .'

She had been going to say he was a desperate-looking ibex. It was what they always said about the boys who made eyes at them on the way to school. But Dandy was watching her in an imploring way, as though their lives depended on the right answer.

'I think he's gifty,' Dandy said quickly. 'I never felt like this about anyone before. I'd do anything for him.'

Nan gaped. She knew she looked foolish but there was nothing she could do. Dandy did not seem to notice. 'He's asked me to go steady. I hope you don't mind.'

She was able to speak again. 'Why should I mind?' she shrugged.

'Well, we won't be able to go around together so much. I'll see him after school and on Saturdays.'

'Oh.'

Dandy squeezed her and gave her a kiss on the cheek. 'You're a pal. You'll cover for me, won't you? I can tell my da I'm with you?' Nan nodded. 'Well, I must get back to Max. Max. It's a nice name, don't you think?' When she turned her eyes sparkled like the glitter on Christmas cards.

She went back to the room where the hairy gorilla lay in wait, turning at the door to give Nan a sympathetic look. 'Say, you're not jealous are you, pal? You'll get your turn too, you know.' She winked. 'Say nerts.'

'Nerts.'

She closed the door behind her. Nan was left alone in the hall which was gathering shadows. She let herself out into the garden and slid over the railing that divided the two houses.

Nellie was in the kitchen in a state. 'Mary's gone,' she wailed.

'Gone where?' Nan went through to the scullery to look for her tea. She was starving. There was a dried-up fry under the grill but when she reached for her plate Nellie came up behind her and slapped her on the wrist.

'For your information your sister's gone missing,' she said. 'Your mother and father went off on a jaunt and I was supposed to be keeping an eye on the child. I slipped out for some cigarettes and the minute me back was turned didn't she scarper.'

'It's all right,' Nan said. 'Mary won't do anything foolish. I'm sure she'll be back soon. Could I have my tea please?'

'I couldn't eat a bite until that child is back in one piece,' Nellie said. Nan sighed. It was clear that Nellie meant business. No one in the kitchen would eat until Mary returned. She could hear sounds from the dining-room which told her that her parents had come back and were going ahead with their tea. Father never allowed anything to interfere with his meals.

'If anything happens to that young one, I'm for the chopper,' Nellie worried.

'What could happen?' Nan said irritably.

Nellie sat down. She held a dish cloth for comfort. 'There's things going on in the world today. I couldn't begin to tell you.'

But she did. She told Nan about a ship's steward called Francis Albert Bressington who carried face powder and a looking glass and colouring for the lips and who sometimes dressed up as a woman. He had lured a boy into a field. The boy was later found dead, his body showing signs of terrible misuse.

Nan found the story confusing. She thought Nellie had got it mixed up but she listened with interest, for it reminded her of the girls at the party, who had powdered their faces and coloured their lips and were dressed up as women.

They sat quite quietly, imprisoned in thoughts, for ten minutes or so until Mary came in and Nellie jumped up and ran at her, beating the air with her dish cloth in anger and relief. 'Well, Lady Muck, step in if you please and eat your leather eggs,' she said.

Then she saw that the little girl had been crying. She patted her on the head. 'Never mind,' she said. 'We'll fry up fresh.'

CHAPTER 8

In the afternoon Mary had been alone in the house. She was at an age when people forgot about her. She found a comic and went to sit on the edge of the sofa by the drawing-room window. The comic was old. It had a burnt smell. She could not compel the characters to mystify her. She sat looking at other children skipping in the street but they too seemed frozen like drawings in a book, their noises scraped on the air. She had no friends. It was always Nan. She did not resent the fact that Nan had been peeled away, leaving her exposed. One was meant to weep and gnash in this valley of tears. She was only shy with people she liked. She would do something if it occurred to her. Sooner or later she would get married.

She went upstairs and fetched the key out of father's boot. She let herself into the Indian room. The room breathed heavily, more alive than the people she knew and she could feel its dark glare on her back when she knelt inside the wardrobe and thrust her arm into the other boot. She clambered out quickly when she had got the key and went like a sleepwalker with her shaky hands pushed outward until she had reached the trunk and pushed aside the tiger skin and unlocked the lid.

The letters were gone.

Gone. The picture of the brown woman was gone. She began to forage through the piles of richly coloured fabric and clothing. There were more clothes underneath, embroidered, a box of beads and a pair of slippers more beautiful than feet. At the bottom of the trunk was a set of painted dishes, some knives and forks with pearl handles and a box of foreign coins. The letters were gone. She continued searching until her breath came out in small tattered pieces. She banged down the lid and locked the trunk shakily. She dropped the key into its black boot and closed the door of the wardrobe. She shut herself out of the vengeful room and ran upstairs to replace the key. Then, when she had looked about for some object that would give her comfort, she ran downstairs and let herself out of the front door, into the bright, lifeless sunlight.

She dragged her pillow-case in one hand along the pavement while her other hand scraped a stick along the painted railings of Hallinan's Mansions. She walked up garden paths, mapped with cracks and creaking with moss, and lifted the steel knockers with her stick for she could not reach them by hand. 'I am making a collection of mixed hair,' she volunteered to each, in turn, of the Lehanes, to Mrs Guilfoyle and her lodger. Mrs Lehane gave her a glass of milk and her daughter, Gladys, who was reputed to be fast, offered to do the splits. They were amused. They appeared never to have heard of hair.

'Have you got any loose hair?' she said to Mrs Guilfoyle. She had been waiting a long time. This neighbour wore a dressing-gown in the house but put on a carnation-pink worsted dress when someone came to the door. Mrs Guilfoyle chuckled. It made her bust wobble. 'You bold little business, you,' she said. 'Your mother'd have your guts for garters.' 'I am collecting loose hair, women's,' Mary began again. It threw Mrs Guilfoyle into a frenzy. She laughed until her teeth clicked. She backed off into the hall. 'Mam-zelle dee Ravelais!' she shrilled. She winked at Mary. 'I have a new woman in my top room. Oh, God, she's gas.' She made a mouth like a shovel and whispered as if it was something rude: 'Foreign.'

There was a clatter on the stairs. A thin woman in a greenish black robe fled along the steps in a sideways motion, like an animal. She had a beige, alarmed face. Her black hair was pinned up with a comb. 'You call, Mrs Guilf . . .'

Mrs Guilfoyle could not contain herself. She swelled like a paper bag that has been blown up and is about to be banged by a boy to make a noise. 'Mlle de Ravelais,' she snorted. 'This is the daughter of my friend, Mrs Cantwell. She wonders if you can help her. She is collecting the hair of loose women.'

Mary held out her pillow-case for the lodger to see. The woman's hands rose to clamp the edges of her foaming black head. 'I will have no part in this,' she said. 'It is very bad luck. I am saving my hair for my fiancé.' Mrs Guilfoyle watched her with amusement. 'Bad luck, do you say?' she jeered. 'Well, maybe I can assist after all. Hold your horses, Mary, child.' She stamped back into the house. Mary and

Mlle de Ravelais were left to regard each other with suspicion.

When Mrs Guilfoyle returned she had something like a silver coin clutched in her fist. Mary's heart beat painfully for it looked like a two-shilling piece.

It was a locket, not even pure silver, going syrupy around the edges. Mrs Guilfoyle prised the catch with a red fingernail. 'The lord and master,' she said, with the same look of a paper bag blown up to burst. 'Bad luck,' she muttered. 'I'll give you bad luck.' Her nail made contact and sliced into the opening and Mary could see a man's terrified face, tobacco-coloured, peering out beyond the scarlet scythe. The face was now fully seen – or at least as much as could be inspected behind a bristling clump of real hair. It was red hair. It clung to the man's face like a military moustache as if it had been placed there to give him courage.

Mrs Guilfoyle snatched it roughly from the photograph, removing as she did so some of the man's features, his nose and upper lip, for the hair had been glued on. She held up the sparse tuft of virility. 'My husband left me this as a memento when he went to fight the wars,' she said. 'This, and nothing more!' She dropped the lock into Mary's pillow-case. 'Use that for your bad luck, dear. See if you can make him squirm, the oul' scald. Pity I have nothing more personal.' She winked at Mlle de Ravelais who looked mortified. 'It's all right Mam-zelle dee,' she said with another terrible wink. 'I won't say another word – not another syllable. Pas devant l'enfant.'

Mary backed off down the path thinking of the man in the locket who looked so lost and faded without his nose and his rigid red lock. Paddy von Longfong. She kept looking into her bag on her way down the drive and along the road. The bright orange swatch looked bravely masculine against the woolly knot of female hair. It was only a little piece. It was hardly a transformation.

She did not go into the next house. It belonged to the McGoverns. Maisie McGovern had beautiful hair but she had lost a baby and a thing had happened to her. She had gone soft in the head. Mary had heard the grown-ups speak of this and her mind surged with a picture of Maisie McGovern's marshy skull, hair drifting from its centre like spun sugar. She began to run. Her expression was grim with unease. She paused at the next gate, remembered that it was Willards', and raced on more urgently than before. When she stopped at the next house she had to sit on the front step for a minute to compose herself. She put her head into the white bag, breathing deeply as if it was oxygen. She concentrated on the lock of Paddy von Longfong. It was the hair of a hero from the wars. It would give her courage. When she looked at it, lying sternly aloof from the other combings, it merely gave her doubt. The advertisement had specified ladies'. Secretly Mary hoped to present the certified hair specialist with a transformation. She did not know what a transformation was but believed that if she put her best into it, it must become one.

When she heard a noise behind her she pulled her head from the pillow-case and turned slowly around. There he was, towering over her, twisting a dish cloth in his hands like a hangman's rope. Hammer! Dread seeped into her. She could feel her knees shaking. 'Hammer's after you!' the children would hiss into each other's ears on the way home from school in the dusk and, although he was said to be harmless, they succeeded in frightening themselves.

His real name was Jasper Sammon and his claim to eccentricity was that he remained indoors and came out to roam the lanes at night. No one had seen him in daylight before. Mary wanted to run away but her bottom was glued to the step. She stared and stared. He was a tall man whose body seemed to have slipped so that all his weight was raddled round his hips. He had small eyes and a wide, drooping mouth. His eyes seemed to take a long time to reach those of his caller. 'Yes,' he said sadly. Mary tried to herd together words in her head. 'I am making a collection of hair,' she said boldly, in her mind. 'I wonder if you would care to contribute.' The words faded on her brain. She stumbled to her feet meaning to run but there was a look on his face, of genuine interest, and she found before she could prevent herself that she had walked toward him, opened the mouth of the pillow-case and held it up for him to see. 'Come inside,' he said hungrily. 'There is something I want to show you.'

It was late when Mary got home. Nan was still in her party dress and Nellie was in the doorway giving out, with relief, that the tea was desecrated.

In the kitchen the table had been dragged back to the window which looked out on a narrow strip of yard with a high grey wall. Nellie objected. There were no flowers, she complained, nothing to look at but the cavortions of tomcats.

Nan and Mary faced each other across the table, their faces stripped of colour by a colourless dusk. Nellie, in the scullery, rattled a pan of sizzling eggs. 'Where were you?' Nan demanded. 'We thought something had happened.' 'You stop, Nan Cantwell!' Nellie called out. 'You're not to torment the child until she's had her tea.' Mary frowned triumphantly at Nan out of one eye. She was rubbing the other eye with a fist. Nellie brought out the salt-smelling plates. Having seen to the children she arranged herself over her meal and gave herself to it with fervour.

'I saw Hammer,' Mary said. 'He took me to his bedroom. He showed me something.'

Nellie looked up, eyebrows arched, her mouth bulging with bread. 'Hammer?'

Mary broke into her egg with a fork and licked the prongs. 'Tell us what happened?' demanded Nellie. Mary said: 'Yes, I will, but you're not to interrupt. I'll tell it from the beginning.'

She told them about the mystery tittering of Mrs Guilfoyle and the lodger, the lock of Paddy von Longfong. She paused between episodes to eat her tea but they did not touch theirs. It was the second time in an evening that a meal had been ruined on her account. She led them circuitously to the front porch of Jasper Sammon, known as Hammer, and watched their faces collapse with horror as she described his appearance in the doorway, studying them with interest for they looked exactly as she must have done.

She had followed him into his dark, sad-smelling house. He brought her into the parlour and told her to sit at the table. The table was covered in mustard-coloured velvet edged in bobbles and the fireplace had no coal or sticks in it, but a most beautiful thing, a fan made of silver paper. There was a picture on the wall, of a dancing bear. She was given a drink of red lemonade that hissed out of a flagon and some wilting biscuits. 'Rubber biscuits,' Mary reminisced, 'without any raisins. I had to eat them. He sat and watched me.' He asked her would she like some more, he liked to see children enjoying themselves; and when she said no he said, 'Something else, then? I'm sure I have something nice for a little girl.' He jumped up in a lively fashion and went to rummage in a press of the sideboard. He cried out, 'I've found some crackers! Do you like crackers?' She thought of more sodden biscuits clotting up her mouth and said 'no!'

in a very firm tone; and he said 'aah!' on a different and less lively note. It was only then that she saw what he had taken from the press – a box of Christmas crackers, good as new, big ones, covered in scarlet crepe paper with gold angels glued on. Her eyes filled with tears again at the memory of this disappointment. She knew that one did not get second chances with adults. She saw the faded red lid go back on top of the crackers and the box was slid in among a collapsing wall of memorabilia. 'Well,' he said with regret, not looking at her; 'there's nothing else. We might as well go into the bedroom.'

'Sacred hour!' Nellie intoned, but Mary gave her a severe look for interrupting.

'It was the big room. The curtains were pulled. It was very dark, but shining.'

'Shining?' Nellie said. 'With no woman in the house?'

'Pictures everywhere, shining in glass.' His mother. Never smiling. On the floor a big square of roses linked, shimmering out of a cold, hard lake of custard.

'The floor?' Nellie said. 'Custard?'

'It wasn't a carpet,' Mary said. 'He said he can't breathe if there's dust. It was like this' – she ran her palm over the oilcloth – 'but hard.'

'Gold Seal Congoleum Squares!' Nellie pronounced with triumph. 'That's very new! I don't think that man's lost his marbles. Cleans in a moment with a damp mop.' Nellie shook her head and gazed out the window, lost in admiration of this labour-saving device, but Nan's grey eyes bore sharply into her sister. 'What happened?' she persisted.

'He showed me his . . .' Mary pursed her lips. She dropped her head and studied the crumbs of bread on her plate.

'That's what you get for talking to strange men,' Nan said.

'He didn't look strange,' Mary protested. Her lower lip trembled. 'He looked ordinary.'

'He showed you what?' Nellie was alert again.

'I can't tell you,' Mary said. 'It's a secret. He made me promise not to tell.'

In the bewildered silence that followed they listened to the distinguished patter of noise that drifted from the dining-room, diminished by distance, kites in the wind. Father's proud drone over mother's placating murmur, the chink of cups, the drizzling insistence of the record machine. 'Drink to me only with thine eyes'.

'Children aren't supposed to keep secrets from grown-ups,' Nellie sulked.

Mary frowned under the burden. 'This is different. This is a secret with a grown-up.'

Nellie captured crumbs under her broad thumb. 'I don't like it,' she said. 'I don't like the cut of his capers.'

Nan remembered this long afterward as the beginning of the changes. It was the first time she had heard a grown-up say anything uncomplimentary about Hammer. They had always been kind about him for he wore a hat on his nightly ramblings and lifted it to any ladies who might be abroad with their husbands. It was the first time she had heard an adult criticize another adult in her hearing. Up to that, it seemed, all the grown-ups were united in their hunt for deceits, defects and signs of ingratitude in children.

Mary still had her lips pursed as if she feared that Nellie might drag the secret from her mouth by physical force and Nellie stared hard into the little girl's face as if studying this possibility. Her features were thickened with thought. 'Well,' she established at length. 'I'll be clearing above so.' When she had gone Nan said, 'You can tell me. I'm not a grown-up.' 'You've got diddies,' Mary argued.

Nellie salvaged a jam roll from the dining-room, scarcely touched, still dappled with icing sugar. Fresh tea was made. While Nan filled the kettle in the scullery, the maid deftly scooped the used dishes from the kitchen table on to the tray. They rose in greasy, sliding piles but none of them fell. The cake was set in the clearing and Mary wet a finger and dabbed it in the sugar covering. Nellie took the tray to the scullery. She heard the dishes being tumbled into the sink in a puddly clash. She had a moment of panic thinking of her weeks of work gone to waste, her collection lost. She heaved a wet choking sigh. Then Nan was back with the tea and Nellie, returned, was sawing thick circles from the cake, a Woodbine poking from her mouth.

Nellie did not bite into her circle of cake the way Nan and Mary did. She unravelled it until it was a long ribbon, wet with jam, and fed this into the foggy cavern of her mouth. It made her look like a human fire-eater. She retained the smoke and the cake behind her teeth while she admitted a gulp of tea. All the time she had a peculiar expression on her face as if she was having difficulty with the contents of her mouth but Nan and Mary took no notice because they were used to her and they knew that this was how she looked when she had something interesting to say. She swallowed more tea and probed at her tongue with her teeth. 'I had a cousint went like that,' she said. She tapped the side of her forehead several times to indicate the way her cousin had gone. 'His mother tried to get him into the harmless lunatics' ward of Ennis County Home but there was no room. The last bed was occupied by a greyhound. They put him in the consumptives' ward. A very dirty ward. His mother took him home again.' She unravelled another slice of cake and dangled it over her mouth, lowering it like a rope into a well. She drew in smoke and tea. The children's eyes loomed over coils of sponge cake. 'The misfortunate creature,' Nellie mourned, 'drank a cup of milk.'

'Your cousin?'

'No, no. The mother. There was a cockroach in the milk and she swallied it down. They had the doctor out but there was nothing he could do. There is only one way to kill a cockroach and that is to smother it. The mother did not care about herself. That is not the way of mothers. "I will pray only," she said, "that my son will not be left alone." Well, God is good.'

'What happened?' Mary's voice was gruff with apprehension.

'Didn't me cousint take a pilla to her in the middle of the night and smother her. After that the doctor was able to get him into the criminal lunatic ward, which was the best of all, so his mother's last wish was granted.'

Nellie loved the newspapers. She could not read but would thrust father's paper at Nan and urge: 'Read us out the news, will you?' She liked to listen while she kneaded dough or did the washing. By news she did not mean the happenings in Dail Eireann or on the stock exchange. She had a preference for items like the story of the Cuban actress, Señorita Ofelia Rivas, whose little dog fell into the sea when the liner *Esperanza*, on which they were passengers, went on the rocks. The actress leaped overboard to save her pet but was attacked by a huge shark and devoured in spite of a frantic struggle. Fishermen who later killed the shark found the jewels and turban of Señorita Rivas in its stomach.

The stories which Nellie told in return mostly concerned her family. She had an endless stock of relations who had lost their marbles. They all belonged in the past. Her favourite stories concerned the Union where poor and homeless people went to live. Some of Nellie's family languished there and dined off diseased horsemeat. The healthy cattle that were driven live into the institution by day, to provide fresh meat for the deprived, were smuggled out at night and sold for the profit of the managers. Putrified horsemeat featured on the plates of the inmates. Nellie always told them this when they complained about the fatty bits on their meat. She never talked about her children. When she went to work she had to lock them into the room where they lived. Susan, who was seven, looked after them. Nan sometimes envied them the convenience of eating in the room where they slept, the freedom of living without a man.

Nellie smoked her last cigarette, her lupin-pink mouth drooping in her face, her bushy eyebrows knitted in thought. She dislodged the last brown dregs of tea from the pot and rinsed her teeth with them, punishing the end of her cigarette into a mash of wet brown shreds in her saucer. She gathered the end of the jam roll into its paper doyley and put it in her handbag. She glared at the children. 'Beggin' your pardons, but if youse have nothing better to do I'll leave yis with the shambles.' She left then, with an air of offence and banged the door. The children did not move or show any change of expression.

Later, when they were washing the dishes, mother looked in. 'What are you doing?' She peered uneasily into the basin of yellowing dish water in the sink, the dull gleam of cutlery from the bottom. 'Oh, well,' she said. 'Someone's got to do it.' She did not care for housework. She liked to read and smoke and gossip with the neighbours. She did some absent-minded sewing. Everyone understood this. Even father rarely held her responsible for domestic matters. 'Tell me what you did today?' she said. She reached into the pocket of her dress and pulled out her cigarettes and matches. She lit a cigarette and leaned against the window, watching her children with a remote smile. 'I went to a party,' Nan said. 'A boy kissed me.' 'Did you like that?' mother said. 'No.' 'You will do a lot of things you don't like when you are a grown-up,' mother reminded her. Mary began to recite the tale of her afternoon of hair raising. Mother showed an interest in Mrs Guilfoyle's lodger but after that she seemed to lose curiosity. She pulled back the piece of net that covered the scullery window and was gazing out at a fuchsia bush in the back yard that was caught in the glare of the bulb that hung from the ceiling.

'Look!' she said. 'Fairy lanterns.'

Mary had reached the end of her tale and she was crying. 'It's all gone,' she grieved.

'What's gone, chicken?' mother said and before Mary had time to answer she added, 'Let's go upstairs. I think there might be some sweets.' She left the scullery swiftly to evade its claims. Nan and Mary flashed each other a look of success.

Their parents' room was a comfortable place with a jumble of furniture and a big bed under a writhing pink eiderdown. There were smells of perfume and cigarette smoke. A dressing table blocked the window, its surface covered with books and scented bottles. Beside this was a chair covered in red velvet. It was where mother spent most of her evenings, reading murder mysteries or the lives of the saints. The children settled themselves on the end of the bed. Mother took off her shoes and curled up in the velvet chair. She pulled some pins from her hair and her heavy plaits collapsed on her shoulders. 'What will we do?' she said. The children sighed happily. On the rare occasions when they were alone with her they wondered why they did not spend more time with their mother. She was kind. Without father, she was full of fun. For a moment Nan wondered wildly if they might all go to the pictures like the Jews but she allowed the thought to die. Father would not like it. She had never seen her mother go against her father's wishes.

Mary said, 'I'd like to have a little bit of your hair.' 'That's very old-fashioned,' mother said. 'We used to do that when we were small.'

She rummaged in an untidy drawer of the dressing table for her scissors. 'No!' Mary said. 'You mustn't cut it. That's not allowed. It's combings.' 'I see,' mother said. She never questioned anything. She turned her chair to the mirror and began rapidly to remove the pins from her hair, dropping them into a little china dish. She pulled at the shining braids. The children helped her, each unravelling a plait, tense with the task. She shook her head. Heavy, waving hair framed her face and shoulders. She looked quite different, she was a queen. The children felt ordinary, excluded. They clawed the ends of her hair to relax the curls. Mother seized a brush and pulled it roughly through her hair. She shook her head forward and dragged the brush from the nape of her neck until it tumbled forward and covered her face. She brushed for an endless minute. She had no face. Her hair flew out in a shimmering spray. She put the brush back on her dressing table and sat with her head down. Her hair flowed into her lap. She sat like this until Mary could stand it no longer and had to search for her, gathering the loops of hair in both hands, clutching and scooping until she had assembled it in a piece and held it up like the severed head of John the Baptist. She sought her mother's face. It was smiling. 'Look!' she said with interest. She picked up the brush and held it out to them. Not a single hair adhered to its bristles. 'I haven't got hair at all. It must be steel wool.'

She reached into a drawer and pulled out a tortoiseshell comb. She wound her hair as one might twist a wet towel to wring out the water and then rolled it into a cone. She jabbed the comb at it. It billowed and settled miraculously. She addressed her reflection critically. 'Your father and I,' she said, 'met at a post box. We were posting letters to other people who were forgotten in that instant. We fell head-over-heels in love. It was the hand of destiny. All things are destined.' Nan had heard the story before. As always she saw, not the meeting of the fated lovers but the two letters dropping into the box, their envelopes blind, as in a dream. It was these that held her curiosity for although father was a mere soldier who might have written and forgotten many letters her mother was, at the time of the meeting, a postulant in a convent.

For a moment mother appeared absent-minded, seeming to lose track of her thoughts, then she pulled open another drawer in which there were books and gloves and a twisted brown paper bag. She chose the bag and shook it experimentally. There was a whisper of different paper, weighted. Mary's face became sharp. Mother opened the bag. Inside were three buttered brazils wrapped in cellophane. She held the bag out to the children and they each took one. 'Three sweets for four of us, thank God there are no more of us,' mother said. 'There's only three of us!' Mary's voice clattered around the golden hump of butterscotch which concealed a whole brazil nut, but mother appeared not to hear. She fidgeted with the wrapper on her own sweet but did not open it.

The children stood awkwardly on either side of her chair, fingering the carved wooden top. Mother picked up a book from the dressing table. She opened it where it had been marked with a piece of ribbon and began to read. She pulled at the paper twist on the sweet with her teeth to open it and it slipped into her mouth where it disappeared completely. Her teeth did not knock against it. It did not bulge in her cheek. It was a skill that adults had. ''Night, mother,' Mary said loudly and with pleading. Nan went to the window and stood with her fingers on the sill looking out at the cool coppery evening. The cries of children rang out from the lane in the back. She wanted to feel the air but it did not occur to her to open a window. No one ever opened a window except Nellie, to bang a teapot against the wall and knock the leaves into the metal strainer in the gutter. There was a feeling of wanting in the pit of her stomach. She could feel its smoky ascent inside her, like the Holy Ghost when she had been confirmed. She became impatient with this yearning. She struck it aside and allowed her head to fill with the imagined clamour of the Four Horsemen, the sound of cannons and their power to rouse to the point of fainting. She turned from the window and she went back to Mary and seized her arm. ''Night, mother,' she said carelessly, dragging the smaller child from the room. Mary's body had grown heavy with the burden of her longing. As usual, they had remembered too late why they did not spend more time with their mother. Mother was not very much in touch with children. She appeared not to know where they had come from and it did not occur to her that there was anything she ought to do about them. She looked pleased when she saw them, but surprised. And after they had been around her for a time she forgot all about them as if, in the force of her own glow, they became dimmer and dimmer and then faded away completely.

When she was in bed Nan said her prayers. She thought that prayers had the quality of bread. The Lord's prayer was a slice of brown bread without butter; the Hail Mary, a half round of sliced pan, thinly buttered. An Act of Contrition had currants. The little prayers, known as aspirations, which were uttered for the granting of a wish or to buy time off the term which awaited one in purgatory, were like pieces of bread thrown out for the birds. She was not terribly fond of bread. 'Lord, I love you, save a soul,' she muttered unfeelingly. This was a prescription taught her by the nuns for the release of holy souls in purgatory. Purgatory was a Godless box where souls were sterilized for entry into heaven. She imagined that it looked like the sullen little back room where she slept with Mary. Although cramped, it had become a depository for family photographs and useless lumps of furniture. The room gathered the sun during the day and compressed it, by evening, into a crouching heat. Heat peeled off the surfaces like old paint. Smells of antiquity curled up into the air.

Around the walls, the ancestors, faded beige, clamoured behind dusty glass, grimly grouped for holidays or weddings or thrusting at the camera the starched parcels of newborn Cantwells. Nellie said it was a queer thing to have in the children's bedroom, this rogues' gallery. Nan liked them. They were her history. Their stories were locked in behind their tortured faces; Great-gran Cantwell who had twelve children and refused to speak ever again after the birth of her youngest; cousin Vesty Harmon who went to The Bad; baby Tess who died of a congested brain at two years and five months. She opened her eyes, as she always did, to say goodnight to them. She was distracted by the sight of Mary bending over the open wardrobe looking for her nightie, her white bottom stuck in the air like a peeled potato. 'Come to bed,' Nan said. Mary found her nightie and scrambled into it. She climbed over Nan to get to her side of the bed, at the wall. She did not lie down but sat on top of the covers hugging her knees.

'Nan?' she said.

'Go to sleep.'

'I wish I was grown-up. Grown-ups can do anything they like. They never have to tell lies. If they die, they go straight to heaven.'

'Don't talk rot,' Nan said, although she knew it was the truth.

Mary crept under the covers and turned her face to the wall. She felt she was going to cry again. It seemed that everyone was growing up except her. Soon even Nan would be grown up. She would be the only one who was small and had nothing. She remembered then that she had something. She had a secret.

'Come in,' Jasper Sammon had said. 'I want to show you something.' He led her into his bedroom. His sandals slid on the Gold Seal Congoleum roses. 'You must promise me,' he had insisted, 'never to tell a living soul.' He led her by the hand to his dressing table and sat her on a stool covered in green brocade. He watched her solemnly while he unhooked from a carved edge of the mirror a small leather bag looped with string. He had widened its mouth with his thumb and forefinger and held it up to where she could see. At first she could identify nothing and had to screw up her eyes. Then she understood. She covered her mouth with the fingers of both hands and listened to the drumming of her heart, under her dress. She had never felt so significant. 'It's not very much,' he said; 'but I've been collecting it since I was thirty. It's all there now.'

It was his hair, every bit of it. The top of his head gleamed like a dish. He looked sad. She could understand why. All his life's hair and it was just a little bit at the bottom of the bag. She still held the pillow-case containing her own collection.

'Here,' she had said. 'You can have this.' He reached in and pulled out the hair in little pieces, as if it was pinches of snuff. He poked it into the smaller bag. When it was all gone he hung it back on the dressing table. Neither of them said anything. Already tears had begun to prick at her eyes for the loss of her own harvest. She climbed down off the stool and walked to the door. He followed her. He stayed in the doorway, watching her as she walked off dragging her empty white bag.

CHAPTER 9

Dandy called for Nan every Saturday at one o'clock. They spent half an hour walking to a cinema in the city and were in time to join the orderly front end of the queue. They whispered secrets and toppled with laughter. Boys gaped at them and were gratified when they bothered to insult them. In the picture house, invisible youths passed sweets to them over their shoulders.

It was after two. Dandy had not come. 'I'll go on my own,' Nan swore. She put on her white linen dress and she sat on the end of her bed. 'When she comes, I shall be gone.' She saw a flash of red hair in the street below and she ran to the window but it was a woman in a polka dot dress who had a little shaved dog on a lead.

'Nan?' Mary had come into the room and was scraping paint from the door with a fingernail. Her voice made no more impression on her sister's white linen back than a feather on snow. 'I have twopence.' She had saved it from her tram fare. She opened and closed her hand several times on the coppery coins. Nan might take her to the matinée if Dandy did not come. Nan always said she would take her next year when she was older, but when a year had passed and she asked again Nan would tease: 'I said *next* year.'

'Nan?' she begged. She wanted to be out of the house. Earlier she had gone up to mother's room for a book. Father was there. He had his head in his hands. He was crying.

Nan turned on her crossly. 'You're not to pester me.'

She dawdled only a little longer and then she went out to the park to look for teeth. She had come across an interesting advertisement in the newspaper from Orgel and Company of Nassau Street. *Old false teeth wanted. Bring or send registered post.* Nellie had once been in service to a family of the gentry that gave garden parties in the summer where little hard biscuits were served with ice-cream. Later, she said, she would have to search the bushes for false teeth which had got lodged in the macaroons and been taken out and concealed.

Afterwards Nan went out. She meant to go to the matinée alone but, without Dandy to amuse her, her sense of purpose was poor. Halfway along Clanbrassil Street she found herself once more spellbound by the names of the shops. Aronovitch, grocer; Baigel, wine merchant; Leopold, poulterer. It wasn't just the strange food in the windows, the tins of cabbage preserved in salt, big green pickles and trays of greyish paste made from liver or herring. The foreign-sounding names were connected with violence. The nuns had told the children that Jesus came on earth to redeem the Jews but they killed Him. They crucified Jesus and this put a mark on them and set them apart. People seeing this mark would say 'pass on, pass on', and Jews had to wander the face of the earth, forever homeless. Nan first heard this when she was six and she looked for the mark on Davey Crabitz, a friend of her father from the garment trade. He had taken her on his knee and it gave her a vantage point from which to explore. She removed his hat and searched all over the beige hill of his head until he inquired, very politely, if he could help. She said, in a whisper – so that father would not hear – that the nuns had told her the Jews murdered Jesus.

'Who murdered Jesus?' he whispered solemnly.

'Pontius Pilate condemned Christ to death at the desire of the Jews,' she recited.

'Ach! Governments!' Mr Crabitz said and he ruffled her hair and gave her threepence.

On Saturdays the street was thronged with people buying delicacies. In spite of their mark and the fact that they were poor, the Jewish people seemed to live well. They were like people in a film, excited by the possibilities of plot. They argued over the price and quality of what was in the shops as if it really mattered what went on the table in front of men and children. They used their large hips, decorated with lace and scraps of dark silk, to steer a course through the noisy, shabby, exciting street, smelling achingly of bread and vinegar and little cakes.

She kept looking out for Gickla and Becca and Mrs Schweitzer. When she did not see them she told herself that she was concerned and she ran through the side streets until she reached the house with the yellow door and boldly raised and dropped the brass letter flap. As soon as she had done it she felt embarrassed and wondered what she would say when the door was opened. Nothing happened. She felt relief, disappointment. After a time she used the knocker again. There was no reply. She stood for a time looking down at her dress which rattled in the hot summer breeze like a flag against the grey pavement and she knew then that she had imagined the magical family of Jews, had made them up. Nothing wonderful really existed. Betty had come from some other source.

The door was opened by Gickla. She wore a blue silk dress and a blue ribbon dangled from her black curls like a prize rosette. 'I'm sorry you had to wait,' she said. 'I was putting on my new dress.'

'Oh, sorry! You're going out!' Nan said awkwardly.

'No, no. I have put on my dress because it is new. Come and see. We have many things that are new.'

Nan was shown a wireless set, a fur boa for mama, a coloured rug. She did not know what to say. Poor people did not buy such luxuries. 'Ivor has got himself a proper job.' Gickla's boast answered the question that was in her head. 'He no longer wheels his cart. He is working for a rich and kind lady.' Nan tried to picture Shyster employed in the house of a rich lady. She saw his ragged clothes, his matted beard. She could not imagine him as a butler or a secretary. A gardener, perhaps. 'What does he do?' 'Oh, I do not know,' Gickla said indifferently. 'His work is secret and confidential. That is all he will say. Don't you think he is clever to have got such an important job?'

'Yes,' Nan said doubtfully.

They went into the kitchen and sat at the table under the radiant montage of picture stars. Gickla was looking at her curiously. 'Why did you come? Have you brought back my scarf? You should not have bothered with that old thing.' She spoke of the scarf with contempt.

'I . . .' Nan was dazed by the photographs. They seemed more alive than she was. 'I forgot your scarf. I was on my way into town. I felt a bit queer. It's so hot. I was going to ask for a drink of water.' The truth was, she did feel strange. It wasn't just the movie stars. She felt weak and achy. Her throat was dry. She felt sticky inside her clothes.

'You look a bit green.' Gickla stared at her.

'I'll just get a glass of water.' She stood up uncomfortably and went to the sink. Her body was throbbing. She felt horrible. She ran the tap and splashed her face with cold water. She drank from her cupped hands.

'Aah!' Gickla exclaimed in dismay. 'Your good dress!'

'My dress?' Nan looked stupidly down at her pristine skirt, letting water fall between her fingers.

'You have a stain. Your monthly flow.'

'What are you talking about?' Nan jiggled against the pain.

'Aah!' It was an outburst at Nan's slow-wittedness. The dark girl prised herself up from the table with a knowing, woman's look. She reached for the back of Nan's skirt and pulled it up where Nan was forced to look on it, the blotch of crimson with its dark outer frill. 'Your period. It has come through.'

She could feel her face scorching crimson. She gazed at the mark until it wobbled in her tears.

'Your period!'

Nan nodded. A tear fell.

'Have you not had your periods before this?'

She shook her head.

'Do you know what I am talking about?'

Nan hesitated. She had heard Nellie mention the curse and when she asked Dandy about it she said yes, she had the curse, worse blasted luck. She never heard anyone talk about it further or call it by any other name and she did not know why but she thought it was something that was not done, like talking through the lavatory door.

Voices bobbed up at the front of the house and there was the crunch of a key. 'Oh,' Nan moaned in alarm. 'It's mama and Becca,' Gickla proudly announced. Nan hurried from the sink and sat rigidly in her chair. 'You must not tell,' she begged. Gickla blinked and waited for the others with the bloated smile of a goddess. The mother and daughter smiled when they entered. They had no nerves. Nan was kissed four times on her cheeks. She wondered how she would get away. Hopefully she turned to Gickla and the lovely girl took her cue. 'Nan has become a woman,' she announced. Becca and her mother beamed. 'See!' She pulled Nan from the chair and turned her around. 'Her first time!' Nan burned with embarrassment but the women exclaimed with wonder as if she was an acrobat in a circus. Mrs Schweitzer hugged her and pinched her cheeks. 'A *woman*!' she pronounced it as something wonderful. 'We must celebrate. Becca, get the sweet wine.'

Becca went to the dining-room and Mrs Schweitzer fetched four long-stemmed glasses and a jar of little biscuits. Gickla whispered to her mama. She took Nan's arm and led her from the room. She fetched, mysteriously, a sewing shears and, more puzzling, introduced Nan to the linen press. From the bottom she removed a sheet, bleached and worn thin. 'It is old,' she instructed. 'No longer in use.' She cut a portion the size of a headscarf and folded in lengthways. 'Go to my bedroom and settle yourself. Borrow a skirt from my wardrobe and wear it over your dress.'

Nan went to a tiny room where the girls shared a bed as she did with Mary. The curtains and the cover of the bed were poor but the dressing table was piled with dolls and when she opened the wardrobe it surged with womanly fabrics. She arranged the piece of sheet as best she could and selected the most ordinary skirt. From the kitchen she could hear cry after cry of mirth like a storm of seagulls that had frightened her when she was small.

They greeted her return with looks of smothered amusement. They held up glasses in which was a liquid of a lovely colour, pale transparent yellow, like a winter sunrise. Wine. No one at home drank wine. There was sherry and whiskey for occasions but meals were haphazard affairs. 'To your womanhood,' the Jews teased. She sat down and peered into the glass that had been filled for her. At school the nuns warned of the evils of drink and when she was confirmed she had made a promise to God to forswear drink for the rest of her life. She watched the fleshy fingers of her hostesses snaked about the crystal stems, their mocking mouths that lapped the rims of their glasses, and the calm, greedy pleasure in their half-closed eyes. She had made that promise when she was a child. Now she was a woman. She wrapped both hands around the glass and raised it to her lips. The sharp sweetness flooded her mouth and she held it there and closed her eyes. She began to feel better. 'Do you like it?' their rich voices pealed with celebration. She nodded. She drank the wine in sips. The film stars on the wall bowed and winked knowingly. Her locked limbs thawed. For a moment she felt that she was a part of something. Someone else came into the room. The women parted their lips and showed their gleaming teeth in welcome and Nan did the same. It was a man. He was young and slight with anxious brown eyes and a long nose. A small, nervous mouth burrowed into a beard. He wore a brown suit of good quality, slightly too big, and a tie of green silk. He looked like a woodland creature peering from a tree.

'Ivor!' they laughed, greeting him with beckoning arms.

'Shyster!' Nan breathed, she was astonished. Gone was the ragged and frightening ruffian, reputed to lure small children and carry them away beneath his rags. His hair was cut and shining, his beard trimmed. The face that emerged was shy and kind and his body was light and graceful. His fingernails were clipped and polished and the hands that had picked so delicately through rags now showed as beautiful hands, sensitive hands. The cloth of his suit was soft and in his alarmed gaze that covered the scene of idle celebration there was also something flexible, a query mixed with the criticism. Made bold by the wine Nan gazed at him as long as she wanted to. She thought he looked nicer than any man she had ever seen.

'Wine?' Shyster pointed an elegant finger, so different to the plump fingers of the women.

'It is a celebration,' his mother dismissed. 'Nan has achieved her womanhood.'

He nodded solemnly. She did not feel ashamed.

When she got home mother was doing something in the scullery. The sight caught her by surprise. Mother stood well back and frowned as water splashed from the tap into a saucepan. There was a plate of fried liver beside the stove. She put this over the saucepan with a lid on top and stood it on the cooker over a low flame. All the while she had the apprehensive look of one handling explosives.

'Hello.'

She turned around and smiled, relieved to see Nan. She wiped her hands on her apron. 'Your father did not come home,' she explained. 'He might be hungry when he gets in.'

She nodded. 'Yes, mother.'

'Your father has provided this home and everything in it,' mother chided automatically.

Nan made tea and put butter and jam on bread. She brought this to the kitchen table. Mother hovered. She brought a cup for herself and held it out like a begging bowl for Nan to fill with tea. 'He's a good man.' She sat down, clutching the cup with both hands. 'He loves us. He has . . . worries.'

They watched each other until Nan could no longer stand the look of hope in her mother's eyes. 'Did you have a nice time at the sales?' she said. 'Did you buy anything?'

'I will tell you a secret,' mother said cunningly. 'I think you are old enough for me to confide in you.' Nan sat up very straight and offered her full attention. 'It is the factory. There are problems.' She was disappointed. The dull business world that filled her father's days was not one she associated with secrets. All the same she was flattered to have her mother's confidence.

'The Cantwell corset no longer reigns supreme. It is losing its place in the market to competitors.'

Mother made the admission with great difficulty as if it was weighted with personal guilt. Nan could not respond. It was not a secret. It was scarcely even news. She had known for some time that father's design 'for the inhibition of female obesity' had been overtaken by newer, more alluring styles. Even Nellie in a brazen fit of treachery, confessed that she no longer tormented herself with the Cantwell but had been converted to the W. B. Rubber Reduso which Kellets were selling at 39/11 as opposed to two guineas for the Cantwell in Pims. 'Healthy and hygienic to wear in a lovely shade of peach pink!' Nellie recited the advertisement provocatively. It was 1925. Women were seeking less restrictive underwear. Father, unable to tolerate the notion of free females, continued to manufacture a heavy, unpopular piece of corsetry.

Nan reached for her mother's hand. 'It will be all right,' she lied. 'Fashions never last.'

'It will be all right, won't it, darling?' mother pleaded.

Nan said. 'Where's Mary?'

'She went up to bed with a book. Poor baby. She came in to her tea looking very put out. She said there were no teeth in the park. She found a hedgehog and put it in the coal shed. Teeth. Perhaps she was looking for the tooth fairy. I suppose I ought to have given her a shilling.' A shilling. 'I'll go up and keep her company,' Nan said. She came around the table to kiss her mother. Mother sniffed. 'I smell wine. Have you been drinking wine?'

'Just a sip. It was a celebration.'

Mother said, 'How nice! What did you celebrate?'

Nan could not help smiling. She had almost forgotten. 'My womanhood!'

Her mother laughed. She looked pretty. 'It's so simple? A sip of wine turns you into a woman?'

'No,' Nan smiled. 'I got my first period today.'

'Period?' Her mother looked amazed. 'Who are these people?'

'They're Jews.'

'Jews?'

'Shyster's mother and sisters.'

Her mother leaned forward urgently. Her face was peaked with distaste. 'You are not to mix with these people,' she instructed. 'These are not nice people. Ordinary women do not speak of such things.'

She could feel herself freezing again, her limbs hinged to rusting metal. 'But, mother . . .'

'If your father had come in! If your father should hear you speak of such things!'

On her way to bed she stopped and ran back to the kitchen.

'Mother?'

'Yes, Nan.' Her mother's face was closed. She had yet to forgive her.

'Do we have any old linen that's not in use? You know.'

Her mother's eyebrows arched and her eyes dipped to examine the texture of the oilcloth on the table. 'All our old linen is donated to the Old Men's Asylum,' she said.

'Mother?'

'Yes.'

'Goodnight, mother.' She came over and she got her kiss but it was on the bone of her jaw and not on her lips.

CHAPTER 10

The following day during lunch father told the family he had an announcement to make. They were glad of the diversion. Nellie was off because it was Sunday and mother had cooked a sheep's head on father's instructions. She boiled it up with an onion and brought it to the table in a serving dish. Bubbles came from the eye sockets and tufts of grey flesh bobbed on the disembodied skull. There was a sirloin of beef to follow but everyone's appetite had been affected.

He told them he had changed his name. Nan could not remember what his name was. She never heard him called anything except father. 'Cecil!' mother protested in fright. Cecil. She could understand.

He had progressed to the syrup pudding. His head was sideways, like Bertie with a bone. He was concentrating. Every few seconds he dabbed at his mouth with a napkin. 'I have decided upon Webster,' he said when his mouth was clear. 'It is a respectable name.'

'*Web*ster!' Their confusion gave the name a special emphasis, as if it had to do with ducks' feet or the homes of spiders. It was not the name of a saint.

He laid down his spoon and placed his hands on the table. 'Cecil Webster.'

She saw it then, the power in those haughty hands. He had taken away their name. It was as if their lives were empty frames of his making within which he had chalked the features. He had taken a duster and wiped them clean. She glanced at her mother and saw, as she expected, a face scrubbed of all expression. Only her eyebrows rose with shock. 'Mother,' she demanded. 'He's trying to change our name.' 'Our name. Yes.' Mother made an effort to sit to attention. There was a look of mild reproach on her face. She hated being made to face things.

Her heart began to beat painfully. Nan Cantwell, Hallinan's Mansions. Nan Cantwell, Hallinan's Mansions. 'What about school?' she said cautiously. 'All the people we know.'

'Your mother will give you a note for the nuns,' he said. 'The matter scarcely concerns you. Children are not entitled to a full address. You will be known, as usual, by your Christian name.' 'Mary!' She tried to involve her sister but Mary was using her spoon to make a syrupy hill in her dish. She was smiling. Nan had to tackle father alone. 'You can't do it,' she said. 'It's our name. It's *ours*!' 'It is already done,' he said. 'Our name has been changed by deed poll.' She had never seen him so calm. 'It was necessary to do it. That is all you need to know. Names do not matter to women. They are only of interest to people in the world. Women do not have a name until they marry.'

She could not argue with him. He was too powerful. He was a storm, blowing them this way and that, shaking loose their hold on ordinary things. He was the one who had ordered their mundane existence, refusing to send the girls to a good school because only boys required an education. It was not that Nan wanted ordinary things. She wanted the extraordinary but when it happened she had still to be enough herself to experience it.

'Why?' she begged.

There was an odd wistful look on father's face as if he was actually considering the question and then he remembered it was a child, giving cheek. 'Because I have said it,' he barked.

The edges of her jaws were clutched by numbness. It was a warning of tears. She folded her napkin carefully and put it on the table. 'The one meal of the week we eat together and she has to cause a barnie,' she heard father's voice complain. She kept her head down when she pushed back her chair and ran out into the street. She felt as if she had been slapped. It was the unfairness that stung. 'Women do not have a name until they marry!' Mother was married and he was taking away her name. Why couldn't they leave him? Why couldn't they find a place to live on their own in peace? Nellie managed. She knew the answer. Mother liked being married. She liked not having to work or to worry about money. Although she was afraid of father, she was proud of him. He gave her stature with the neighbours. There were details of marriage that disturbed her but she liked being Mrs Cantwell. 'Oh, mother,' Nan thought. 'How will you face your neighbours without your name?' It was her only vanity.

Running along the warm pavement, her head ducked. Nan made

up her mind that she would never go back. 'I shall run away. I shall make my own way in the world.' She had a vague, exciting picture of boats and restaurants, a group of working girls with sweaters, one of them with her face. There intruded on this an image of mother peering uneasily into a saucepan while water gushed menacingly from the tap. She would have turned there and then and raced back to her had it not been for another disturbance to her thoughts.

'Hello.'

She looked up. 'Dandy!'

'Walk?' Dandy's hair fell across her face and she slouched in an indifferent fashion.

Nan had not intended to talk to her ever again but she had to talk to someone and mother had said she must not see the Jews. Dandy knew about life. She would know if it was normal for the curse to go on for a second day. She would have something to say about fathers who gave and took names as they pleased. 'Where will we go?' she said.

Dandy thought. 'We could go to the morgue.'

They walked in silence. Once Dandy stopped to say, 'I saw you from the window. I ran after you.'

The morgue was half a mile from Hallinan's Mansions. It was attached to a nursing home run by nuns. The dead had been old. They had exhausted their contributory role. Few people came to mourn them. An occasional clump of relatives studied one from a distance.

A nun looked up when the children came in, a dark figure in a corner on a hard chair supplying the creak and rustle of continuous prayer. They kept their heads lowered and joined their hands piously and she let them pass. They walked between the high narrow beds of the dead and looked into their faces. The corpses were not like ordinary old people. They had been laid out in the blue and brown habits of the Legion of Mary or the Order of St Francis to coax them into spiritual company. All the cunning and anger was gone from their faces. They were like shrivelled babies, paper-thin, perplexed. One could tell at a glance that their souls, black or white, had taken flight.

'My da took a strap to me,' Dandy mumbled at the polite remains of an old gentleman.

'What?'

'You heard. He leathered me.' For the first time that day Nan looked straight at her. Dandy had a black eye like a scrapping boy and the side of her jaw was the colour of an orchid.

'Oh, Lord, Dandy, why?'

'I came home late. I was out on a date.'

'You can't let him treat you like that,' she whispered angrily. 'Just because he's your father he can't do what he wants.' She stopped, remembering. Fathers. Dandy was crying. Tears poured over her blackened face, she snuffled over the old man. Nan put out a hand. 'Dandy – my father's awful too. He's done something terrible. He's changed our name.'

'Your name?' Dandy's swimming eyes widened with interest.

'He's done it by deed poll. I'm not Nan Cantwell any more. He's change our name to Webster.' She found she was crying too. The nun glared at them with sharp suspicion seeing the old man so richly mourned.

'Let's get out of here,' Dandy sniffed and she steered Nan into the bright sunlight.

They went to the park. They pulled hawthorn from the hedges and adorned their hair with sprigs. 'Let's run away,' Nan begged.

Dandy made a face. 'We're too young.'

'Nobody cares about that. We could get jobs in shops or factories. We could stay in boarding houses.' It was like a light inside her, the thought of adventure. Once again her head swam as when she had tasted wine. 'If we ate very little food we could save some money. We could send for Mary and our mothers.'

'We could get fellas to take us out to high tea.'

'Well. Yes.'

Dandy laughed, a careless explosion that creased her damaged face. 'You eejit! You baby! You wouldn't last a day.'

'I'm not a baby!' Nan protested. 'I'm just like you.' She pulled at lumps of grass. 'I've got the curse.' She waited excitedly for her friend to react. Dandy lay down in the grass. She glared at the sky. She rolled over and the little spiky blossoms hopped from her hair.

'You're as green as mouldy cheese,' she said. She watched Nan sadly through her puffy eyes. 'Do you really think I'd go away?'

'You can't stay.'

'I live in the real world. I always have. There's nowhere else.'

'I'm always looking for the real world. Hardly anything seems real,' Nan said.

'You're a liar, Nan Cantwell. Why do you wrap your bust? You've got a lovely figure. You could have your pick.'

'I don't want my pick.' Nan's voice was high and bleak. 'I don't like fellows. You never liked them either.'

'Well, I can tell you they're the only thing. When a fellow puts his arms around you and kisses you, you float away – it's like your first Communion.'

Nan looked at her for a long time. She did not seem happier for all this floating away. The bruises on her face made her older and harder. She seemed restless and defiant. She could not see it but her fellow was just like any other man causing trouble. She reached for Dandy's hand. 'They're not the only thing,' she said. 'There's still me – your best friend.'

Dandy thought about this and she shook her head. 'But you ran after me!' Nan insisted. 'You wanted to see me.'

'I had to *see* you,' Dandy said. 'I needed an excuse to get out of the house. It was all right to be with you. My da likes you.'

'But it helped, didn't it, to talk?'

Dandy shrugged. 'It helped to pass the time. Max won't be here until three.' She frowned. 'It must be nearly that now. I'm meeting Max here. You have to go now.'

Nan scrambled to her feet and ran.

'Na-an!' Dandy's voice was full of penitence. She knew she ought to take no notice but she slowed down and then she looked back and was bewildered to see a little girl with red hair and a yellow dress sprawled in the grass. 'What do you want?' she shouted back. 'Don't go home,' Dandy begged. 'Please don't go home.'

Nan scuffed her boots in the grass. She walked back nonchalantly.

'Oh, go away!' Dandy contradicted in anguish. 'You can't stay here. Just wait for me somewhere. If I come home without you I'll be killed.'

'Get killed,' Nan bawled. 'See if I care.' She raced away as if something was chasing her. The low branches of a tree clawed her face. After a time she was out of breath and she sat down among ferns in a shady place beneath the trees. She was not waiting for Dandy.

She was resting because she was tired. Soon she saw the dark and stiff-limbed figure of a boy walk across the green part of the park, his arms swinging like socks on a clothes line. When Dandy saw him she stood up and waited for him and they stalked off into a valley of shrubs and brambles. Nan wanted to cry. She wrapped her arms around her legs and rocked back and forth to help herself but it only made her sleepy and after a few minutes she put her head down and sucked on her knee and dozed. She dreamed that she was in the park and was being watched by an Indian woman who sat on a bench and stared at her. The woman had a small jewel in the side of her nose. She was eating an ice-cream cone. A group of children stood in a half-circle and gaped at her, partly in envy of the ice but more because of the novelty of a mahogany-coloured lady on a park bench, parcelled in gold and purple from head to foot when everyone else was showing off their arms to the sun.

She woke when Dandy shook her shoulders. 'It's me,' she grinned. 'Wakey. Time to go home.' Nan peered at her sleepily. Her face seemed softer, more healed, in spite of the ugly marks that were scribbled on her flushed face; she looked soft and pretty now.

Dandy pulled Nan to her feet. 'Thanks, pal. I'll do the same for you sometime.' Nan detached herself coldly. 'I'm not speaking to you,' she said. She walked ahead. When they came to the shops Nan was impeded by a young woman with a pram staring longingly into a sweet shop. Dandy caught up with her. 'I know how it's done,' she hissed. 'I know the facts.' 'The facts?' Nan stared at an arrangement of Clarnico Iced Caramels. 'Men and women. He told me. It's awful.' The words sat on the back of Nan's neck where they pricked her with ice-cold curiosity. She hurried on. Dandy followed her, all the way to her gate, skittish with her blasted awful secrets. She was trying to shut the gate when Dandy said: 'What did you make of the darkie in the park? Ali Baba and her ice-cream cone?'

'She wasn't Arabian,' Nan murmured coolly. 'She was Indian.' A pulse began to beat in her throat. She frowned at Dandy in alarm. She shook her head. 'There was no one there. It was a dream. You imagined it.'

'Not me. I live in the real world, remember? So long, Sou'Webster!' She laughed and raced back to her own house. She didn't care about anything.

She kept thinking of the faces she had seen in the morgue. She felt that she was one of them, that her soul had been taken away with her name. Resentment confined and pinched her like her party frock that was too small. She cooked a meal for herself without bothering to ask Mary if she was hungry. When she had fed the leftover scraps of rasher and egg to Bertie, she picked him up and brought him, under her arm, to the coal shed. She told herself that she had fetched him for company but in truth she wanted to see if the hen or the cat could be provoked. Mary was in the shed. She squatted on the piles of sacking near the hen. She had something in the lap of her dress that looked like a pine cone. She was smiling and crooning to herself. When Nan pushed in the door she cupped her hands over the thing in her lap and pushed it behind her.

'What have you got there?' Nan said.

'Nothing. Only a hedgehog.'

Nan dropped the cat and it fled into the garden gratefully. 'Mary Webster,' she taunted spitefully. Mary beamed. She picked up the hen and stroked its head. 'Mary *Hilda* Webster,' Nan inserted the hated middle name. Mary made a good-humoured face. Nan glared at her and then stormed back into the house. She went upstairs. There was a light showing under her mother's door but she did not go in. She went to the lavatory. She still had the curse.

She was woken after midnight by father coming in with a truculent banging of doors. Mary was asleep beside her. Her harmless plaits poked out on to the pillow. She felt sorry for having been so mean. She put an arm around her. Mary's sleeping arm instantly embraced her with forgiveness.

There was another disturbance sometime before morning. The silence of the night was slashed by a scream. It was like the night of the cats, only it wasn't cats; it was a woman's voice, terrible, a ragged shriek ending with a gurgle as if her throat had been severed with a knife. Nan awoke sighing with dread. She had been in the middle of a dream. She was in the morgue, walking between the mortuary beds. She stopped to look at the face of a departed one and found that she was gazing into the black open eyes of the Indian woman which were alert and full of spite. She sat trembling until she heard, with relief, the eager clatter of father's bare feet on the stairs. They crept down after him, Mary, Nan and mother, holding each other for bravery.

They were disappointed to find that it was only Elizabeth the hen, protesting because Mary's hedgehog had snuggled under her wing for warmth.

CHAPTER 11

In the morning mother kept Nan home from school. It was her day for the hairdresser. Nan brought tea on a tray. She served mother and brought her own cup to the red chair at the dressing table. They watched one another and listened to father's destructive exit for work.

Mother did not need to have her hair styled. She always wore it in plaits. She went for the neighbours. Mrs Guilfoyle and Mrs Lehane visited the tongs shop every second Monday – Mrs Bradish, Doris Chandler, Mamie Butler. Mother liked the atmosphere, the eggy smell of perms, the sourness of gas jets, the glamourizing process which stripped the women of their trappings of glamour. Red-faced and streaming with soap, the housewives lacked incentive for pretence. It was a true saying, mother often commented, about letting your hair down.

When she was finished mother held out her cup to be taken away. Nan took it and, on the insistence of mother's gentle gaze, she went and looked out of the window while the slim figure reefed off her billowing nightgown and loyally strapped herself into a Cantwell corset. When she was sheathed in a long white petticoat she said remotely, 'Do you suppose it will still be called The Cantwell? It is unwise to change an established name.'

Nan returned from the window. She tucked herself into the chair and watched while her mother put on the rest of her clothes. She brought out a navy dress from the wardrobe and surveyed it critically. It was long past fashion. When she seemed satisfied she put this on. She wound her plaits and pinned them under a navy hat. Her oval face and large eyes contested bravely with the mournful outfit. The hat was like a basin. It would not contain the waves of her hair. Inky fronds collapsed around her face and she pushed at them with a brittle hand. Nan sighed. Mother normally wore her best hat to the hairdresser, a black straw with squashed linen flowers.

'We don't have to go to Mr Kelly,' she said. 'It's a lovely day. We could go for a walk.'

'It is important to keep up appearances. You will realize that when you are older,' mother said. It was a dislocated argument. Mother's hair was not suited to the fashion of the times. Mr Kelly only knew one style and he obligingly fried her beautiful hair into rigid waves the same as everyone else's. As soon as she got home the waves were banished back into her severe plaits.

They found themselves outside the dingy shop exterior of the hair stylist at half-past nine. The neighbours were already there. She could see them through the glass, pink inside the cubicles that were divided with sagging loops of red curtain. Mrs Bradish's fat hand waved enticingly. Mother seemed not to notice. She looked cold in the sunshine. She was in a trance, frowning, locked into some private conflict. Nan pushed at the glass door provoking an angry little bell and mother looked up, startled. 'Why does he always call me Mags?' she complained. 'Mags. As long as I've known him. My name is Marguerite.'

When they went inside, the row of boiling red faces raised in affectionate grins. 'Morning, Mrs Cantwell!' Mother took no notice. She went to the cash desk which was overlooked by a wilted woman in her thirties. 'I have an appointment,' she said.

'Name?' the woman challenged, although mother had been a customer for years.

'Mrs Webster.'

She looked at her book. 'I have no Webster.'

'Nevertheless,' mother said firmly. 'I have an appointment.'

Mr Kelly came over then, gnashing a fizzing tongs in the air in greeting. 'Morning, darling,' he said. Names presented no difficulty to Mr Kelly. All women were darling.

He escorted mother to a washbasin to have her hair soaped. She passed the row of neighbours. They eyed her with critical bewilderment. 'Good morning,' said Nan, who had followed her mother. Mrs Guilfoyle's small eyes bore sharply into the navy hat. 'Good morning, Mrs Cantwell,' she said in a significant way. Mother ignored her. Her face showed that it was an effort. 'Come and meet my new lady,' Mrs Guilfoyle persisted. Mother tilted her head slowly to look at the foreigner whose greenish black hair had been trapped by many brightly coloured pegs. 'Mamzelle de Ravelais,' Mrs Guilfoyle presented. Mlle de Ravelais' white hand floated up nervously to protect her chest but mother turned and grasped the hand with confidence. 'I am pleased to meet you,' she said. 'I am Mrs Webster.' The neighbours coughed and shifted and raised their eyes with awe. It was a while before the lodger noticed. She had been secure in mother's grasp, and comforted. She began to feel the unease in the company. She snatched away her fingers. Mother watched the fleeting hand with a despairing grin. She turned that clown's look on Nan who stood uselessly. 'My!' mother mocked. 'What hapless creatures young girls are. Look at you!' She pulled at Nan's soft yellow hair. Nan backed away. 'Look at her,' mother invited the neighbours. She could feel it, the hateful flood of pink to her cheeks that had lately become companion to her embarrassment. Mother laughed nervously. She had her black bag clenched against her like a shield. 'Well, one must make the best of things. I think we shall have the child's hair done for a change.' Nan's face jerked up, full of shock. 'Would you like that, Nan?' 'Yes,' Nan said quickly. She thought of the film stars on the kitchen wall. She looked at Mr Kelly's red-tiled floor, furred with snails of singed trimmings. Her eyes itched with tears, not because of the humiliation, but because of the unexpected treat, with which she was not equipped to cope. 'Mr Kelly!' mother summoned. 'We would like a wave for the little girl.' Mr Kelly responded effortlessly. 'The young lady!' he corrected, wagging his eyebrows merrily. She paid Mr Kelly from her purse – it was a shilling – and said that she had business to attend to. She left quickly. Nan tried to turn and watch her go. She wanted to see her safely past the neighbours. Mr Kelly already had her head between his hands and was thrusting her into the basin.

It took hours. She could smell her hair burning and she felt the red iron close to her scalp. Her head ached from the strange smells, the fearful frizzling sensation. Her eyes watered and her skin settled down to a permanent ragged pink like a spoiled ham. All this pleased her for it made her more vividly aware of each moment of her transformation.

'Look, darling!' Mr Kelly said. 'What a beauty!'

There was a mirror on the wall, rust-speckled, and she gazed into this. Rigid yellow waves marched down either side of her round, excited face. Mr Kelly held a hand mirror behind her head so that she could see this artifice continued around the back of her skull. The effect on Nan was partly the fault of the mirror. It had been placed high on the wall for the benefit of taller customers and for the hairdresser's own use. It gave her a reflection of her face only. She forgot about her gymslip, the rounded shoulders, inky hands that made defiant fists. She was a young lady, exceedingly lovely. She kept turning her head from side to side. Her grey eyes swam in the spotted mirror whose very flaws enhanced her own perfection. She was utterly transformed.

'It's very nice,' she said. 'Thank you.' She would have liked to give the man a tip, to impress on him her worldliness, but she had no little bag from which to slide a threepenny piece. In any case he was high-spirited enough. His face was squashed into a smile. He kept looking at her face and then down, below the range of the mirror, and up again. 'What a razzle dazzler,' he said.

The neighbours were gone. Mr Kelly had left Miss Keane from the cash desk to comb them out while he attended to Nan. Nan's mother was blamed for this as well as other things. It was a talking point for weeks, until more interesting events took over.

'What a razzle dazzler,' she said to herself when she was outside. She had assumed a special walk as if she was wearing the new high heels or a dress in the latest Mousseline de Soie. She was light as a bird. Even the withdrawal of her name, the continuation of the curse, scarcely mattered. She was a razzle dazzler, capable of pleasing people by her appearance alone. She would not have to make an effort any more. It made her gracious. On the wall of Gickla's kitchen there was a golden-haired star of particular beauty, pictured dancing on a spiral of stars and it was with her that she identified. The old feelings of irritation had vanished. 'I have grown up,' she thought. The thought did not strike her with rage.

All around her, things looked as they had always done. She found this reassuring for it meant she did not imagine her own transformation. As she turned into Hallinan's Mansions she spotted in the gutter the remains of a cat which had run under the wheels of a motor car. It had the stiff, unreal look of a lost glove. She met Doll Cotter pushing a pram. She stopped without encouragement and rifled through the sticky pink and blue blankets to admire the baby. Doll did not appear to appreciate the gesture. She let out a sigh, full of misery and sniffed.

'What's the matter?' Nan said. Doll gazed, listless with despair. 'Gawny!' she said. 'Your hair's gifty.' 'Thanks,' Nan said. She tried to move on. The heaviness of Doll's heart weighed badly on the lightness of her own. Doll manoeuvred the pram expertly so that it blocked her path. 'He's getting a tooth,' she said. 'Yes. You told me.' 'Little hairs.' Doll's chin trembled and she stretched her mouth downward to keep it steady. 'What is it?' Nan said. 'Behind the hedge,' Doll wept. 'Minnie Willard.'

Minnie Willard, rich and pretty, the meanest child that ever lived. She used her pocket money to bribe other children to join her in tormenting the most ready victims.

She recovered her financial losses selling awful information about men and women.

'I have to go,' Nan said. 'Oh, God,' Doll whispered. Nan pushed past, shaking her golden curls which did not move at all.

She did not go home, merely to a point some yards away with good viewing vantage and for a piece of vital equipment which she picked up with distaste. Doll was leaning over the pram, pretending to settle the baby, but Nan guessed it was merely to hide her tears. 'You leave me alone!' Her lonely, frustrated cry was her only gesture as Willard's gang commenced their chorus from their hiding place. 'Dirty Doll! Dirty Doll!'

Doll had no advantage. From the back, with her untidy white-gold hair and a big cardigan of her mother's draped on her shoulders, she could have been a shawlie from Moore Street, pushing a pram of fish. Made bolder by Doll's acceptance, Minnie Willard came out of hiding. Her head of shining ringlets popped up from behind the hedge, her smiling, angel's face. 'Dirty Doll! Dirty Doll!' she taunted.

'Hello, Minnie,' Nan called out. 'How are you?'

Minnie turned around. 'Game ball,' she said. 'What happened to your hair? It looks a fright.'

Nan shrugged and came forward nonchalantly, her hands held behind her back. 'Tell us, Minnie, have you ever been kissed by a boy?'

Minnie stared at her. Her eyes went very pale, the colour of plain glass marbles. Doll looked from one to the other in bewilderment. 'Yes,' Minnie said. 'I know everything. If you want to know, it will cost you twopence.'

Nan shook her head. 'No thanks, I only wanted to know, have you ever been kissed by a dead cat?'

Minnie's pale eyes diminished to pin-points. She frowned. 'No-aaooo!' The little dead cat sailed through the air, steered by its matted tail. Halfway through its unnatural flight an amazing thing happened. The tail, which had been damaged in the accident, came away and the cat flew straight into the arms of Minnie Willard so that they stared at each other, snarling and appalled, until Minnie managed to fling the animal's body to the ground and run into the house, shrieking with panic.

That day there was no proper dinner. When Nan got home she found Nellie sitting at the table pulling shreds of corned beef from a limp square of greaseproof. Mary was eating mixed pickles from a jar. A loaf of bread crumbled into the oilcloth from its sawn end. When Nan asked about the meal Nellie moaned that she wasn't up to full-scale catering. It was a queer thing to come in after years of unstinting service and find yourself treated like a thief in the night.

'Mother would not speak to her,' Mary said.

'Did you call her Mrs Cantwell?' Nan wondered. Nellie nodded warily. 'Our name has been changed,' Nan explained. 'Father has changed our name to Webster. Mother won't answer to Cantwell any more. It's loyalty.'

'Like common crimnils,' Nellie denounced.

It turned out there had been a rumpus. The change of an ordinary thing like a name so agitated Nellie that she felt the need of a fire. She was sitting over her modest blaze when father came in and pointed furiously at the little knot of roasting coals. 'Best Wigan coal,' he ranted. 'Forty-nine bob a ton. Bloody sun outside scorching your eyeballs. You women think I've got money to burn.' And he had stormed into the scullery and seized the kettle that was warming for Nellie's tea. He poured it straight on to the fire so that a viper of grey smoke reeled out and hissed at his face. He would not stay for his dinner and mother was not up to eating. Nellie did not feel inspired to cook for the children alone.

'Someone should stand up to him,' Nan dared. 'You ought to threaten to leave.'

'That's rich. Me adding fuel to the bee he already has in his bonnet,' Nellie snapped. 'Where am I going to get me good-looking ten bob a week?'

There was silence until Mary reached out curiously to touch Nan's scorched curls. 'Your hair's lovely,' she said.

'It's a Marcel,' Nan said. 'It's the latest.'

Nellie lit a cigarette and gave leisurely criticisms to the hairdo. 'I knew a woman once,' she said, 'blondied up her hair.' She put a hand out and explored the glacial curtain of waves, interested to note that the child's silky hair now had the same wiry texture as her own. 'The yella seeped through the roots into her pores. Her skin all went yella, eyeballs, tongue. Bilious yella.'

'What happened?' Mary said.

'They shaved her hair off and waited for the yella to grow out through the roots.'

'I didn't get my hair coloured,' Nan said. 'It's a wave.'

'All the same,' said Nellie, 'you never can tell.'

Mother came back from a visit to town and told Nellie to set the table for four. The children were to have tea with her. She had bought a chocolate cake. She seemed in a festive mood.

There was an air of nervousness around the table which made it seem like a birthday. There was tinned salmon and salad. Everyone knew something was wrong. Father kept watching mother in a worried way. She scarcely touched her food. She watched until the cake had been divided and then formed her fingers into a spire under her chin. 'I have decided,' she said, 'to take a holiday.'

The children looked up anxiously, not at mother but at father, to see what he would do. Mother went on quickly, 'I am going to Europe. I have booked a three-week tour with Mr Thomas Cook.'

There was a wild and terrible look in father's eye.

'I have paid five pounds,' mother said. 'I shall need another thirty.'

He leaped from his chair and rushed at her. The children looked away. They thought he was going to strike her or strangle her. Instead he seized her joined hands in his own and said, 'How would you like to go and live in Paris? Say "yes", Mags. Just bugger off, start again. We could! The foundation business in Paris could use a breath of fresh air.' Mother's mouth dropped open. She shook her head in a panic. 'No! Oh, no! You must not try me further. My home! My friends! I only meant a holiday. A little rest.'

He sighed and let go her hands. He seemed utterly exhausted. He went back to his place and frowned at the crumbs of cake on his plate. The children watched him spellbound. To their amazement, when he looked up again his face was perfectly composed, indifferently polite. 'When do you sail?' he inquired mildly.

'On Friday week.'

'I shall give you fifty pounds. You must lodge in the best hotels.'

CHAPTER 12

It shook them, the extent to which mother was missed. After the excitement of packing, the journey in a cab to Dun Laoghaire pier, where she said nothing all the way but clenched the children's hands and stared ahead with a mystical look, the house settled down to a dreary wanting. Extraordinary. She never had anything to do with it. Father kept the children home from school to fill the gap. They were swallowed by it. Nan spent her time in front of mirrors, admiring her hair, wetting her fingers and smoothing her waves with spit. Nothing got done. Nellie drank tea all day and demanded news from the papers. She was full of contempt for the world's catastrophes. Nothing could match up to mother's defection. Nan read out that the popular Spanish actress Raquel Mellor had come under the displeasure of the Vatican for a song in which a young girl blasphemes the Church and afterwards repents. The actress was on her way to Rome to seek the Pope's forgiveness.

'Them oul' clerics,' Nellie snapped around her cigarette.

Father was subdued. He ate alone in the dining-room. Much of the time he listened to a record he had bought for mother, 'Pale Hands I loved beside the Shalimar'. She used to play it, watching her own pretty hands in her lap with a smile, but then she forgot about it.

Every morning he ran to the hall to see if there was word. There was nothing for a week. When he came down to breakfast on Saturday he found a postcard on the mat. 'Word from mother!' he shouted out, making the children scramble from bed, hysterical with hope.

They clustered around the card for comfort. When they read it they were confused. 'The Eiffel Tower is very shabby. I am so happy here.' It was signed Marguérite, with an accent on the first 'e'. 'When's she coming home?' Mary whined. Father turned the card carefully and studied the soup-coloured picture of Paris streets for this information. 'Nothing,' Nan declared. He turned the card over again and tapped the inky loops which were skewy with excitement. 'It's word,' he said.

It was word. Perched on the mantelpiece it helped to fill the void. It stirred father to action. He brought a friend home to tea so that he could flick at the sinister message and say: 'Wife's in Paris for a spot of shopping.'

He summoned the children from the kitchen to meet his friend. They were in their school clothes. Although they were not attending school they had worn them since mother went away. Normally they changed into dresses at home in the hope that she would notice them. 'This is my friend, Mr Archie Shipham,' he introduced the guest. 'He is a piano tuner.' He made it sound like a great calling. The man had a dark face and rampant hair. His black eyes gleamed with sadness. He fascinated the children. They stared and stared. He did not make a joke nor take sweets from his pocket. He stared back at them. He appeared to be interested in them, curious, like an animal peering from its cage in the zoo. He quickly lost interest in Mary and concentrated on Nan. He winked at her in an intent and melancholy way. Father was extremely excited by the outcome of this confrontation. 'She is getting to look quite all right,' he boasted and he told Nan to serve them their tea.

'What an old ibex,' Nan said crossly when she was setting the tray in the kitchen, but she felt pleased at being singled out for attention. She went to trouble with the meal. She made a salad from cold chicken, and Queen of Puddings. Before bringing up the tea she changed into a pale yellow frock with short sleeves and a fluted collar. As she entered the room, Mr Archie Shipham gave her a strange look, a sort of warning, as if they shared a secret which she must contain.

When the men had finished eating father said he would fetch them each a good cigar. 'I'll get them,' Nan offered, for she knew the little drawer in the dressing-table where the biscuit-coloured box was kept. But Mr Shipham said, 'No, you stay and talk to me,' and father bounded off delightedly to his room.

'What age are you?' said Mr Shipham.

'I'm fourteen.'

'Nearer fifteen.'

'How do you know?'

'I know.'

She walked over to him and held the edge of the table, fingering the cloth and staring into his face. 'Go away,' he said. She could not move. He put out a finger and stroked the bare inside of her arm, from the warm and damp part underneath her sleeve down to her waist. 'Little girls,' he said, 'are such shameless animals.' She knew that something else would happen. He stretched that long finger again. He touched her chest. It was the kindest touch she had ever known. She smiled at him.

'Here's a find,' father burst through the door. 'Cubans at five shillings a box!'

Mr Shipham gave her a slap on the behind, so sharp that she cried out with pain and ran from the room with tears stinging her eyes. She could hear the barking laughter of the two men behind her.

CHAPTER 13

She went back to school. It was only a week until the holidays. There were exams and then there was the summer concert. Nan felt a sense of relief when she heard the clang of the school bell and saw the forbidding grey building. There was nothing in it that she did not know. She ran up the steps as she heard the shouts and giggles, subdued into the lovely grainy chorus of the prayers in the corridor, and flew straight into the arms of a nun. 'She can't kill me, she can't kill me,' she thought giddily, biting down a smile which the nun mistook for impudence and called her a brazen hussy.

She was surprised to see Dandy at her desk. Dandy had grown up so quickly that she imagined by now she must have flown down the drainpipe after Primmy, her sister who had run away to England. In spite of her determination never to speak to her again, she was glad to see her and anxious for a chat, but they were made to sit alone during exams. The folded papers rustling with mysteries were already being scattered on the desks.

Nan had always found it hard to concentrate. She used to spend the months coming up to exams with a book obediently held in front of her nose, memorizing facts and sentences and pages. When she sat down to answer the questions she found she could only remember the interesting bits, the loss of Red Hugh O'Neill's toes through frostbite, the thunderous verses of *Morte d'Arthur*. This year was different. She had neglected her books completely.

The other girls were starting on their papers, their faces tortured with thought and lumps of hair falling over their eyes. Nan sat perfectly still in front of her pages of foolscap, her inky pen in its little ditch, the folded question paper waiting like a gift. There was no sing-song knowledge locked into her head, no answering chorus like the prayers in the corridor to leap from her brain to examiners' demands. She did not care. Lately she had run into questions that had more than one answer or did not have an answer at all. When she finally opened the paper, under the deeply threatening gaze of the supervising nun, it was like pulling back the curtain on one of those rare winter mornings when the sky is pink and the snow a ballroom floor for gliding on. The questions were easy. Who had killed whom in what battle. What king followed which. Unfettered by the weighty prose of history books, she found the answers readily. The basic information did not fill up the long pages so she improvised with thoughts on power and greed; she employed the blood of Sister Immaculata's martyrs and added a quote from *Morte d'Arthur*.

Nan went through an English paper in a placid and detached way, as a boy might eat a whole chocolate cake. There was an essay question on 'my most unforgettable character'. She glanced around. She could tell by the look of studious boredom on the faces around her that other girls were writing about Daniel O'Connell or an aunt who had gone to Africa on the missions. She caught Dandy's eye. Dandy winked at her. She did not know why but it made her feel reckless and she quickly covered pages writing about Nellie. She no longer felt like a child at school but like someone plucked from adult life and compelled to sit at a little desk for a class reunion. Sums and verbs tugged the imagination instead of the memory. She enjoyed the game, particularly since it could have no possible consequence.

She sat in the shed in the playground during lunch eating cheese sandwiches. She closed her eyes and saw in her head the intent monkey eyes of the piano tuner and she was washed by echoes of his touch. She concentrated on this until it almost became real and it frightened her and made her open her eyes. 'Hello, cob-Webster,' said Dandy, who had pushed her lightly to wake her up. 'Hello,' Nan said. 'How've you been?'

'Game ball.'

'How's . . . ?' Nan struggled in her brain for the name of the bull-like boy who had claimed her friend's attention. '. . . Max?'

Dandy shrugged. 'We're all washed up,' she said stylishly.

'Oh. I'm sorry.'

'Don't be. I gave him the old heave-ho.'

'Why?' Nan was astonished.

'I had better things to do.' The satisfied way she grinned made it easier to believe. Nan felt hurt. 'What things?'

'Bookworming.' Dandy laughed, embarrassed.

'You?'

'I did it for my ma,' she said quickly. 'She found out about Max.'

'Oh, hell's bells,' Nan said.

Dandy shook her head. 'She never made a fuss. She said, "Oh, you're just the age I was when I met your father. Is there no end?"'

She stretched her arms over her head and Nan could see she was getting a lovely figure; she really was a stunner. 'I gave the boyo the raspberry,' she yawned. 'Plenty more where he came from. I've been shut up with my books for weeks. God, I'd love to run up the mountains and scream my head off. I just thought I'd do something for my ma – give her a fright if nothing else.'

'You gave *me* a fright,' Nan said. 'Are we friends again?'

Dandy laughed. 'You are a desperate baby,' she said.

The bell went then, its mad, formless song emphasized by a tickly little bell which a nun shook in their faces. Nan had no time to question Dandy further and soon she was tackling a tangle of sums with a resumption of her earlier soothing remoteness that made her forget about her changeable friend altogether.

She was looking for Mary on her way home when she was arrested by Sister Immaculata. 'Oh, yes, miss,' the nun said. 'You're a nice example. A very nice example.' Her expression did not match this opinion.

'I . . .' Nan did not know for which of her failures to apologize.

'Two weeks you've been missing without so much as a by-your-leave.'

'My mother's away. I was kept home to look after my father.'

'Changing our name, waving our hair – we've got too big for our boots since we were made the fairy.'

Nan blushed. She had completely forgotten the importance and prestige of being chosen as fairy for the concert. She scarcely remembered the childish little routine that was at the heart of this honour.

'I've got my eyes on you, miss. Don't think you can pull the wool over my eyes. Tomorrow there will be two hundred parents, thirty-four sisters, six priests and a mon-see-neeor gathered in the school hall. If your performance is anything less than impeccable you need never show your face in these corridors again.'

CHAPTER 14

By morning, Nan's disdain had deserted her and Mary shivered with fright. They could not eat their breakfast. Father prescribed an egg and treacle nog. He beat eggs in a bowl and sloughed treacle from a tin with a wooden spoon. A measure of brandy was dribbled in for vitamins and the lot was energetically beaten over a flame. 'It needs a light touch to stop it curdling,' he confessed as he spooned the vile brown scrambled eggs on to their plates. They gazed mournfully at their plates, warped with resistance inside their nighties. 'Runts!' he complained bitterly. 'Skin and blasted bones!' He poked at them in disgust and was confounded to discover that it was not so.

'You've got a figure!' His accusing finger wagged at Nan. 'What have you been up to?'

She wriggled in annoyance. 'Nothing.'

'Nothing? You're a bloody liar.'

'I'm growing. Everyone grows.'

'Don't give me cheek, miss. You've been up to something. You've been influenced by the fashions.'

'Fashions?' she looked amazed.

'Oh, you're brazen. Flaunting yourself, flat as a washboard. You've been interfering with your chest, haven't you?' His colour exploded and he froze, as if struck by lightning 'My God! You've been and bought a brassiere. You've paid out three and eleven for a Fitu.'

'Fitu?' Nan echoed in bewilderment. She did not know that it was the fashion of the year for the stylish woman to flatten her chest with a brassiere of this name which was an unseamed cotton bandeau.

'Here, you!' Father picked on Mary. 'What's she been at? What's she been doing to her chest?'

'She wraps herself in bandages,' Mary blurted, hoping to end the interrogation and win their release.

He shook his head, exhausted by the responsibility of daughters. 'My child tying down her chest like common women in the street.

My child making an exhibition of herself, parading herself for men.'

'That's not true!' Nan cried.

'As if you didn't know that every common trollop is tying her bosom this year. It's the fashion.' He spat the word. 'Lewd and unnatural. Oh, I'll have my eye on you.'

Mary had her eyes on the checked oilcloth but she could only see the time speeding past as if she was sitting on a train and it was fields and lakes and cows being pulled past on a rippling frieze. Already the tap dancers would have pulled on the black hose and the posies were being stitched into tutus of red and blue crepe. She began to cry. It was the last straw for father. 'Weak-minded women,' he cried out in despair, 'are a grievous responsibility. Well, I'll not leave you to make more mischief. You're coming with me. Get up those stairs and get dressed – and leave your body as God made it.'

Mary's dread of the nuns overcame her fear of father's passionate state. '*Please*, father,' she whined bravely. 'It's the school concert. We have to be in time. We'll be *murdered*.'

'I'll give you murder,' he promised. 'Get up those stairs or I'll break every bone in your body.' He advanced with a reckless swiping motion of his arm. They scraped back their chairs and fled.

'Now we're for it,' Nan said gloomily when they were safely locked in their room. 'What did you have to go and tell for?'

'I had to say something quick. He would have killed us.'

'He'll probably kill us anyway with his horrible concoctions. And the nuns will finish us.'

'What'll we do?'

'Don't worry. I'll think up a good lie.' She rooted in the wardrobe for her blue party dress. She untied her nightdress and dropped the dress over her head, without attending to her breasts. The frock settled itself to her shape. She frowned in the wardrobe mirror, seeing how her body bullied the childish little silk shift to suit itself, altering its appearance completely.

'A lie?' said Mary anxiously, struggling into a yellow cotton smock in which her body vanished harmlessly.

'I'll say I had a fainting fit and you had to get the doctor as there was no one else in the house. You can say that sort of thing when you get to my age.' She turned this way and that, looking at her strangely shaped summer-brown legs, the way the front of her dress rippled when she moved. She would look like a little girl again, she promised herself, when she put on the long white socks Etta Gorman had knitted and the flat satin dancing shoes. 'Father will soon grow tired of us,' she assured Mary generously. 'We'll get to school in time for the concert. We're only missing rehearsal.'

He brought them to the factory. 'It is modern times,' he consoled himself aloud as they were fanned by breezes on the top of the tram. 'Little girls can no longer be sheltered from the ways of the world. One must guide their paths. It is time you found out about the facts of life. Foundation wear is what sets a certain class of woman apart. I will say no more. I know it will not interest you but the factory is also your heritage. If I had a son . . .' He sighed, an accomplished lament. 'One of you may aspire to the outer office.'

It was a low dusty red building in a collection of faded, uneven boxes like boxes on a high shelf in a hardware shop. There was a compound of small factories in the poor part of the city, dependent on cheap labour for the production of mantles or boots or biscuits. The buildings bore painted signs and sometimes a slogan. 'Cantwell Corsets,' said the flaking letters on a sign painted dark green, 'first in foundations around the world.' The children were impressed by this flair and comforted to see their old name anchored to a hoarding. They were prepared to overlook the sooty meanness of the building with a heap of bicycles tangled in front. Other factories had a motor car outside. They had not visited the corset company before. They had only seen the little heap of factories from the tram. When they were small, mother would point it out as something to be proud of.

He would not immediately let them in. He ran a critical finger over a decayed brass letter box and said solemnly, 'Listen! Listen to my ladies.'

He used to say the factory was a refuge for poor women down on their luck – not a place to hang up their hats, but a decent establishment with employment suited to the fair sex. Needlework. He had raised them out of the gutter, clad them properly, set them on the right paths. It impressed on their minds a picture of ladies seated in a circle dressed in white starched smocks and stitching at samplers of lawn. Now, when he invited them to listen they expected to hear a chorus of light voices raised in song, but there was only an angry whine and rattle. It puzzled them because it was familiar but unexpected. 'Sewing machines!' Nan said in surprise.

The other thing that affected them, once they had been let into the building, was the smell. There were smells of cotton and rubber that flew up into the nose like talcum powder but a darker odour seeped through the sickly beige walls. They passed a number of small offices on a corridor. At the end of this passage was a tall wooden door which parted in the centre. It had a small window, set high for adult eyes. Beyond this were contained the salvaged women. Father peered through the glass. He swung open the door. The noise and the smell intensified. At the last minute the children were afraid but father's arm shot out and swept them through.

There were about forty women. Some sat at benches cutting or sewing and others were crouched over sewing machines. Nan found herself staring at a woman whose boot flapped each time she stamped the pedal of her machine. The workers glanced indifferently at the visitors. So dead was their gaze that they seemed to have no eyes. Their skin was like old mushrooms. They worked at an extraordinary speed over pink rubbery lengths into which they stitched the bones of fishes and loops of elastic and steel. Nan's displeased nose told her that the sourish smell came from the women. Neglect. Horrible. She averted her gaze to the ceiling and saw that there were no windows in the room, only spidery beams from which were suspended tin shades and yellowish bulbs.

'They are dressed in rags,' Mary whispered.

'They are poor women,' father murmured back. 'They do not expect to have silk on their hides.'

'But you said,' she persisted, 'that they were decently clad.'

'They are decent where it matters. I have made each of my ladies a present of the Cantwell.'

She said nothing after that. She was puzzled. Foundation garments were what set a certain type of woman apart. The ladies did not look proud. Most of them wore several cardigans, held at the front with safety pins. She began to grow uncomfortable. She got a queer feeling. She was being watched. She looked up slowly. At the back of the room, almost hidden by the taller figures in front, was a row of rat-like eyes strung out along the darkest wall. It struck at her heart. Children! She stood on her toes to peer at them. There were eight of them, lined along a bench like class dunces, sewing very fast with needles and thread. Thin white arms rose and fell, sharp fingers sewed hooks on to finished corsets and they snapped thread with their teeth. They never took their eyes from her. White faces kept suspicious watch. Red hands worked with fretful hurry.

'Look, father,' Mary whispered, for it seemed to her that he must, like her, have overlooked them until now.

'They are the finishers,' he said.

They were not much older than she was. 'They're children!' Mary said.

'They do their work,' he said.

She could not tell what Nan was thinking. She leaned against the wall in a bored and sullen way. Mary was left to work it out by herself. These were the facts of life. They were shocking, as Nan had often hinted they would be. But what were they? What were the facts? This was the factory where father worked his hands to the bone to keep a houseful of women in idle luxury. The salvaged ladies were not idle and they were not luxurious. She had imagined the factory as a glamorous place with mirrors and silver cash registers and mannequins in their underwear. She had pictured father sitting down to tea and biscuits on a little tray. There was nothing like that, only the squirming pieces of pink rubber and the withered ladies. She understood at last. Father was responsible for women everywhere. He looked after the women here and made sure they were decently clad in corsets. He paid for mother and Nan and even Nellie. There was Etta Gorman and Miss Graham – all the poor buggers. She looked up at his tense face and for the first time she understood him. Everywhere he went, people depended on him. No wonder he was angry, he dared not smile for fear of attracting yet more dependants. She moved closer and held his hand. He glared down in amazement. 'I understand, father,' she said.

'I very much doubt that you do.' He took back his hand and used it to push them out of the workroom. Before he released them he brought them to a tiny office which he called the showroom and pointed silently to the pale torso of a plaster model. It was dressed in the strangest garment they had ever seen, a tanklike construction of rubber and steel with straps and buckles, as if meant to contain a madman.

It wasn't for a man. It was for a woman. Two shrivelled pink pudding cloths billowed gently over the modest mounds of the model's chest.

CHAPTER 15

'Here she is, sister!'

'Spawn of the devil! Sacred Heart, let me not damage her until she's done her dance.'

The nuns were on the lookout. They had had the rest of their little girls dressed and trembling with fear for an hour. They plucked Mary from Nan's arm and pushed her in the direction of the improvised dressing-room. 'Run along, child! Into your costume! *Quickly!*' The blast of their anger was saved for Nan. She had been picked to play the fairy. It was an honour.

'Well, miss?' She could see the outline of their knuckles in their deep black sleeves. 'What have you to say for yourself?'

'I had a fainting fit.'

'Could you not have sent word that you were indisposed? Would that have been too much trouble?'

Nan knew she was not expected to answer. It was the tradition for girls who were in really bad disgrace to hang their heads until tears came, until their faces swelled with repentance and trails of remorse bubbled from the nose. She wasn't going to let this happen. She would not go on the stage with a scaldy face and pig eyes. 'I won't talk now,' she said. 'You can do what you like afterwards but I'm saying nothing until I've done my act.'

'The impudence!' whispered one skewer-like figure in admiration.

The nuns did not know what to do. They murmured and swayed like firs in the wind. It became evident after a time that their dilemma had not solely to do with her mutiny for there was a new note to their conference.

'The cut of her . . .'

'Big beast of a woman . . .'

'Downright immodest . . .'

She folded her arms and pretended to look out a little high window that was opaque like an acid drop. Her face was burning and she could feel the pressure of tears high up in her nose. 'I don't care,' she told herself. 'I can't help it if I'm growing up. I never wanted to grow up. I never even wanted to be the blasted fairy.'

'Sisters, sisters!' cried a frail, disembodied voice. It was Mother Ignatius. She could not be seen because of her lack of height. 'The hall is full and we are due to begin. The little girls are waiting to be put in order.' She pushed her way through the younger, stiffer sisters and looked sadly at Nan. 'Is my little Nan in trouble again?' One of the sisters mouthed an explanation. The old nun frowned. 'What is this? Are you intent on giving the child airs and graces because of her figure? A chicken would be praised for its plump breast. Indeed, foolish, clucking hens you resemble more than women of God.' She flapped her sleeves to be rid of them and took Nan by the arm. 'Go and get ready now. Do your very best dance and offer it up for God's intentions. Don't be self-conscious for that is a symptom of vanity and unbecoming in a young girl.'

Nan looked at her with gratitude. 'I don't mean to be disobedient,' she said. 'I would prefer to be good.'

'Deeds, not words,' said the old nun patting her very kindly. 'Go and do your best.'

The art class was being used as a dressing-room because of its nearness to the school hall. The room was full of school uniforms, slung over the backs of chairs where they had been shed by other children. A slab of mirror was balanced on a desk by the window. Nan sat on the desk and investigated its unlikely display of womanly effects: powder and rouge, sticks of black colouring and pots of blue stuff for the eyes, an assortment of lipsticks. She could hear the sickly scrape and sigh of the orchestra tuning up in the hall. In a few minutes they would begin a wilting rendition of 'O, Mother, I could weep for mirth', to accompany a tableau depicting a scene from the life of the convent's founder, Mother Geraldine Lazarre. A line of girls had their skins darkened with black boot polish and tea cloths swathed around their heads and they held out, in supplicant pose, black dolls for conversion.

There was a tempting red stalk of lipstick, glistening out of its gold tunnel. Nan rolled it up and down experimentally. She pouted her lips and drew over them heavily in *Mexican Fire*. It was surprisingly hard to follow the outline of her own lips. There was a furry edge, like a crayonned scribble. She found a piece of paper and blotted her mouth against it. She had seen grown-up young women do this. Her lips now had a fierce and parched look but the outline was still not even. With a very careful hand she drew again, this time going a little outside her mouth's natural border. The effect, if extravagant, was tidy.

There was a thunderous noise like rocks falling down a mountain. The Irish dancers were on stage. Nan was unsure of her reflection. She had hoped to assume just a shadow of the cake-like perfection of the stars in the Jews' kitchen. Instead she looked larger than life. All the goodness was gone from her face. Her eyes beamed out an exhausted vividness.

'Gawny Mac, aren't you ready yet? There'll be *stink*!'

'Hang on a sec. Do I look okay?' Nan whirled around to catch the messenger, but the child had fled.

Veronica Fannigan's 'Rustle of Spring' was prancing along the piano. The fairy was next. There was no time for adjustments. Her fingers had begun to shake. She would just put on Etta Gorman's white stockings and her dancing shoes, which she had carried all morning in brown paper bags. Etta's bag had an abandoned look. No one had disturbed it since it was first deposited on the mantelpiece. Nan peeked into the greasy-looking carrier. 'Oh my God, I am heartily sorry for having offended Thee . . .' she began to gabble.

'You're on! You're on!' screamed a terrified messenger. Nan pulled on the snake-like lengths of knitting and slipped into her dancing shoes.

She ran to the door, then turned round, facing the mirror, as if to catch a thief. To tell the truth, the effect was not so bad. Only the little dress was out of place. It quivered inconsequentially like a piece of sheep's fluff on a barbed wire fence; hopeless to try to cover such a wild-looking woman. 'Oh, my!' Nan murmured. She raced along the corridor and stumbled into the backstage gloom.

The posies were on stage. They whirled about in bewildered circlets crying out that one should pity not the flowers, standing all their lonely hours, for there dwelt within their bowers, little folk with magic powers.

The posies were the smallest children in the school. Nothing more was expected of them than that they should please their parents with their appearance. After they had finished their squealing melody they formed a line along the back of the stage, making way for the flies. The flies were older girls who carried lighted Hallowe'en fire crackers. They were meant to be elves, but they wore black hose and had greaseproof paper wings sewn on to their backs, and they looked so like a swarm of flies that they became so termed. 'Ooooh!' cried the audience as splinters of light from the sparklers spattered the darkened stage and the flies finished their crouching dance. 'Go on!' came an encouraging murmur in Nan's ear; and then a rush of excited whispers.

'The fairy queen!'

'Good luck, child!'

'Good luck, Nan!'

In a second she was seized by the full burden of her privilege and her limbs locked; she was paralysed. Hands brushed and pushed at the back of her dress, not knowing she was petrified, and then her feet from their remote reaches stirred and made a sudden reckless dash so that she found herself carried toward the centre of the stage making the series of small leaps and then one grand leap, right in the spotlight.

'Ooh!' went the audience.

It was an exclamation on several levels and contained, as well as some genuine admiration from the younger children in the audience, cries of amusement, appreciation of an uncultured kind and actual screams of horror. Her leap fell away to nothing. She felt terrified. She swivelled her head for a glance into the wings, seeking some smiling face to reassure, but all she could make out was a single figure austere as a church spire, a thunderous whisper: 'You are the bane of my life!'

It was the stockings. Nan could not tell if her mother's vagueness had wiped from her memory the fact that they had to be white or if her romantic nature had driven her to embellish. Etta Gorman's socks were a sulphurous yellow, banded with black like a wasp. There were red garters ornamented with rosebuds for their support.

'Get-her-off!' she heard the nun hiss from the shadows. Her dance toppled and she peered down into the little pile of pebbles that was the audience. 'We are the spirits of the glen . . .' She started to sing, very loud, for she was alone in the dark and she was frightened. 'Fairy ladies, fairy men.' She had a good voice although she was often criticized for singing into her boots. Now she threw her head back and sang very loudly and defiantly and surprised even herself with the true way her voice rang out.

After the first verse she did another elaborate dance which involved high leg kicks and touching elves and posies on the head with her wand. Nan had always considered it a stern dance for a fairy. It lacked lightness and grace. She had an inspiration to relieve it a bit, slow down the movements so as to lull the audience out of its dismay. As models of grace she chose the stars in the photographs. She raised her arms in a sinuous movement and then languorously raised a leg, turning slowly to face her critics. She imitated the rapt, dreamlike smile of the cinema ladies and made her hips move in a way that did not disturb the top of her body. The elves and posies rose to resume their dance and Nan returned to the centre of the stage, waving her arms gently while the smaller children gambolled about. Her eyes grew accustomed to the light. She found she could identify individual faces in the front rows of the audience. The mothers looked bemused. Their hats seem placed abnormally low on their brows and their chins were raised at an angle, as if they could smell burning. The men in the audience, monsignors and fathers, were transformed. The irritable dullness, the mottled predictability, had been washed away. They all looked extraordinarily young and innocent, clutching their hats in a pleading fashion, eyes wide open and wondrous, as if the childhood promise of magic had at last been realized.

There was a moment in which Nan met their gaze and swept her wand over them and felt genuinely possessed of some deep and mysterious power. It was the best – the absolute, gifty, tin lid best moment of her life. She sang another verse, improvising new snake movements. By now they came as second nature. The elves and posies sang a chorus and Nan danced again until, in a bitterly mortal moment, the curtains were pulled across on a clatter of metal rings and the stage went dark.

She stood shivering with delight and disappointment while the smaller children gathered up the exhausted fire crackers and scurried offstage.

She did not want to go away. She wanted to stay on the stage forever. There was a glorious reprieve when the curtains were swept back once more and the stage lights came on and a tiny girl ran up to

Nan and gave her a real posy – from a shop – of flowers. Nan wanted to undo the wrapping and throw the flowers one by one to the crowd. Instead she bowed gravely and waited for the advancing billow of curtain to consume her.

She was a star, elevated as the lovely ladies of America who wore coatees of mink and ermine and walked on spirals of celestial stars. How beautiful to be a woman, to have power without having to shout and go red in the face. She was a magnet, able to draw away all the gloom and disgust from the faces of grown men while she, in the gathering of their years, could transfer to herself the knowledge of ages. And she knew. She knew. She ran offstage with a curious lightness and separateness of her limbs as did the film actresses. She knew now why they used each limb with individual purpose when they walked instead of pooling the whole body to a single purpose of destination. She had seen it in the eyes of the men, now gawkish on her knees, now on her face, now on her bosom. She could feel the power in each separate portion of her body – even the parts she had never thought about before – as one feels in a pebble from the beach at the bottom of one's pocket, the crumbled cliffs, the captive insects, the frothing tides.

CHAPTER 16

'My cousin's here! My cousin's come to stay!'

A few days after the concert when boredom had set in and the children were almost wishing to be back at school, Nan was surprised to see Doll Cotter running toward her, waving her arms. It wasn't just Doll's excitement that interested her, it was the sight of those thin arms clawing the air like a swimmer. She couldn't remember having seen her before without her hands harnessed to the handle of a pram. She was glad of an event. She had not been able to settle since the concert. She sensed that a glorious future would come and claim her and it was difficult putting in the time until it did. Once or twice she had called on the Tallons but the twins seemed to have lost interest in fun and she did not like Dandy's new game which was to borrow schoolbooks from her older sisters who had now left school and to spend the day in the park with a book and an apple. She was suspicious of the treacherous manoeuvres of growth. It was only a few weeks since she had been a child and Dandy was adventurous and womanly. Now Dandy was burrowing back into childhood while she was exhausted by the stretch of her years. She felt isolated. Even Mary seemed preoccupied, impossible to provoke. She was not actually doing anything, but she had a busy air, like a bird that is thinking of building a nest. She longed for mother to return with gifts and stories and the scent of foreign places.

'Hi, Doll!' She climbed on to the concrete ledge in which the railings were rooted and swung herself around, holding the spike at the top with one hand. She wanted shoes. It was a part of the dissatisfaction of getting older, she discovered, to want a different thing, a more expensive thing, before the fulfilment of each previous desire. Her dancing feet, her lady's legs, were contemptuous of the splay-toed summer sandals or the hobnailers, which were standard footwear for children. She wanted bright red leather shoes with tiny heels and thin straps fastened with buttons.

Doll's white-gold hair flew out like ropes of pearls; her face was flushed from running and the delicate pink of her cheeks was matched by the fluffy strands of her jumper. Nan stopped swinging and clung to the railing, watching with interest. Doll was normally dressed in cut-down clothes that had belonged to her mother or been purchased from a cart. The jumper was new. It was palest pink, softest wool, embroidered with tiny deep pink rosebuds. It was nicer than any jumper Nan owned.

'My cousin Anastasia!' She slowed down, panting. 'Anastasia's here!'

'Where is she?' Nan said. 'Why isn't she with you?'

'She's at home. She's with the babies.'

'What's she like?'

'She is superb,' Doll said, without having to stop and think.

Nan jumped from her perch and followed Doll back to her house. She was disappointed, when they got there, to see a square-looking girl, about Doll's age, with a plain face.

'This is Anastasia, my cousin,' Doll presented proudly. 'This is my friend, Nan.'

'How do you do?' Nan said.

'Game ball,' the cousin said, but she did not lift her eyes from her knitting needles which rubbed and crossed busily like little animals washing their paws.

They watched from the gate, Doll with a look of respect and Nan with a frown. The girl had knees like rubber balls. She had tight curls and little squinty eyes. Anastasia took no notice but occasionally extended a large foot to rock the pram beside her on the porch. The baby did not make a sound. There was no noise but the clash of knitting needles.

'I have to go now,' Nan said.

'Don't you want to stay?' Doll was surprised that Nan was not content to remain and admire the cousin.

'I'm wanted at home.'

There was nothing to do at home. Nan ate some ham and tomatoes that Nellie had put out for lunch. She fed the hen and washed mottled milk from the cat's saucer, pouring in fresh from the jug on the table. 'Mary!' she called out in boredom. 'Yiss!' a clenched and muffled voice from the drawing-room. Nan went to find her, not sure if she wanted to play with her or persecute her. She found the child standing on top of a bookcase pinning Christmas decorations to the wall, her closed lips studded with drawing pins.

'Have you gone crackers?' she said.

'Nerts.' Mary threw her a little red rectangle like a prayer book which opened into a paper accordion and grew into a multi-coloured paper snake as it fell. She spat pins into the palm of her hand. 'Put those up, would you?'

'For what?'

'The concert.'

'Concert . . . ?'

'I told you.'

She remembered then, the night after the school concert Mary, in bed, had revealed a plan. She would organize a concert in the drawing-room, performed by local children and attended by their parents, the neighbours. Mary had been impressed by the commercial success of the school concert. The hall was packed with parents who had each paid a shilling for the privilege of watching their children's talents. Parents would pay anything to admire their children. Her own parents had never come to the school concert but she hoped they would be attracted by the convenient location. Father, anyway. They had no exact date for mother's return but she calculated that it ought to coincide with the concert which was planned to double as a welcoming celebration.

Nan was surprised to discover that the younger girl had already knocked upon the doors of neighbours and rounded up talents. There was to be an admission charge of twopence. A sale of tea and rock cakes would cover expenses. Mary was confident of a clear profit of five shillings.

'That's good,' Nan was forced to admit. On a generous impulse she volunteered her fairy dance for the programme. The thought of doing her dance again made her feel light-hearted and she helped Mary to pin red crepe paper around the light bulbs.

Later Nellie lent a hand. She opened the dividing doors and dragged the dining table across two floors to slot it in against the bay windows of the drawing-room where it made a lovely circular stage. She pushed the piano in against its edge for the convenience of the accompanist. Then she had a brilliant stroke. She untied the clothes line in the back yard and suspended it across the drawing-room ceiling between light fittings, draping it with two large brocade bedspreads for stage curtains. There weren't enough chairs in the house for the anticipated attendance so they decided they would ask each performer to bring two chairs for their own parents. The house could be made to yield sufficient seating for additional friends.

They finished at four. They were exhausted and covered with dirt but they still had to face another ordeal.

'We've got to ask permission from father,' Mary remembered.

Nellie wiped her nose with the back of her hand, leaving a grey streak. 'There bei'nt much he can do about it now, short of bust a gut,' she said philosophically.

'All the same,' Mary said firmly, 'he's got to be asked. We'd best wait outside for him, then we can let him know before he comes in and finds out by accident.'

'Well, he won't be in yet so we might as well have a cup of tea,' said Nellie, giving Nan a friendly slap on the arm to direct her to the kitchen.

They traipsed around the opened rooms with cups of tea, wondering if they should roll up the carpets, where ashtrays ought to be placed. Nellie was proud of her efforts. 'There's a thing, now, bringing theatricals to Hallinan's Mansions. There's a marvel.' She sank into an armchair and eyed the misplaced table as idly as if it was a stage at Covent Garden and she the holder of a box. 'I used to do a turn meself,' she released. 'Did you?' the children were avid. 'What did you do?' 'I'd chew up eggshells and then I'd swally them.' 'What for?' they were disappointed. 'It'd turn people's stummicks.' Nellie left her seat and went to inspect the stage. She stroked the surface of the table, playing with the dust. 'Dermot Seery took me to the seaside – a tram conductor from Gardiner Street – and treated me to me tea in a hotel with entertainments in Bettystown. There was an oul' divil on the piana and he was invitin' anyone to get up and sing a song. A one got up with a voice like a bag of drowned cats. I wanted to have a go but Dermot Seery was a very dry class of individual an' he hung on to me wrist as if I was a convicted crimnil. I would of given me two big toes to get up on that stage. Stagestruck. That's what it's called. I never got over that. I always felt I'd missed me true focation.'

'You should have gone back to the hotel with entertainments,' Mary said, 'without Dermot Seery.'

'An' who, may I ask, would pay for me high tea?' Nellie demanded with scorn. 'Any road, I didn't fancy the sea no more. When we came out after our tea I got a terrible fright for Jesus, God, wasn't the water all gone.' 'It's the tide,' Nan said but Nellie drowned out her reason. 'Oh . . . I do like to be beside the seaside,' she sang in a low growl, like Bertie when he was afraid. 'I do like to be beside the sea . . .' With no warning she hiked up her skirts and scrambled on to the table. She there executed an elephantine prance, heaving her slippered legs into the air and singing with threatening volume: 'I do like to be beside the tee-tee-tee-diddlydee-diddlydee-diddlydum-dum-dee. Oh, I do like to pee beside the seaside. I do like to pee into the sea . . .'

The children joined in, plunging about the floor, excited by the rudeness. There was a warm, dusty disorganized feel about the room and a reckless red sun flushed their faces. They all felt as happy as it was possible to feel and powerful too, having extended their territory to the drawing-room which was meant for a drier class of individual.

There was a dreadful knocking at the front door.

'It's father,' Nan whispered. The table rattled as Nellie's legs were claimed from the air. 'Oh, well,' Mary said quietly. 'He'll kill us.'

'Yis better answer it.' Nellie slid grimly to the ground, as the door was once more subjected to a bashing.

'Why hasn't he got a key?' Nan debated, reluctant to hasten the confrontation.

'Why hasn't he got a child with a ha'pworth of sense?' Nellie snapped unfairly, thinking of the reprisal due to herself. 'Let in your father.'

It wasn't father. It was Doll Cotter who stood on the step trembling, her eyes big and black as inkwells, when Nan gingerly pulled back the door. 'It's Minnie Willard,' Doll gasped. 'Come quick.' 'What's wrong?' Nan wanted to know but Doll just continued to plead and seized her arm and threatened to pull it from its socket. 'Oh, please come quickly or it will all be over,' she said. Nan went with her. 'I'll be back in a mo,' she called over her shoulder to Nellie and Mary, who cowered in the hall unable to shed their fear. What would be over, Nan wondered, as she panted after Doll and noted that her hair no longer flew about in strands but plopped on her back in a neat gold bunch that was held by a crochet ribbon in a shade of pink that exactly matched her pretty jumper. She could see Minnie Willard at the Cotters' gate. Was she trying to torture or kill one of the babies? Was she saying her awful insults to poor, sick Mrs Cotter? When they got to the house she saw that Anastasia was still on the front step. 'Oh, blazes,' she thought in dismay. It was Doll's precious cousin that Willard had come to torment. If Willard had her way, Anastasia would be driven away, leaving Doll once more the full burden of the babies.

Minnie and the cousin were watching each other. For the moment there seemed to be some sort of truce. Nothing to be heard but the clash of Anastasia's needles. Then Nan noticed an astonishing thing. Willard was crying. Her hands were curled into rosy fists and she scrubbed at her eyes. She made a thready whine of complaint. Anastasia watched complacently. 'An' that,' she said, 'is a scientific fact.'

'What is?' Nan interrupted.

Anastasia sniffed. 'Red-haired kids have loose blood,' she said. 'If they're brung up rough they sometimes last. Lots of potatoes and cabbage to tie up the veins. But *rich* red-haired kids are all natural born goners.'

'What happens to their blood?' Nan studied Minnie Willard with new interest.

'Left to their own devices they go consumptive.' Nan was beginning to understand Doll's admiration of the cousin. The gnashing rhythm of her knitting needles never altered, not even when she took her eyes off them for quite a long time to look at Willard with menace. 'If a red-haired kid got in someone's way and there might be a class of minor accident, like, say a jab of a knitting needle – then their blood all just falls out. There's no dryin' in red-haired blood. It just all falls out.' Anastasia turned her expressionless and slightly squinty eyes on Nan. 'I betcha now, you never seen her with a scab on her, like any normal kid. No dryin'.'

The children were silent with respect for it was true, they had never seen Minnie with a scab, like anyone else.

'You leave me alone!' Minnie squealed.

Anastasia pursed her large mouth. 'You get yourself an' your lavatorial language offa our doorstep or I'm warnin' you . . .' and for a moment she stopped knitting to point a needle at Minnie. The child let out a yelp and ran away toward home. The others remained admiring Anastasia over the bars of the gate. 'I'm going to a party,' Doll said.

'Whose?' Nan was amazed.

'Maddy Hafner's.'

Maddy Hafner was noted for the sophistication of her parties. She had all the latest gramophone records, such as 'Bye bye blackbird'. Nan had never been asked. Dandy had once gone in her boldest phase. 'When did she ask you?' Nan wondered.

'She didn't,' Doll said. 'She just told me she was having a party. It was Anastasia got me asked.'

'Anastasia?' The square, impassive cousin did not look as if she would fit in with Maddy Hafner's smart set.

'I didn't ask,' Anastasia corrected mildly. 'I told her I'd poke out her eye with me needle if Doll wasn't at her party.'

In the evening Nan had tea in the kitchen with Mary and Nellie. Nellie told them about a woman she had worked with who had three legs. 'One little short leg growin' out of the middle. She wore her skirts long to keep it hid. She didn't wear a shoe on it, only a woollen sock. We never knew. She never told no one she had a superfillous limb. One day a man came with a dog. The animal took a figary agin the poor creature as she was taking its owner's hat, an' didn't it make a set at her. The misfortunate cripple took a lep up the stairs on her three legs, using the short one for levveridge, like a boy on a pogo stick. Men went mad for her after the word got around. She told me once, they'd pay fourpence for a look and sixpence for a feel.'

Father had not returned. Nan put his tea to warm in the oven and left a note on the kitchen table. She set a cup and saucer and cutlery on the green baize table in the drawing-room. When the dishes from their own tea had been washed, she brought Mary out for a walk.

This did not follow their usual direction but took them away from the shops into a more select set of streets where the doors and railings of the houses were painted white and palms waved from little wooden tubs on the porches. Here the houses had names instead of numbers, Glenville, Sorrento, Ashleigh.

'Oh, look,' Mary said, 'there's a party.'

They stood beneath the lighted window, listening to music strained through a gravel of voices. Couples rolled past the window like horses on a merry-go-round. Mary was open-mouthed with enchantment. The girls inside were like angels, gliding and glowing, vanishing at the waist into puffs of chiffon and taffeta skirts. 'Oh, *look*!' the child said again. It really was an angel that came into view, unearthly pale with her white-gold hair puffed into curls and tied at the top with tiny pink ribbons. Doll wore the fluffy pink jumper that Anastasia had made for her and, underneath, a silky pink skirt.

'Come on, now,' Nan said. 'There's something else.' Mary did not want to go. She dared not believe that anything – except, perhaps, the Four Horsemen – could be better to watch. Nan had to pluck her fingers from the white railings. She brought her to see Anastasia. 'There y'are,' greeted the squat figure on the doorstep. She was counting stitches. Mary waited for something interesting to happen. The older girl did not look up again. Her needles made a noise like someone's false teeth. 'Who is she?' she whispered.

'It's Doll's cousin. It's Anastasia.'

'Oh.' Mary's tone limped with disappointment. 'Oh, come on, then.' Nan gave her an impatient tug, annoyed at having wasted on Mary the wonderful cousin who knitted and crocheted in party shades, who used her needles to orchestrate parties and subdue bullies.

Father was home before them. They heard the lonely pecking of fork at plate from the drawing-room as they let themselves into the hall. 'He's in there,' Mary whispered. 'Shh!' Nan cautioned. They waited for some clue to his mood from the noises of his dining until Nan, dreading her own imagination most of all, shouted out: 'We're home, father!'

There was a pause. They strained acutely. The dreary tap of cutlery resumed. 'Nothing!' Nan said. 'You wait.' Mary wagged her eyebrows. 'Murder will be done.' She pattered down the hall.

'Where are you off to?' Nan felt deserted.

'I'm going to dig a slug for the hedgehog.'

Tea rattled to a halt. There was still no sign of violence. Nan sighed and waited. She heard his chair being scraped back and then mouse-like shiftings. To her surprise there came a thin stream of noise. The

Ave Maria. He was playing the Ave Maria. She couldn't understand him. The drawing-room had been turned into bedlam and he had nowhere to eat his tea in peace after ten hours of hell at the factory. He was playing the Ave Maria.

'I'll do something to please him,' she thought, and was dismayed by how little came to her mind, how little she knew about his pleasures. Mother was all that came to mind and mother was not there. 'I'll tidy their room,' she decided, 'for mother's return.' She collected a little bouquet of brushes and clothes from the polish press beneath the stairs and she went up. The room had, as she expected, a restless and turbulent look. The eiderdown fell in an exhausted way over lumps of blanket and important items of gentleman's assembly drowned uselessly in dust on the surface of the dressing-table. Nellie said she got no inspiration doing for a man. Her heart wasn't in it.

Nan straightened the bed and pushed a huddle of shoes beneath it. She rubbed polish on the wooden bedhead to make a clean smell. She buffed the mirror on the dressing-table and scooped father's studs and pins into one of the little drawers. There was a piece of notepaper folded in this drawer and Nan took it out to arrange the items neatly. It had a single word scrawled across it in green ink, grandly, like someone's signature – 'Saturday' – and underneath, an initial, M. She looked at it for a moment. Perhaps father had put it there to remind him of mother's return. It was not his writing. It was writing she had not seen before. She put the paper back in its drawer and employed elbow grease to banish the dust and bring up a shine on the dressing-table's surface. She arranged mother's brushes and a bottle of perfume on this shining surface to take away the lost look of male occupation. The room looked better. Something niggled. She could not think what it might be. She thought she ought to check the sheets to see if they had been changed. Nellie might have invented the saying, 'what the eye cannot see . . .' She pulled back an edge of the coverlet and saw that the folded edge of sheet had a wilted and grappled look. She replaced it quickly and went downstairs, wishing she had not looked.

The music had stopped. There was a quietness so thick that it seeped out under the door, like a fog or a ghost. She waited until she could stand it no longer and was forced to risk his anger.

'Goodnight, father.'

He sat at the card table over some neglected part of his meal. He was looking unseeingly over the makeshift stage, out of the window.

'Goodnight, father.'

He turned to her. There was a terrifying look in his eye, as if it was some central part of his body not meant to be revealed, as if he had been cut open on an operating table and she was made to gaze deep into the wound. 'Nan,' he said. 'I have to talk to you.'

She stiffened with unease. He did not want to give her a talking to. He wanted to talk to her.

'I have to talk to someone. You're old enough, aren't you?'

It was not right. Children are not meant to carry the weight of adult hearts. She made no move into the room. They stayed watching each other until her light grey eyes became shaded with the look of closure he had seen so often in her mother's brown eyes. 'Oh, Nan,' he said. 'I've made a desperate hash of things.'

She closed the door and ran up to bed.

CHAPTER 17

The concert was a great success. One thing failed to go according to plan but it was not a thing that could have been foreseen.

In the days leading to the entertainment word spread like fleas at a circus. Talent presented itself from all parts of the parish, from walled residences to alleys, with ringlets and ballet shoes, with running noses and bare feet. Mary was able to vary her cast list. She could pick and choose. She sat on a step ladder with a jotter and a laundry marker, giving auditions. Boys had the most impressive talents. There was a boy who could play the harmonica with his nose and one with a 'singing' dog that howled when he sang. There was a Joseph Brady who did magic, taking nuts out of his ears and making a white mouse vanish up one sleeve and reappear from the other. Looking back it was easy to say that if they had confined the programme to such demonstrations the trouble would not have occurred but looking back was easy and the boys did terrible damage to the table with their boots.

The girls sang songs, did Irish dances or recited poetry with their elbows stuck out and their hands knotted into rosettes in the centre of their chests. They might have been just as nimble at pulling nuts out of their ears but they had to respond to their upbringing.

Artistes were to be paid with a glass of lemonade and a bun in the kitchen. To this end and for the refreshment of the audience during the interval, Nellie toiled over trays of grit-like knobs which came out of the oven looking exactly as when they had gone in, grey and serious, peppered with dried fruit. There was a sign on the front door. 'Gala concert. Admission Twopence. See the Astounding Talents of your Children!' It was a nice day. Elizabeth had been sitting on the porch all morning to avail of the scratching and petting fingers of visiting children. As a further intimation of the attractions to come, Mary hung a notice around the hen's neck. 'Something to crow about! Roll up!' It was considered an original idea but, as the first of the mothers arrived with their clacking heels, their snapping handbags and their fleshy laughter, the hen took fright and ran about, catching in their ankles, causing them to trip. The bird thought it was being used as a football and it screamed and dropped feathers and other unmentionables on the clean step until Nellie caught it under the meat safe where it was left all day, making little 'ark ark' noises of sadness or relief.

At ten to two the seats were full and there was five and fourpence in the money box. Behind the artily suspended bedspreads, Alice Devlin waited with her medals winking on her chest and her toe pointed.

They would have started only Veronica Fannigan had not yet arrived and she was to accompany on the piano. Mary peered into the dining-room at the audience. She wished she could have installed benches to make room for more. Hardly any of the fathers came but all the mothers were there, as well as aunts, sisters, observers. Mrs Guilfoyle had come even though she had no son or daughter in whom to invest pride. She had brought Mlle de Ravelais who was dressed for the occasion in an extraordinary dress made from layers of dull-coloured chiffon, grey, rust, black, giving the effect of some lighter-shaded garment that had been damaged in a fire. Only Mary's own parents had failed to arrive. Father had not been home the previous night and there was no message from mother, although Mary kept back the plush red chair in her bedroom for her viewing comfort, should she arrive.

In the kitchen they were starting to panic. 'We'll have to do without the piano,' Nan decided. 'Yis can't,' Nellie said. 'It's a perfessional concert. People have paid good money.'

The boy who played the harmonica with his nose said he would accompany but Nan thought an accompanist should have more dignity. 'We'll change the programme around,' she said. 'We'll put on the acts that don't need music in the first half. Dancers and singers after the tea break. The pianist is bound to have come by then.'

The boy with the harmonica opened the show. Then came the magician who caused screams of delighted fright when he pretended that his mouse had run away and he had sighted it vanishing up Mrs Bradish's skirt. He was really very good. The Tallon sisters' comedy act was not up to scratch but the audience had warmed up and was receptive to their cracks. The Martindale girls sang a song in harmony. It was decided that the boy who sang with his dog did not require competition from the piano so he too was pushed on stage before the interval. While this was going on a very small boy came and knocked loudly on the door. 'Me sister's got the mumps,' he panted. 'You want the doctor, son,' Nellie told him and was about to close the door in his face when he protested: 'Me sister! Veronica Fannigan! She's meant to be on the piano.'

The show was going remarkably well. The women's knees had fallen at relaxed angles and the gritty wash of their laughter mocked and praised the performers. Even Nellie had run from her arrangement of cups and buns to have a smoke and snigger in the doorway. When the time came for the interval they were so parched with mirth that some went back for second helpings of tea – although they did not demand additional buns – and pennies piled up in the separate box that was earmarked for expenses.

When they were settled back in their seats and the boys in the kitchen had commenced a war with the remnants of Nellie's rock cakes, the children decided they would have to go ahead without the piano. The boy with the mouth organ was accepted as accompanist, although he was to stay out of sight behind the curtains for fear of provoking hysterics.

'Quiet, please! Everyone resume places!' Mary organized her cast. Two small children seized the stage curtain at each of its inner corners and ran back rapidly so that the stage was revealed. The audience coughed in appreciation of Alice Devlin's pink cheeks and dimpled knees. They waited attentively. After a time they heard, somewhere in the distance, a mouth organ. They frowned and gripped their handbags. They were beginning to feel the after-effects of Nellie's buns. They needed music to keep them going. The mouth organ, swaddled in dust and brocade, was no more than the provocative echo of some remote and alternative celebration. Alice began to dance. Her feet hammered the top of the table. Her medals clattered. 'She needs a piano!' grumbled Mrs Mulvey, who was sitting at the back. 'Give us a belt of the joanna,' seconded Mrs Guilfoyle. Mary watched anxiously. Things were not going well. She was alarmed when Mrs Hanlon, with a rebellious wink at her friends, stood up.

'This won't do! This calls for action!' She thrust herself between the jammed chairs and discontented bodies. 'They're going to ask for their money back,' Mary thought. She wondered if she could get away with giving them each a penny since they had already enjoyed a good half of the concert. To her surprise the woman did not make for the door with a mouthful of complaints but headed for the stage. Mary thought she was going to take it out on poor, nervous Alice but she did not. With an arch wriggle of her behind she installed herself at the vacant chair by the piano, yanked back the lid and commenced to plunder the keys. She was accomplished. Mrs Hanlon's reel had none of Veronica Fannigan's exam-conscious prissiness. It was a rollicking sound, as meaty as the woman's laugh. Alice responded with some sensational kicks and soon the audience was clapping in time with the piano and the few men were making the required whooping and whistling noises. 'Oh, thank you, thank you,' Mary breathed silently. She vowed that if the woman made to leave the piano she would beg her personally to stay but when Alice went down the step ladder behind the table, it was clear that Mrs Hanlon meant to remain. After a brief and dutiful smattering of applause for the child, the audience directed a storm of clapping at the pianist, whose features were pink with joy.

Doll Cotter clambered on to the stage. She had not been invited for her talent. She had a tiny, chalky voice, barely tuneful. Nan had picked her because she wanted to show her off.

She looked beautiful in her new pink sweater and skirt. Her hair had been curled with tongs and Nan had borrowed her mother's pearls, which were never worn, and arranged them in her hair like a hairband. She was still not self-possessed. She stood on the table breathing heavily, wringing her hands. 'If I were a blackbird,' she mused aloud, as a clue to the pianist, and with no further delay she launched into her song. Mrs Hanlon used her elbows in the accompaniment, as if she was washing the collar of a boy's shirt. The tune rose like a whole flock of birds in fright. Doll could hardly be heard. 'Sing up, girlie,' complained Mrs Guilfoyle. Doll swallowed nervously and it appeared she had swallowed her voice in fright for now no sound came at all. 'Eef I wore a blackbirrrd . . .' Mrs Guilfoyle encouraged. She waved her arms like the bishop giving his blessing. The women heaved up their voices obediently. After a while Mrs

Guilfoyle rose like a blackbird and fluttered through the crowd. She ascended the table and there sang the whole of the song, leaving Doll standing timidly at the table's edge.

The volume of her voice pitched against the beating of the piano was like the battle of the Titans. They were Titans, these adults. The children sensed the day was lost. When Peggy Sullivan stood up to sing 'The Last Rose of Summer' dressed in a long frock and a wide-brimmed hat with flowers, Mr St John the auctioneer, who had been apparently dozing, suddenly stood up and seized his wife's overcoat. He borrowed plain hats from two of the ladies and pushed these into the chest of the coat. He took a swing at the stage so that his trousered legs and his mean little feet in black shoes could be seen beneath his wife's cherry wool. The child on the stage stepped back in fright and did not even cry when the man took the hat from her head and put it on himself. He began to sing. He kept rolling his eyes under that hat and pushing up the extra hats hidden in his chest. The audience shrieked with laughter; it rocked. Children ran up from the kitchen and huddled, mystified, in the doorway. Mr St John wiggled his behind. The ordinary women, the housewives, so set in their respectability, were cackling and crumpled with delight. The children knew they must do something. They felt as if the house had been set on fire.

'What will we do?' 'Who'll go next?' They consulted in worried whispers. 'Nan! The fairy dance!' Mary proposed, remembering the effect of the fairy dance on the parents at the school. She had unselfishly decided to scrap her own performance of the Ballad of Paddy von Longfong. The mood was not right for poetry. A dramatic remedy was called for. Even the pianist no longer played but slumped over the instrument twitching, attacked by mirth as if by machine-gun fire.

Nan put on lipstick and arranged her hair while Mr St John brought his astonishing performance to an end and leaped triumphantly from the table. Mary had been waiting on the step-ladder. She climbed to the stage and made her announcement. 'We are now going to have a fabulous dance.' The women whimpered with glee and rubbed tears from their tragic eyes. The contemptuous faces grew gradually composed. 'Mamzelle de Rav. used to be some class of a dancer,' commented Mrs Guilfoyle to no one in particular. '*I* was a fabulous dancer,' Mlle de Ravelais said severely. 'I was a prima ballerina. I did the dance of the gazelle.'

Immediately the audience began to applaud, raising their hands, clapping the lodger to action. 'Oh, please hurry, Nan,' Mary prayed and, while Nan was arriving at the foot of the steps, Mlle de Ravelais had stood up and was bowing to her neighbours with a look of great hostility. She traversed the room in little mincing steps and then with an astonishing leap she was standing on top of the table. She bowed again. Her dance commenced with a slow pirouette and she began to whirl, faster and faster, brushing up the layers of her dress to show warm underwear beneath. She began to prance, holding her head at a challenging angle. The pianist improvised with some sounds that were like light carpentry.

Mlle de Ravelais spun violently and then she made a great leap, rising like an arrow shot from a bow, descending with both legs spread far apart. It was meant to be the splits. To be fair, her dance did show signs of some much earlier experience and it was largely due to the size of the table that the choreography was not successful. There was not room for both of her legs. She pitched to the floor like a stick flung for a dog. Cries of dismay mingled with the scraping sounds of laughter. 'Oh, sacred hour is she dead?' cried a woman in a voice strangled with delight. 'I'm nearly killed myself.'

It was clear that the concert was at an end. No one else could go on, not with Mlle de Ravelais stretched limply and at such peculiar angles among the rags of her chiffon. Nan hurried to fetch Nellie. Nellie stole some rum from father's store and held it to the Frenchwoman's lips. The pale mouth nuzzled greedily at the glass. 'She's coming back,' cried a woman. 'She's all right.' 'We ought to wait and see if her leg is broken,' said another witness doubtfully but already the audience was straightening itself for the street and beginning to push each other to the hall, with last amused looks over their shoulder to remind them of the gas of the afternoon.

'Are you all right?' Nellie shook the prostrate woman. Mlle de Ravelais finished the rum in slow, considered sips. Only Mrs Guilfoyle and a few of the children now remained. 'I am all right,' the lodger said faintly. 'I am yoomeeliated.'

'Yerra, come on home, dear,' said Mrs Guilfoyle. 'If your bones are in one piece there's nothing to detain you.'

The woman scrambled to her feet. She was obviously not injured. 'There ees!' she protested.

'There ees what?' Mary straightened the extraordinary cobwebby panels of chiffon.

'There ees a thing to detain me.'

'What thing?' Mrs Guilfoyle said.

'There ees the matter of my fee.'

'Fee?'

'I am a professional dancer. Always I command the highest fee.' She held out her hand.

'How much?' Mary had gone white.

'Ten shillings.'

Mrs Guilfoyle rattled with laughter but no one else did.

'We haven't got ten shillings,' Nan said, astonished.

'Eight shillings.'

'There isn't much more than six shillings,' Nan said, 'and . . .'

'Six shillings.' The woman's hand was still extended. Her eye was like steel.

Mary sighed. 'The box,' she said. 'On the hall table.'

Mlle de Ravelais stamped out and collected the money box. 'How much?' She rattled it.

'Five and fourpence.'

'Six shillings.'

They had to go to the kitchen and open the expenses box for the other eightpence.

'Put it down to experience,' Nellie said much later. 'Experience is useful.' They were having a makeshift tea with toast in the kitchen. They had to light the fire to comfort themselves. They were tired. They had tidied up the dining-room and drawing-room, pulled down the curtains and decorations and restored the furniture to its proper setting. The performing artistes – some of them in tears – had been sent home with the borrowed chairs. The remains of the buns had been swept up and emptied into the coal shed for the animals. There was a fry under the grill for father although they did not really expect him home. They had given up hope of mother's return that evening. There was nothing to do but mope.

'Nothing is any use,' Mary sighed. 'I'm never going to do anything again until I'm grown up.'

'You might be right,' Nellie said.

'It was a good concert,' Nan said. 'It would have been all right with the proper pianist.'

Nellie gave a little yelp of laughter. She pulled a sod of blackened bread from the toasting fork and blew on it. 'I used to work for a very superior sort of woman in Sandymount, with a young fella, three or four. Them people was so respectable they invented their own language. The young fella always referred to his micky as a "pianis". "Don't you be foolish," says I, "a 'pianis' is a man that plays the piana".' She chuckled softly. The children huddled over the fire, comforted by the sound.

There was a knock at the door. 'It's father,' they said.

'No t'isn't,' Nellie said. 'An' you're not to be putting the heart across me again. Your father always has his key. It must be your mother.'

'Mother! Mother!' the children cried out. The hopelessness of the day was forgotten as they raced each other to the hall and pulled open the door. In the thickening dusk they stood watching the dark figure on the step, waiting patiently for their eyes to adjust to the gloom and relieve the baggage-burdened figure of her blackness. They wondered why, after all the time away, she did not drop her bags and throw out her arms to them. They stood shyly blinking until their accustomed stare lightened the sky and confirmed the darkness of their visitor.

CHAPTER 18

Mother came home the following day. She was confused because no one had come to meet her. 'Didn't you get my postcard?' she said. 'I sent a postcard from a foreign city.' She handed Nan a startling hat, recently nested on her hair. 'All the women in Europe are having their hair bobbed. It is the latest thing. The Marcel is dead.' Then, seeing the windblown look of the children, she said, 'Father?'

It was Nellie who stepped out of the gloom of the hall, pitching forward as if there was a force against her. 'There is a visitor, ma'am, to see you.'

'Who is it? Is it one of the neighbours? I have not yet stepped through the door.' She had the look of a bird, eager yet apprehensive. Nan held the festive hat over her mouth.

'Where is father?' mother said. She was tired. Coming home tired her. For the past weeks she had enjoyed the sharp taste of freedom. It had a taste, actually. It was like a lime. She had sat down on her own at tables dressed in pink linen with gay baskets of fruit and tiny childish posies. Once she had taken lunch at a table in the street. Lovely meals, the vegetables half cooked in separate little dishes! She enjoyed the ceremony. She had not been lonely, never once wondered what to do. Foreign men were so attentive. One had begged her, begged her to be his wife. Ridiculous. It made her laugh, the strange man with his absurdly miserable face and his wagging moustache. 'I have . . . loved ones . . . at home.' That is what she said. 'If you would let your hair down and allow me to touch it, I would remember it all my life,' he said. And she did, although she would never tell this to anyone. When she came down to dinner next evening her hair flooded the collar of her lace blouse. She had not let him touch it, of course. She chose a table at the furthest end of the restaurant and watched his panic-stricken eye above a pile of prawns while she ate a big white fish.

'Loved ones.' She loved the sound. She did not miss them. It was only a matter of weeks. She would have liked the little girls to be more flower-like in their clothing. She had done her best in this respect. Her husband's pink face appeared in her head. A god. She loved him. She always had. He was the handsomest man she had ever met. If she could frame his face, divide it from the chaos of his person.

A man stepped past her into the hall, warped with baggage. It was her cab driver. The bang of the cases on the hall runner alerted her to the present. 'Who is this person who wishes to see me?'

She startled Nellie with her imperative tone. The maid scraped her feet like a dog.' 'It's a woman, ma'am. It's most peculiar.'

'Oh,' mother sighed. 'One of father's friends. I'm not sure I can . . . .' She took off her navy overcoat. She was wearing a dress of brown crêpe de chine, a yellow flower clenched at her breast. Her legs showed. She glanced down at them and at her small feet which were encased in neat shoes instead of the familiar boots. She allowed the children a small smile – perhaps she was amused by their astonishment. 'A cup of tea, Nellie,' she said. 'We will all feel better when we have had a cup of tea. Our visitor will not mind waiting until I have drawn breath.'

'Oh, ma'am!' Nellie clutched the blue coat like a person. 'It is most terrible. This person has been in the drawing-room since yesterday. She will not remove herself. Mister has not been home.'

'You have not offered her a bed in the Indian room?' Mother was reproving.

'No ma'am, I have not. It is a darkie. Black as the ace of spades.'

'I have been to Europe, Nellie. I have seen people of all hues and persuasions.' But mother looked unsure of herself. The shrug of her shoulders became a shudder. 'Put the kettle on at once. We must get this over with.' She went to the drawing-room. Nellie hung at her heels, unable to abandon the horror for it was very interesting. The children were compelled as far as the doorway.

The woman sat on the sofa. She had a jewel in her nose. Over a many-coloured sari she wore an Aran cardigan.

Mother said hello. The Indian stared at her. 'So,' she said. 'There you are.'

'Can I help you?' mother said.

The woman considered 'I do not see you as an ally. We must each help ourselves.'

She turned to Nellie but Nellie jerked her head to convey ignorance. 'Who are you?' she said.

'I am Missis Cantwell,' the Indian said in a little dark, drawstrung voice.

'Lord save us, another of God's demented,' Nellie whispered.

'Who are you?' mother said patiently. 'What is your business?' She wanted to say, 'I am Mrs Cantwell, let us have no more of this nonsense.' But she was not, and it made her head spin.

'I am Missis Mumtaz Cantwell of Calcutta. I wish to see my husband.'

Mother studied the furniture critically and selected a hard chair with a seat covered in stripes of satin. She sat down and stared past the visitor, out of the window, with a preoccupied air. When she returned her attention at length it was with an obvious effort, as if extreme boredom or extreme tiredness claimed her. 'Your husband . . . ?' she said politely.

'My husband, Mr Cecil Cantwell of the horse regiment of the army of the British Empire. We were married in Calcutta in nineteen hundred and six. Six months later he left me and did not return. Since then I have been seeking him. What else was there for me to do?'

Mother's eyebrows had shot up and her eyes were large but her mouth remained calm. 'This is a sorry story,' she said, 'but I cannot see how it concerns me. My husband is Mr Webster. He has a business in the city.'

'I know him and he knows me,' the woman said.

'Take no notice, ma'am,' Nellie encouraged. 'She's not the full shilling.'

'I have here a photograph.' The woman was rooting in a big bag embroidered with beads.

'No!'

The boy in the photograph looked cross but the curve of his jaw was soft out of the rigid neck of his uniform. His hair was almost white and his skin tanned as it had been when mother met him. The savage eyes of the girl pierced a storm of white lace. Both Nellie and mother were surprised by the white lace because it meant something different to them, something unconnected to heathen continents.

Mother put a hand to her mouth and rocked her body. Nan's eyes were on the hem of the brown dress which lapped her calves with each movement, forward, back, forward, back. She unshielded her lips. They were pale in her golden skin. 'I must lie down,' she said. 'Will you bring up my bags, Nellie, and show this lady to her proper quarters?' She left the room quickly, brushing past the children who watched her chalky lips jealously, for they had not had their kiss. They slipped down the hall and out the back door, running crookedly along the yard to the shed where they clambered on to the coal and felt in the dark for the hen and the hedgehog.

'Black as the ace of spades,' Nellie grumbled as she hauled mother's two soft velvet grips up the stairs to her room. The light was off but she switched it on thoughtlessly for she could tell no one was there. 'Ma'am?' she called, frightened. 'Oh, Sacred Mother of Jesus.' She ran to the bathroom, cursing its black emptiness. 'Don't you be ridicklis,' she scolded her hammering heart, dropping the cases to clutch at it as she burst into the children's bedroom. It wore the day's veneer of haphazard tidying. There was no one there. 'Where are you, ma'am? Answer me.' No one answered.

The moon gaped directly in the window of the Indian room and she did not need to exert the light switch. The leaves of a leathery tree gyrated like a shower of pennies at the glass. Their dotted light struck the big trunk with its tiger-skin rug and lit up the bed. She saw the small, peaceful hump beneath the blankets. 'Ma'am?' Nellie yelped softly, like a cat. There wasn't an answer. Mother was sound asleep.

Some time after midnight father came home. He woke Nan with his furtive entry and she sat up in bed trying to remember what terrible thing it was that she had to accommodate in her mind. His frightened footsteps squeezed the steps; dry wood-grunts.

He went into his room. There was silence – and then a shout. A single cry, short. She heard him coming out of the room and then running down the five steps to the return landing where he flung open the door of the Indian room. 'Mags!' he cried. 'Mags!' He stayed in there a long time. Nan could hear nothing. Eventually, when she had lain down again and was drifting into sleep, she was disturbed by him coming out of the room, sneaking down the stairs.

In the morning, when she came down, he was sitting rigid in an armchair, wrapped up in a blanket like a baby, his face thunderous with self-pity.

CHAPTER 19

Nellie would not cook for the visitor. It was the matter of station. She defiantly ferried the plates of fried food to the dining-room in sets of two and then stamped back to the kitchen cursing about the pot calling the kettle black.

The Indian criticized her. She intimated that she herself had been brought up in a house of many servants who would, had their mistress desired it, have eaten a live snake. Nellie muttered that the venom was maybe contagious. The Indian's nostrils flared and her jewel twinkled. 'You have no authority in this household,' she accused mother. 'You are unable to command peace for the master.' Nellie banged down chops and mashed potatoes in front of mother and father. Mother said nothing. She had retreated into a dreamlike state. Most of her time now was spent in the Indian room with her books. She came down to meals and ate what was put before her. In spite of Nellie's poor hospitality the Indian too attended mealtimes. She did not suffer from lack of food for she had anticipated a problem with catering and had brought in her packing a small spirit stove upon which she wrought pungent messes in her bedroom.

Father was divided. Most of his mealtimes were spent staring at mother in an agony of wistfulness and regret. Occasionally his glance was torn away to attach itself to the Indian in admiration. She was the only woman he had ever heard mention the debt of respect due to him, although he had always imagined such a debt.

He could hardly remember her. She bore no resemblance to the thin exciting girl he had married because of the dry heat she exuded, which was like the climate of the country. Years later when he was seriously married and had the children he won a competition in a magazine. He was photographed holding his prize and identified with his military past and a portion of his address. There came, three months afterwards, a letter in vengeful green ink: '. . . at last I have found you. Soon I will come . . .'

'How the devil?' he would demand of himself as the green letters pursued him in subsequent years, the postmarks drawing closer. It was not a real question, merely a complaint. He knew very well that people find what they need, just as they get what they deserve.

There was a terrible incident. Nellie tried to murder the Indian with a kitchen knife.

It was about a week after her arrival, a hot, dull Saturday. The quiet of the house was sundered by a fearful sequence of screams. The noise disturbed mother's reading and she sat on the edge of the bed with a thumping heart, a hand touching her throat, wondering if anyone would expect her to do anything. She followed the noise cautiously to the kitchen and stood in the doorway watching the two large women, the brown one and the white one, wrestling to the death. The Indian punched Nellie's face and Nellie pulled her hair. They bashed one another around the kitchen table; but it was Nellie who had the handle of the knife gripped in her fist and was working, stubborn-jawed, to get the point of its blade between the dark woman's breasts. Mother kept very quiet for she did not wish to interrupt Nellie. It was then she noticed that the assailants were also intently silent. The screams came from the hen. It was on the kitchen table, running up and down in a panic, its feet slipping on little piles of coconut and saffron and dried fruit, its feathers flying in a helpless storm.

The noise drew outside attention. Children came in from the Mad Lane. The Martindale girls crammed the doorway of the kitchen. Mrs Bradish rattled her rosary. No one knew what to do.

It was the Martindale girls who came to the rescue. They began to titter. The sound, sniggery at first, took on a sawing pitch as they held each other for support and jiggled with mirth at the sight of the two women trying to kill each other. Nellie, distracted, rounded on the onlookers with her weapon. They all backed away. Mother, seeing that she was supported by witnesses, reached out a pale hand. 'Hand me that, like a good girl, Nellie.' She hoped Nellie would know by the tone of her voice that she was not giving out. Mrs Bradish reeled into the kitchen and collapsed on one of the settle beds which had been introduced to the kitchen. 'Oh, God help us,' she wailed. 'What atrocities are under this roof?' Nellie and mother looked uncomfortable. It was a general question rather than one tied to the incident. The Indian had been with them almost three weeks. All the neighbours were becoming impatient. Nellie handed the knife to mother. 'Thank you,' mother said. 'Now, you must not go around committing murder because of simple domestic disagreements.' 'As God is me witness I never done murder in me life,' Nellie said. 'It's this misbegotten Maharanny that's of a murderous intent.' She pointed furiously at the Indian.

'Did she try to kill you?' Nan said.

'She done worse,' Nellie accused. 'She attempted to dissimilate an innocent hen!'

'Oh, Elizabeth!' Mary cried. She ran to seize the bird, squeezing it fiercely. It screamed in outrage and terror.

It turned out that the Indian had attempted to convert the hen into a curry for the table. She had developed a custom of going to the shed each morning to feel under its idle bottom for an egg. The children kept up their pretence with an egg from the larder for father's breakfast. The Indian spied on them. She perceived their game. She was not amused.

'The master's money is being wasted on food for a useless bird,' she said. 'I attempt only to recompense his loss with a pleasing dinner.' She flung a contemptuous hand in Nellie's direction. 'What this woman puts in front of the master ought not to be offered to goats. This is a rebellious and ungrateful household.'

The scene was being witnessed with flawless attention. The black eyes of the Martindale women swivelled from one astonishing confession to the next.

'If you're not going to offer us a cup of tea, missus, you might introduce us to your visitor,' said Mrs Bradish. Gladys and Dilys tittered. Mother waved a vague hand at the Indian. 'It is our new cook.'

'What is her name?' Mrs Bradish pursued. 'Has Nellie got too good to do the cooking?'

Nellie stepped forward. 'Her name is Mrs Mumtaz,' she offered with surprising presence of mind. 'She is from Calcutta.'

'Mr Webster served in India, you know.' Mother had recovered. 'He missed the hot dishes. Our new cook is fiery, like the food she cooks but she is . . . loyal.' She managed a smile for the Indian. Astonishingly the woman offered no protest. She gave mother a dark glance but she only set about tidying the ruin of her spices from the kitchen table, sweeping them from one palm to the other. Then she went into the scullery. Nellie looked pleased. Her expression was even bolder than usual. 'Put on the kettle, Mrs Mum!' she called out cheekily. 'We could all use a cup.' She put a hand over her mouth to cover her audacity. There was a tense silence and then they heard, with relief, the splatter from the tap into the tin kettle.

'Astonishing really,' mother said, 'that such an ordinary thing as tea comes all the way from India.'

She came to be known as Mrs Mum. She did take over the cooking, except in the morning, when she stayed in bed. After the horror of its strangeness, they grew to look forward to the interesting food. They were all afraid of her but they were able to relegate her to a place in their minds where she exerted no emotional sway. She was like Sister Immaculata or like Hammer, before Mary had met him, when he was only a ghoulish figment of Nellie's imagination.

Father no longer slept with mother. At first he had spent all his evenings sitting on the edge of her bed in the Indian room, holding her hand, whispering, trying to make her understand. She did understand. She smiled and patted his suit, anxious to get back to her book. She felt no real loss of her nights without him. He used to groan in his sleep and argue with himself, plunging about until he woke and clung to her for comfort. She liked waking up to see the quilt of the bed barely disturbed. The full enormity of the situation was too great for her mind to even consider it. Something would happen. She could not criticize father. Her mind was pitched to accommodate weaknesses in men.

Father did not argue with his usual persistence. He knew all along there wasn't a choice. The loss of mother by his side was appalling but had she accepted him, under the circumstances, she would not have lived up to his expectation. He took over the children's room, putting settle beds in the kitchen for them. He grew quiet.

The children felt like Nellie's children, living in one room. It was nice to sit up in bed on the long evenings listening to the wireless and eating bread and jam from the scullery. There were other benefits. Because mother had more time to herself, she allowed them to visit her room, so long as they were quiet. The change in father meant that the house was more peaceful, even at breakfast. Only Nellie kept up a pretence of mutiny. She would not eat the curries. She murmured about plots and poison. Relieved of most of the cooking duties, she did not know what to do with her time. It was too late for her to turn into a conscientious housekeeper. She took the children for walks, introducing them to places of interest: the house of a nurse who murdered unborn babies, a restaurant where the chef had been charged with knocking rats from the rafters into the pots of soup.

The mystery was so large that Nan felt a child again. It was a relief to be able to play ball in the lane, to eat bread and sugar when she felt depressed. Most of her time was spent out of doors to avoid Mrs Mum. She grew thin and brown. Deprived of her reflection in her wardrobe mirror, she forgot about her hair. It bleached in the sun, the Marcel was now just a crisp hem at the end of the soft yellow waves.

A boy she had met at a party, Nat Hurd, was in love with her. He threatened to climb up the drainpipe to her bedroom window but she told him that, if he did, he would come face to face with her father and was forced to add that she slept in the kitchen. Every night he climbed over her garden wall and clawed on the outside of the window. When he came she got out of bed and went to watch him through the glass. He mouthed passionate cravings at her. Sometimes it was raining and his face was blurred by ribbons of water. She could easily have let him into the passage and given him a kiss or she could have told him to go away but he was good-looking and she looked forward to his visits. He told her that he loved her, that he would die for her, that he would wait forever to marry her, or so it seemed to her, for the boy was terrified to speak aloud and the only sound that came was Mary's torpid breathing and occasional cries of discomfort from the hen which Mary now, sensibly, took to bed with her.

CHAPTER 20

Mlle de Ravelais' fiancé came to visit. It was a triumphal occasion because people had not believed in their hearts that the thin, highly strung spinster in the mildewed clothes was admired by a man. People reacted well. They commented on the angle of his beret and the nobility of his name, which was Gaston de Droff. In spite of this the Frenchwoman had been in tears since her lover's arrival.

'He hasn't been attempting anything out of the ordinary?' quizzed Mrs Guilfoyle. Apart from a violent shake of her head which scattered tears over Mrs Guilfoyle's pink wool bosom, the woman was too distraught to respond. It was very curious. Monsieur le Droff was not disturbed. He seemed to find such emotion agreeable in a lady. He attached her to his arm and wheeled her around the streets, turning every now and then to pat her hand or gaze into her exhausted face. Mrs Guilfoyle and the other women of the neighbourhood did their best to uncover the unpleasantness but it wasn't any use. They decided to take the case to mother. The neighbours had not been close to her since the episode at the hairdresser but they missed her and they all agreed that there was no one like her in a crisis. It wasn't that she said much, but she provided an angle of listening that made you talk, extracted the sap of the dilemma.

Mlle de Ravelais was marched in between Mrs Guilfoyle and Mrs Lehane. She was left sighing in the drawing-room while the married women went to look for Nellie and after a series of consultations the visitors were brought to the Indian room. When they saw it, the location gave the neighbours a temporary setback. They left Mlle de Ravelais to gaze out of the window and suck on her knuckles while their eyes whipped about the room, taking in the single bed, the pieces of mother's toiletry, her pile of books on top of the tiger-skin. Mother was watching them. 'Good afternoon, Mrs Guilfoyle, Mrs Lehane,' she said. 'Good day, missus,' said Mrs Guilfoyle. She still could not bring herself to say Webster. 'I am so pleased to see you,' mother said. 'I have been a little low. I am longing to hear your news. Children, give the ladies a place to sit. Run along and get some air.'

Mary had been curled up in the red armchair which mother had brought from her old bedroom and Nan was on a footstool. They gave up their places reluctantly. They were jealous in regard to time spent with mother. As the married women settled into the seats and a sense of communion brewed up among the adults they saw that they need not carry out mother's instruction fully, for no one noticed them. They sat on an edge of the trunk in attitudes of exemplary boredom so common with girls of the day that they became completely invisible.

'Is something the matter?' With a glance, mother indicated the wretched figure at the window. She stood beside Mary and the child could not help staring. When they had last met, the woman had been shabby and slightly batty but she had the authority of a grown-up. Now she seemed furred and decayed with disillusion, like an old kettle ready for the bin. It was strange to see an enemy so reduced, an adult so low on spite. She thought that she ought to be able to love her now but she only saw her misery like stones in a stream; she was no longer unsurpassable.

'It is Mamzelle de Rav.,' said Mrs Guilfoyle. 'She is grievously afflicted.'

'You must sit beside me, mademoiselle,' mother said. 'I will make good company.'

The woman seemed improved by this prospect. She scurried across the room and leaped on to the bed like an animal. She leaned against mother.

'It is to do with a man,' Mrs Lehane hinted.

'No,' mother said. 'Let her speak for herself.'

They waited. A minute was punctuated by long wet sighs. Mother stroked the woman's dry waves. 'Eet ees Gaston.' Her voice was chalky, tremulous. 'Five years I wait for my marriage. He goes to Dieppe to work and save for a home. And now . . .' the words rose to a yelp, 'he has come.'

'It sounds quite satisfactory,' mother said.

'Oh, no! You do not understand!' she shook her head in protest.

'As a man he is . . .' she made a murmuring noise with her tongue and her teeth while she sought the word '. . . incomplete.'

'Paddy von . . .' Mrs Guilfoyle recalled, but Mrs Lehane held the stitching. 'Incomplete?' she said on four or five syllables.

'Ah, yes,' said the lodger. 'Five years I screemp in solitude and misery for a man' – her voice went down to a dangerous growl and she made a yawning face and pointed into the dark cavern of her mouth – 'who will not trouble to put in his teeth.'

'His teeth?' the women looked at each other in bewilderment. They were used to quantifying the defects of men in terms of deprivation and brutality. Physical imperfections scarcely counted.

'They sit on the dresser and they scorn me,' the woman moaned. 'He only puts them in to smile at strangers. For me – the gums!'

Mother was wholly attentive. As always, the only time she seemed fully alert was when talking to the neighbours. 'You are a young woman,' she said earnestly to Mlle de Ravelais. 'It is natural that you should concern yourself with physical superficialities. But you must not allow them to ruin your prospect of marriage.' The woman made a moan of protest. 'Appearances are not everything,' mother pressed. 'Often, the rough diamond is the truest prize.' She herself did not believe this to be true but it seemed the right sort of thing to say. 'Your young man has been saving up for his marriage. His mind has been on serious matters. He had not had time to apply himself to the frivolous aspects of courtship.'

This had a bad effect on the woman. She flung her head about as if she needed to be rid of it. 'You do not understand,' she cried. 'He has saved no money. He has come for my money. He wishes to borrow my life's savings of fifty pounds.'

There was silence. Mother sighed. She took the lodger's pale hands and shook them gently. 'Gaston le Droff is no good,' she said with regret. 'You must have nothing more to do with him. Tell him now before he weakens your resolve. Inform him that you will not marry him.'

'But, Meeses Webster!' the woman wailed piteously, 'I am twenty-nine.'

It was a useful moment. It asserted mother's new name. After that the neighbours had no trouble addressing her as Mrs Webster and even the children began to think of themselves as Websters. At the same time Nan and Mary acquired a view of female life as a brief, colourful rainbow, an arc which ran to earth at twenty-nine.

CHAPTER 21

Mrs Mumtaz took to waiting for father on the landing. She was there each night when he went to bed. 'It is not good for a full-blooded man to sleep alone,' she whispered. 'When the blood boils and is not soothed, it turns to poison. You do not sleep well, sir. That room is an unfit place. I hear you toss and turn in the night, pitched about by its unsavoury elements. Your face becomes bruised like a sky before a storm.' She stood very close to him. Her warm breath was on his face, her perfume in his head. 'No,' he said. 'You know nothing of my life. I sleep perfectly well. I have . . . financial worries.'

But when he climbed into the children's bed, he could not sleep. The room was suffocatingly hot. The ancestors creaked and murmured in their frames. He did not know how to sleep on his own. He had never imagined a time when there would not be the soft offering of a woman's body, laid out beside him. His blood boiled. He was pestered by the thought of it turning to poison. He could not comfort himself for he was a fastidious man and he was under the gaze of the ancestors who had shaped him.

He leaped out of bed and went to the window where he leaned against the glass and gave voice to his deep confusion. 'Bloody hell,' he said. 'Bloody hell.'

He could no longer bear the room. She had haunted it for him. He went back to his old room and there she was, waiting for him.

CHAPTER 22

Mary had two and ninepence.

'Who gave you that?'

'No one gave it. I made it.'

The children were in the garden having a race with caterpillars. They had a wooden chopping board from the kitchen and stalks of cabbage. 'You can't *make* money,' Nan said. 'I earned it,' Mary said. 'It's mine.' She poked gently at her caterpillar with a stick and it convulsed into a furry ball.

In bed that night she grew fretful. Nan tucked in her blanket and went to the window to wait for her admirer. Mary jerked in her sleep. 'Mine,' she whimpered and the word came from her dry mouth on a grizzled thread of spit. 'Wake up,' Nan called over her shoulder. 'You're having a nightmare.' But when the child opened her eyes she was taken by a fit of sobbing that shook her body like the laughing policeman at the fun palace when you put in a farthing. Nan was upset by the noises Mary made. After Nat Hurd had climbed back over the wall she lay awake and the choking noises were still in her head.

It was a shock to hear the same cries entering the house the following day. It wasn't Mary. Mary was with her in the kitchen making a furtive panful of chips while Mrs Mum was at the shops. She no longer wept though she looked puffy and cheerless. Nan ran up the return stairs to the hall, holding a scarred potato in her hand. 'Your mammy?' Mrs Guilfoyle demanded, supporting a distraught Mlle de Ravelais. Mother had already come to the top of the stairs and was beaming hospitably at the visitors. 'Good girl, make us some tea,' she said to Nan.

'It's the mad ballet dancer,' Nan told Mary while she filled the kettle. 'She's in a dreadful state.' Mary did not seem impressed by the news. She looked away. She hacked intently at a pile of blackening potatoes.

'It is the very last piece of hay,' came Mlle de Ravelais' shrill complaint as Nan pushed open the door with her back and entered the Indian room with a tray of tea and Nice biscuits. 'You must be calm,' mother urged. 'Close your eyes and take a deep breath.' The woman clamped her eyes obediently and swept air through her nose. Mother tenderly pushed the limp black hair from her forehead. She would never do this for her children. She always assumed there were other people to do such things for children.

Nan set down the tray and began pouring, arranging a biscuit on the edge of each saucer. The lodger took her tea. Her eyes were moist but not brimming. She dipped her sad lips into the liquid and shuddered, as always, to find it was not coffee. She was obediently calm. 'My fiancé's teeth,' she said quietly, 'have been stolen.'

There was silence. Little offended clinks and the wet working of lips and the rasp of biscuits. 'His teeth,' mother ventured. 'It seems, my dear, unlikely . . .'

'I had told him that I must leave him because of the gums –' Mlle de Ravelais' own secure teeth took a mouselike nibble at the biscuit and she paused to explore it – 'and when at last he had agreed to install them and went to look for them they were gone. Pouf! Stolen!'

'I see.' Mother fell into a dazed silence.

At last there was a sort of snorting noise and they all looked around. Mrs Guilfoyle was weeping. She was pink and had covered her mouth politely to mask the noises that came out unavoidably, little grunts and squeals. It wasn't proper tears. She was laughing. 'Oh, the Lord save us! Oh, I'm sorry. I'm banjaxed.' She pulled a handkerchief from her hip pocket and pressed it to each eye in turn, winking hugely at mother with one eye when it had been blotted. Mother smiled quickly in a wild sort of way, then lowered her face to conceal her expression. Mlle de Ravelais was turning sharply from one to the other and with each turn her chin rose a little and her lips tightened. 'Someone stole my fiancé's teeth,' she said angrily.

'Oh, mamzelle, you're a turn,' Mrs Guilfoyle doubled over and clutched at her bust to steady her leaping heart. 'You're a tonic.'

Nan did not wait to see what happened next. She slipped from the room and pattered quietly down the stairs. 'Mary?' Mary was not in the kitchen. An abandoned pile of crooked chips bled their starch into the wood surface of the table. She ran down the garden and pulled open the door of the coal shed. She was at the back, bunched over the hen. Muddy tears dripped into its feathers. Nan crawled in and squatted down beside her. After a while she made a stiff movement to stroke back Mary's hair. 'Where's the money?' she said. 'Here!' Mary pulled the money from her pocket and flung it into the mound of coal. She felt better the minute she was rid of it even though Nan had to scramble in the black dust to retrieve the large coin and the little one.

'You must tell me everything,' Nan said.

'You'll boss.'

'I won't.'

They took the tram to Mr Orgel's premises in Nassau Street. They got the twopence for the tram from Nellie, who was on the front step polishing the brasses on the door and washing its glass panels with a rag. Lately she had taken to doing strange extravagant jobs while the ordinary dirt multiplied in neglect.

They got a poor welcome in the city. Mr Orgel's man was unwilling to part with the teeth. He had got them for a good price. He could tell they were very little used. 'I am afraid they are sold,' he said but Nan cried out bravely: 'Then you are duty bound to inform the police as they are stolen property.' Mary held out the two and ninepence and the man fetched the teeth and wrapped them up in tissue paper. 'You may be sure I will inform the police,' he said. 'I shall give them your description.' He laughed. Nan took the package and steered Mary from the shop before her trembling jaw could start to wail. 'It was a joke,' she said. 'See how he laughed.'

Mary had procured the teeth by calling at Monsieur le Droff's lodgings and telling him that she was making a collection of hair. While he was in his bedroom inspecting his hairbrush, she took his teeth from their glass by the sink. They did not dare to return the teeth in the same way but Nan parcelled them up in a clean envelope and since neither knew how to spell his name they printed very neatly with her fountain pen 'to whom it may concern' and posted the package in the letter slot.

The episode ended satisfactorily. Monsieur le Droff was so relieved by the return of his teeth – and so apprehensive of their further disappearance – that he kept them in his mouth at all times. Mademoiselle de Ravelais loaned him her money, on condition that he lodge as security – himself. She had a becoming hat from Miss

Flynn of Nassau Street for her wedding. Mrs Guilfoyle said it cost thirty-seven and eleven.

'Why did you do it?' Nan asked Mary in bed that night.

'I wanted to bring you to The Horsemen.'

'You just can't take things. It's stealing.'

'But she took all our concert money. I only got back what was mine.'

'You took nothing from her. The teeth belonged to Monsieur le Droff.'

'Yes, but he belongs to her,' Mary reasoned.

'You mustn't do such a thing again,' Nan warned. 'You have enough without taking other people's property.'

'I have nothing.'

Nan's mind rose in protest to catalogue Mary's personal effects and she was surprised to find herself in a desert. 'You have me,' she said doubtfully. The settle beds were placed end to end so that Mary's hand, when it reached out, only touched Nan's foot. It comforted them both, even though they would not have been so foolish as to admit it for in the morning they would be at each other tooth and tongs, as Nellie said, as usual.

CHAPTER 23

There was a Nellie in almost every household. They shaped generations with their curious speech and cooking although the people who employed them never knew anything about their lives. They came and went quickly and for very good reason; one became pregnant, another stole a glass of porter.

'It is not personal,' father assured Nellie. 'We are all fond of you but we no longer have the work for a full-time domestic.'

Nellie was used to his capers. She blew out a stream of smoke and gave him her scornful look. She picked a scab of food from her apron. 'Am I getting the bullet?' she provoked. 'You may leave at the end of the week,' he said. 'I shall give you two extra weeks' pay and a character.' She stared at him stupidly. 'With Mrs Mum to see to the cooking and the girls at home for the summer I fear I cannot justify the expense.' She kept watching him, waiting for the look that would release her and let her curse him for a tease. He had taken his stiff, indignant stance. Even Nellie had to see he didn't look in a joking mood. She shook her head from side to side. 'Oh, you black bastard,' she swore. 'I'm straight to missus.' She pushed at him with her fists and he teetered backwards. She ran up the stairs in a clatter of loose slippers.

He sat down and closed his eyes. His fingers moved blindly on the table, trapping crumbs and pulverizing them. He was perturbed by a picture in his mind. It was Nellie, when the children were small and she was able to lift both of them up in her arms; the three grinning, the children's jam-smeared faces reflecting the girl's vivid lipstick. 'The storm before the calm,' he said. He repeated this to himself over and over until he remembered that it was the other way round, the calm came before a storm.

'He's after firing me!' Nellie had taken a dramatic pose in the doorway to the Indian room. She had entered without knocking. Mother did not look pleased. 'Come in and tell me what you are talking about,' she said, although she was already informed. 'He's after tellin' me to pack me bags.' Nellie kept rubbing at her hair in an irritating manner. 'Mr Webster . . .' mother interrupted, attempting to impress on her a proper respect for her betters. Nellie misunderstood and thought it was a query. 'That's right, ma'am. The oul' bastard. An' me with three childher. I told him I was going straight to you.' She joined her hands in front of her in a distraught fist and mother, watching this, thought she looks like a slave, begging for mercy. 'I see,' she said.

Nellie sat by the window on the trunk. She looked out absent-mindedly. She took her cigarettes from her apron pocket and lit one. She crossed her legs. 'Oh, God!' She blew air from her cheeks and scratched her knee. 'Oh, jersiful maysus, he's after puttin' the heart across me. I don't know what's got into me. I should have took no notice. It was only one of his moods.'

'Mr Webster pays for his house and everything in it,' mother explained. 'He has not got money to burn. With his new cook . . .' Nellie looked back, astonished. She jerked her head from side to side, as if to swat fresh treacheries as they flew through the air. She stood up, ready for battle. 'His fancy woman!' she flared. 'Aw, missus, you can't still be dishin' up that oul' tripe after what he done to you. You can't let that jumped-up jiggle-o walk all over everyone.' Mother got on her feet. Her pale gold skin was whitened by a rare seizure of emotion. 'Silence!' she ordered. 'You will say no more. You will leave now before you say something we shall both regret.'

'I can't go,' Nellie said more quietly. 'What about me kids?'

'I think,' mother said, 'that you must go.'

'He said I could stay on till the end of the week.'

'Your money will be sent on. You are dismissed.'

So she went. She walked quietly down the stairs and into the kitchen. She did not look at father, who sat at the table with his eyes closed, but collected from the scullery her hat and her coat and her blue Russian leather handbag. On her way out she glanced guiltily at the disarray of cups and saucers and crumbs on the table and then she remembered that the children always did them.

When she got to Sullivan's Cross she did not know what to do. It seemed all wrong to go home in the middle of the day. She had left without a reference. She hadn't enough money to last until the end of the week. Mary came out of the Argus Palace, with a half-penny-worth of bull's-eyes in a newspaper cone. 'Where are you going?' she asked Nellie. 'I don't know. Home, I suppose.' 'Going home?' 'I'm after gettin' the sack,' Nellie said. They watched each other hopelessly. 'What are you going to do?' Mary said. Nellie thought. 'I think I'll get meself some chips.'

The newspaper package warmed her hands and she stood outside the fish restaurant, to enjoy this luxury, reluctant to leave the place where she hadn't ever had to think or worry. She scraped at a corner of the paper until she could pull out a chip. The first one she handed to Mary. She kept the second one for herself, blowing on it in short bursts as if she was whistling a tune.

'It was father, wasn't it?' Mary said.

'Men,' Nellie said. 'I never knew one worth a curse. They go around pestering and pontificating until they've scourged the life outa every woman in sight.' She drove a chip into her mouth and chewed angrily. 'I can see right through them, clear as day, as if they was empty milk bottles. They're all the same, that's one fact you have to get straight in your head.' It was a queer fact since the men she had known had all been so extreme. She couldn't figure it out because they hadn't really the imagination for adventure. She could only suppose they all ran on the same track, and were wound up and set on it before they were born. 'Your father now, spit of me own husband.' She handed Mary another chip. Mary hawed and chewed. 'Good looking, of course, which Eustace Murphy was not.' She thought about him with his gingery hair and his pale blue laughing eyes. 'Good gas when he'd had a jar. He could play the mouth organ.'

He had gone to England on a boat after he was laid off at the factory. At first the money came home in brown envelopes, regular as clockwork. There was enough for her and the two babies. He himself came home at Christmas. That was how she got caught for Josie, her third. Josie was four months when the money stopped. She got a woman to write letters for her, to the house where he lodged and the boss on the building site, but both said he'd moved on. Various do-gooders made efforts to trace him. She herself had been too busy, doing the houses to keep the kids fed.

'Eustace Murphy,' Mary mused. 'Why have you never said anything about him before?'

'I used to,' Nellie said. 'I did when I first started work. They didn't believe me. They thought I was on the cadge. Anyways, I seen enough to make me think that having a husband wasn't that much of a boast.'

'Didn't you miss him?'

'I dunno. Tell you the truth, I forgot all about him.'

It was the truth. She had not thought about him in years. She did not know if he was alive or dead. Nellie found herself thinking more now than she had done in years. Released from the grip of security, her mind was freed for thought. It was a small source of comfort. Once you isolated the enemy, you could go into battle.

'I'll tell you this much.' She squeezed the last chip in half to share it with Mary. 'I'll find meself a job where there's no men to mess me around. From now on I'm only going to work for nuns, widas and spinnisters. I was happy working for your mammy. I loved your mammy.' She began, suddenly, to cry, big bawling tears that fell on her newspaper parcel and made passers-by stop. 'Don't cry,' Mary begged. 'Come home with me. Father will probably change his mind. He doesn't always mean what he says.' Nellie knew this was true but it brought no comfort. It was not father who had thrown her out. She had looked after mother, defended her against father, against his poor buggers, the housework, the demands of the children. It was natural to her to heap her devotion on mother, to take it for granted she would always need her protection. Mother no longer needed her. Mother had dismissed her. Only Nellie was at a loss.

A number of the neighbours was there to witness Nellie's breakdown. They had been buying ingredients for the dinner. Mrs Guilfoyle spoke first. 'What ails you, Nellie?' She shouted in case the woman had gone mad. Nellie wiped her face with her sleeve. 'I'm after gettin' the push.'

'Why, Nellie, dear?'

'For no reason at all,' Nellie's voice was gruff, 'only that himself has brought in his black fancy woman to poison the family and herself is gone demented. I never missed a morning's work, nor stole sup nor silver spoon.'

The neighbours had known that something was going on in the house. Now they felt, under pinafores and solemn jumpers, a wild thrill of excitement. It gave the morning a festive air.

* * *

Father remained seated at the table with his eyes shut until Mrs Mumtaz came down to make the tea. He heard her arranging things on the table. Eggs, flour, meat, he guessed from her trips between kitchen and scullery. 'I have done it,' he said. There were little clinks and the delicate snap of eggshell on china; soon, a dull, slapping noise. She was making some sort of dough. He had come to hate her cooking. The spices in her food and her own spicy scent not only pursued him but now emanated from within him. 'It is done!' he exclaimed angrily. She made a little grunt of acknowledgement and went on patting the dough. That was all. He could not believe it. After the tortuous weeks in which she dogged him so closely that her breath stung his neck, hissing at him, 'Is it done? Have you got rid of that useless servant? Are you still wasting money on that embodiment of insolence? Do it now or I personally shall be forced to take action!' After all she showed no more interest than if he had emptied the teapot or carried out the cat. He felt rebuffed. 'I've got rid of Nellie.' He opened his eyes to regard her indignantly. 'Say something.'

'It is a start,' Mrs Mumtaz said calmly.

He gripped the edge of his chair. 'What did you say? What are you talking about? I did what you wanted.'

'Good,' she said; 'so you will not be afraid to do what else you must do.'

'What else?' He was shouting at her.

'Do you think I am content to cook for another woman's children when I have no child of my own? To be a servant under my husband's roof?'

'Mags? The children?'

'Do not look at me with such eyes. What is, is of your doing.'

'Mags! The little girls! They belong here.'

She did not look at him and he was glad. She was busy preparing his meal.

'In that case,' she pulled out little pieces of dough and shaped them neatly, 'you may leave them here and come away with me.'

'It is not,' said the neighbours, as they returned from their morning's shopping, 'that we wish to interfere.' This was true.

Clearly it was a dreadful carry-on. It required no rearrangement.

Women who stay at home and look after men and children are dependent on the disturbance of this order in other homes for their livelihood. Otherwise they would have nothing to talk about and nothing to give thanks for in their prayers. It is no harm. So long as the scandal does not imply gratification of one of their number, they are kind. They always bring something useful, like a cake, or a bone jelly.

The first delegation was Mrs Lehane and Mrs Bradish. They brought a tart. They planned to say they thought Nellie's cooking might be missed. It was a way of putting her on the agenda. The situation was more difficult than they had envisaged. Mother did not wish to see them. For the first time in all the years she had lived on the street, she did not welcome the neighbours. She did not want to see anyone outside the family. Her problems had become too complex. She had run out of things to say. She could no longer think of ways to defend father and she did not know what else to do. 'It is good of you to come,' she said, 'but I am resting.' She sat up in her single bed in the Indian room. She was eating sweets from a paper bag. 'You need taking out of yourself,' Mrs Bradish said. 'Oh,' mother said, 'no!' She had been at such pains to live within herself. She would not be taken out. 'My head!' she excused, seeing their strange looks.

They went away. They meant to take the tart with them but passing by the drawing-room on their way through the hall they were apprehended by a view of father seated near the window, his face wrenched with dismay, as if he had had a vision of a saint. They had a glimpse of the Indian woman bending over him, whispering at his face. The neighbours worried one another with their elbows and then Mrs Lehane made a tiny noise in her throat, a bird's cough. The occupants of the room looked up. The neighbours noted how the foreign cook's eyes still flashed with a dangerous glare. Father's look held only the miserable reproach of a cowardly dog.

'Ladies?' His greeting was bleak and dismissive. They stayed where they were, hands resting upon their stomachs, anchored by handbags and paper bags, until the foreigner had taken the hint and stormed out. 'Mrs Webster thought you might like a slice of tart,' said Mrs Bradish cunningly. She took the tart out of its bag and set it in front of him on the card table. He looked up hopefully at the mention of mother's name and then gazed down at the tart, its bumpy plainness mocking him. He seemed overcome. 'Yes,' he said. 'I would.' He looked helpless. They were disturbed. His eyes moved fractionally and he shuddered. The neighbours looked back rudely in the wake of his glance and saw the hem of a purple garment edged with gold, a long brown sandalled foot intruding in the doorway. He reached out and trapped Mrs Bradish's fleshy wrist. 'I am glad you have called,' he said. 'You must join me in a glass of punch and a game of cards.' He left them to get the cards and to knock together a pitcher of brew. The neighbours turned and smiled at each other, such sad smiles, barely a shadow of mirth. 'It is hard on a man,' said Mrs Lehane, 'when his wife is not herself.'

Card nights became a regular event. The children had never known the house to be so full of people, except at Christmas. The neighbours came in sixes and sevens. They brought husbands, an unheard-of thing. Men with red faces and gleaming suits grew lyrical on father's brew. Father invited people from the factory; he tainted the festive air with poor buggers. The house appeared to ring out with merriment. Only those who stayed on after the drink had been dispensed knew that it billowed at its edges, with darkness. Nan was confused by the outburst of hospitality. If there wasn't enough money to pay Nellie, how could he afford parties every night of the week? Father said it was business, she was too young to understand, and sent her from the room for pots of tea and fresh plates of cheese and corned beef sandwiches. He knew what he was doing. The parties kept Mrs Mum in her room until it was time for bed. He hoped that in due course, perhaps if Mrs Hanlon played the piano, mother would be drawn down to join them.

There were card games from tea-time until the moment when Mrs Mum knocked on the door and poked her head in. People looked up under their eyebrows or over fans of cards, at the dark figure in silk pyjamas, the diamond winking in her nose. She did not speak, merely glanced at father. He would play out his hand and then tap his cards into a crisp slice. 'Mags is asking for me,' he would say, looking painfully at the green baize.

Sighs and whispers rose to fill the hole left by his departure.

'Pas devant les enfants,' warned Mrs Guilfoyle while the children collected empty plates and glasses and fetched overcoats.

There was a lot of talk. Some of it went over their heads but some flew into doors of their minds, half open. Curious words, frightening beat around them. Sometimes Nan found herself standing stock still, surrounded by these, unable to move or breathe while scraps of gossip tore at the pristine fabric of her mind. She was reminded of a time before Mary was born when mother had taken her to the sea on the tram and she had whined for an ice-cream cone. It was too early in the year for the tea shops and ice-cream booths and she stamped her feet on the sodden grey mud in anger. Mother was not annoyed. She was abstracted, caught up in the dilemma. 'I know,' she said. 'We will have cream horns from the cake shop. We will lick them and think they are ice cornets.' Their palms were powdered with icing sugar and white grains drifted up their nostrils. They walked along the blasted shore, mother in her black boots on the strand and Nan barefoot, her little feet iodine blue under wicked icy wavelets. On a distant island of sand a scattering of seagulls jeered – wah, wah, wah! Nan bit off the point of her horn. Red jam burbled out on to her chin and the top of her tongue. She closed her eyes to enjoy the crunch of flaky pastry and the sting of raspberry. When she looked again the gulls were coming in with scavenging cries. She nibbled around the crater of sticky biscuit and thought of the pillow of cream that would collapse into her mouth when she had eroded the pastry to a finely calculated point. 'Wah! Wah!' The birds tore the air with their common screeching. She took another bite. The cream sagged into a relaxed fatness. 'Wah, wah, wah!' In an instant the creatures were around her, flapping like yellowed nappies. She could feel their feet in her hair, their wings slapping her face. 'Oh, Moses!' mother cried out, alarmed. She ran into the storm of hammering birds and pulled Nan clear. She wrapped her arms around her to ward off the evil cloud of rag birds but Nan peeked. She could see one bird, lower than the rest, his perfectly round eye angry with concentration as he bore in his beak a small saucer of pastry surmounted by a shivering hill of cream.

'I'd say the darkie is getting a rub of the oul' relic,' said Mrs Mulhall as she stacked the cards. 'Paddy von . . .' hissed Mrs Guilfoyle. Mrs Two-eggs looked up mournfully from her empty glass. 'Poor Mags,' she lamented. 'That man has her heart scalded.' Of all the whispers, this one struck most deeply to Nan. She could not stand by and let him scald her mother's heart. She could picture her lying flat and patient, her brown dress unbuttoned at the chest while father, egged on by Mrs Mum, tilted a kettle of boiling water over her heart. She left the dishes and ran up the stairs, two steps at a time. She knocked and ran into the Indian room. Mother sat in her chair by the window, her back and neck curved over a book. 'Mother?' Nan said softly.

Mother looked around with her faint, distant smile. 'Yes, pet.' Nan came closer to examine her, for signs of distress or erosion of her beautiful golden skin. 'What are you reading?' She overturned the book to show the matt yellows and reds of a penny library paperback, a girl transfixed in terror with some sharp implement skewered through her breast. 'The usual,' mother said. 'A mystery. I love a mystery.'

CHAPTER 24

It had been Nellie's practice every second Friday to fill the wooden washtub with kettle after kettle of boiling water and, when it was full almost to the top, in were tumbled sheets and knitwear, dresses, underwear, towels. These were pounded with a wooden pole until they imparted to the water a nice pasty greyness and then individual items were lifted and squeezed and rubbed, on their worst patches, with Sunlight soap. The practice resulted in some integration of dyes and a tightening of woollens but it was Nellie's area and no one thought to protest. Clothes were never rinsed. When the washing had gone on the line the thick, warmish water was hived off into different buckets and basins. One was ferried upstairs to be slopped around the bath and other washable surfaces. Another, with a dangerous addition of soda, was used to attack the cooker. The remains were emptied on to the kitchen floor and spread about vigorously with a scrubbing brush and cloth.

With Nellie gone there was no one to do the scrubbing. This surprised everyone. They never thought of Nellie as having a practical function. Washdays were just another violent demonstration against the world.

At first father seemed not to notice the absence of this domestic discipline. His shirts had always been done to his liking by a Miss Kelp, an epileptic, who called to the door on Monday. It was three weeks before he appeared in the kitchen doorway one morning holding out a dead-looking thing and demanding of the children, in hostile tones, if they called it a towel.

For a long time they sat at the gritty oilcloth with their pot of breakfast tea and then they rose with wordless sighs and went to the garden to fetch the great rotting wooden tub which they carried in between them by the iron rings on its sides. Nan filled kettles and pots and dumped them hissing on to claws of blue flame on the stove. Mary went from room to room, gathering up sheets and pillow cases, towels and trails of dropped clothing. The clothes rose in a mountain on the kitchen floor. The windows wept with gathering steam and little tendrils snaked in from the bubbling scullery. It was terrible work. By the time they had carried all the boiling water and managed to transfer it to the tub without killing themselves, they were already tired. They held the pole between them to beat the dirt from the fabric. For all the impact they made they might have been pushing with a little finger. Even Nellie found this hard work and called out constantly for cups of tea. Their faces went red and shiny and worms of wet hair got in their eyes and mouths. Their arms ached.

On his way to work, father dropped in to see how they were getting along. 'He's come to criticize,' Nan thought, furious. She pulled the pole free of the clawing drapery and drove it down fiercely. Mary made little grunting noises with this renewed effort. He said nothing. He stood there frowning. He appeared to be waiting for some message from the 'schloy, schloy' of the pounding pole – and when it came he stepped forward and said in distress: 'This is women's work!' Nan stopped pounding. She turned on him angrily and wiped hair and sweat from her face. 'We're doing it, aren't we?' 'Yes, but . . .' he looked into the tub, 'I get confused, you know.' He reached out and touched each of them cautiously on the shoulder. 'You're only lasses. You're only little twerps.' He pulled his hands away and began violently to wrench at his jacket, flinging it carelessly on a chair. He removed the links from his cuffs and pushed up his sleeves. He took the pole roughly from Mary and began hammering the washing. Muscles swelled in his arm and his hair went lank and his face crimson. He washed each item with soap and twisted the captive water from it and flung it in the waiting tin bucket. 'There,' he said. They watched in astonishment. He picked up the bucket and they followed him to the clothes-line in the yard and waited for him to shake loose the clothing, piece by piece, and stake it to the line. 'There,' he said.

On the twentieth of August Mrs Mumtaz fell ill. Nan remembered the date because it was the day her examination results arrived in a thin egg-coloured envelope, written upon in delicate purple. She sat on the front step to read it. She had got very good marks. More than eighty in every subject. This interested her because she had done less well in other years when she had worked harder. She was studying her results when Dandy came crashing through the front gate and threw herself down on the step beside her. 'Guess what? I've done it!' she announced. Nan looked up. 'Hello. Done what?' From the pocket of her frock Dandy pulled an envelope similar to the one Nan had received. She shook out the sliver of paper inside and opened it to show her friend. 'See that!' On the top corner of the result sheet was a carelessly scrawled comment: 'Possibly university material.' Nan studied Dandy's marks. She had done even better. Some of her marks were in the nineties. She passed her own result to Dandy. Dandy put an arm around her. 'Oh, how beautiful!' she said. 'You've turned out brainy too. Our whole lives have changed. We'll go to university together.'

Nan had only the vaguest notion of university. Like sport, she connected it in her mind with men. She knew that the universities kept some seats for women, but they were spinsters who had no choice but to be clever.

'I don't know,' she said. 'It might be very dull. I just wanted to finish school.' 'It's not like school,' Dandy said. 'Not at all. You wear a long scarf with stripes. You read books and poems. The men there aren't yobbos. They talk about, oh, life and the world and things. You don't ever have to get married. It's like circles in a pond that get wider and wider. You travel the world learning more and more. You meet more and more interesting people. You wear kimonos and smoke cigars and have affairs when you're forty.'

Nan had the clearest picture of herself and Dandy standing on a verandah overlooking a lake in some foreign place, dressed in kimonos and discussing poems and affairs. She began, in her head, to count the years, to establish the length of time that she must wait: 'Oh, but, Dandy!' with sudden disappointment she recalled an earlier discussion with her friend. 'I wanted us to go away together before and you called me an infant. You told me to live in the real world.' 'This is different,' Dandy promised. 'This is real. You wanted to go away with no money and no learning. That was just dreaming. When you've learnt enough you can teach, you can travel – you can do anything.'

The figures on the verandah lifted glasses with long stems and sipped honey-coloured liquid. One of them quoted a line from *Morte d'Arthur*. 'Oh, but, Dandy!' Nan could no longer tolerate the objections that crammed her head. 'You need money to go to university. Where will we get the money?'

'I don't know about that. I'll get the money. You watch me. I got the marks, didn't I, pal?'

Mrs Mumtaz had a cold. She had never had a cold before. For three days she had lain terrified in bed. The atmosphere downstairs lightened. Mother began to venture from her room. Father became spirited and critical. They might have forgotten about the Indian altogether except that every time she sneezed she emitted a great, piteous wail. 'I shall boil her up some of my brew,' father promised, speculating upon the ceiling. He did not. He was happy to forget about her during the day. Nan had to take over the cooking and it was she who, when she remembered, brought up bowls of soup or rice. 'Laaa!' cried the woman in despair as she sneezed and blew her nose. She looked a sorry sight. Her entire nose and one side of her face was raw and swollen. Nan saw at once what had happened. Each time she blew her nose, she damaged it with the gem. 'If you took it out,' Nan ventured, 'if it comes out, it would no longer hurt.' The Indian viewed her with suspicion but she did take out the diamond. Nan was disappointed to see that it was not an unusual oriental jewel, but a little diamond stud earring, which screwed on and off. She fetched from the dressing-table a china dish that was meant for father's cuff-links. 'You can put it there,' she said. 'I'll leave it on the dressing-table.'

'No,' Mrs Mum said firmly. 'Put it on the window ledge. I want to watch its fire in the fire of the sun.'

She did what she was told. She wriggled the dish about to catch the sun but it looked small and hardly worth the trouble, like a lost tooth. The window was dusty so she opened it to let in more light, but it made no difference. It must have taken all its earlier fire from the eye of its owner.

Father brought home ice-cream and meringues: 'For my ladies!' He kissed each in turn, mother and Nan and Mary. Mother looked frightened at first. She held on to her heart and laughed nervously. Then when father was pouring out whiskey for two she went away and when she returned she was wearing a white voile blouse with flowers embroidered into it, and covered buttons, and a blue skirt. He gave her her drink. She took it and looked down at her hands. He touched her hair and went to put on a record: 'Pale Hands I Loved Beside The Shalimar.' All the time they were drinking they kept their eyes on each other.

Over tea he told them he had a surprise. They all looked uneasy until he said he was planning an outing – a day of pleasure – just for the four of them. 'At the weekend?' mother wondered. 'No,' he said. 'I thought we might go tomorrow. I've made arrangements at work. You never can tell how long the weather will hold,' and his eye glowered at the ceiling.

'Where shall we go?' mother said. 'Wherever you like,' he said magnanimously. 'You choose.'

Nan would have liked to suggest the hotel with entertainments in Bettystown, where Nellie had been stagestruck. Mary wondered, since father was in such uncharacteristic mood, if she dare mention *The Four Horsemen of the Apocalypse.* Neither of them expected mother to say anything but it was she who contributed, in quite a determined tone, that Mrs Bradish had had a trip to Howth and had taken a walk along the cliffs and had lunch in a tea shop and she said afterwards that it was a day to remember.

It happened that it was a day that stayed in the mind, although only partly due to the location of the outing. At ten in the morning when the house was filled with the pleasant tension of hats being pinned and baskets and buckets being gathered, there came, quite suddenly, a single deep cry of rage. It had a doomlike quality, a resonance like a funeral bell. It might have signified murder or any other sort of violent death, but for a while no one made any move to investigate, they just stood frozen with sashes half-tied or socks at half-mast until father gave a noisy sigh and moved off as painfully as the boy on the burning deck. It turned out that Mrs Mumtaz had lost her diamond. When father went in she was pointing rigidly at the little saucer on the sill, summoning woe to those who had interfered with her treasure. 'Someone stole my valuable,' she accused, 'no one will leave this house until the thief has been snared.'

The family was summoned. Nan and Mary and mother stood in front of the window where the diamond had been. Father thought they looked very pretty, in white and yellow and blue. Mrs Mum's method of interrogation was to point a finger at each of the accused in turn and to glare at them for a period of ten seconds or so. The culprit would undoubtedly go red and move her feet about. While she was putting her truth spell on mother a terrible thought occurred to Nan and she tugged sharply at Mary's skirt and frowned at her. Perhaps she had stolen the diamond to get money for the pictures. Mary's face looked round and empty as a plate. Nan was convinced that it contained no residue of recent sin.

At length, when the foreigner had studied each of them in turn, father said: 'You are losing your reason. There are no thieves in this house. We are going out, madam.'

They went on the train. They had a compartment to themselves. The children sat at the window watching fields fluttering past and trees shooting up and down like the needle of a sewing machine. Mother too looked out the window. She wanted to hide her cigarette. 'What are you thinking?' Father put a hand on the fabric of her sleeve. 'We should have had more notice,' mother said. 'I would have made the children something bright to wear.'

When they got to the sea they were discouraged to find other people already there. They stood on the road looking down on the shore at infants, blind under bowls of white cotton, flailing over the hot stones toward the quenching sea; women abandoned in shrouds of flowered cotton. It had not occurred to them that other people would have the initiative. Mother looked interested. She suspected that there might be housewives. 'You'll not mix with the riff-raff, Mags,' father assured her. 'I shall apply strategy. Go and play on the beach,' he ordered the children. 'Take a swim. Here. You may have twopence each for an ice. Your mother and I will take a walk on the cliffs.'

They ran to the shingle strand and wriggled into swimming costumes beneath their dresses. Neither of them was drawn to the water but they were propelled by strategy. Just before they were sucked on to the cold, sliding floor of the sea they turned to wave to their parents so that their obedience would be noted and cheered. They stood shivering in a cowardly fashion, shading their eyes with their hands, looking for their mother and father on the curving path above. There was no one who resembled them, only lovers, preening and admiring. Then Mary recognized mother's hat, and she waved and shouted. The woman who turned around, pale golden and smiling, threw a brief, uninterested glance at the colourless children and returned her attention to the fair-haired lover who had possession of her arm. The children looked at each other and then glanced down disconsolately at the little pile of their summer frocks, wilting into the wet stones. 'She saw us,' Mary said. 'She didn't,' Nan argued. 'We only recognized her hat.' They waited for the couple to vanish around the bend that led to the cliff road but instead they walked on further and they went into a tall white hotel.

Father made it up to them later. He brought them a souvenir, a little net bag of chocolate coins wrapped in gold foil. They had lunch in a tea shop, soup and salad and trifle. Mother and father looked pink and well as if they, instead of the children, had spent hours under the blazing sun of the beach. They kept smiling at each other. Their amusement made the children happy and boisterous. They were astonished by the change in father. All the starch had been taken out of him. Although they had been bored on the beach, they now felt that the day was a heavenly one, that life had grown perfect. Mary said so and her parents looked on her fondly. 'We will have many more days like this,' father promised. She was taken aback. It made her forget her manners. 'Not when Mrs Mum is back on the warpath,' she said, and then she recoiled, expecting to be clouted. To her dismay her parents merely laughed. 'You need not worry about Mrs Mum,' father promised. 'I shall apply strategy'; and they laughed and laughed.

Mother and Mary fell asleep in the train on the way home. Nan and father sat beside each other. They were silent but it was a warm silence. It melted her feelings of resentment. 'I passed my exam,' she said, in an effort at conversation.

'Did you? Good child.'

'I got very good marks.'

He laughed. 'Ought I to do something? Should I give you a present?'

Her heart began to beat wildly. 'I would like to go to university. I would like to hope for that.' He studied her with a half-smile, a look of respect. 'You are a bugger, you are,' he said.

'Aren't you going to eat your last chocolate?' Nan said to Mary when they were getting ready for bed that night. Mary held the last chocolate, the smallest one – a sovereign or a mite – against her face like an earring. 'No. I'll keep it as a memento.' She put it on the window ledge. 'We won't need mementoes,' Nan said. 'There will be other outings. Father said so.'

The outing seemed to give father new heart. When Mrs Mumtaz had not improved the following day, he energetically set about making her some brew. It wasn't just a random mixture from the bottles in the living-room. He paid a visit to the chemist. He used a pestle and mortar and an egg spoon to prepare the powder he measured into the bottom of a large glass. He topped up with a mixture of regular brew, rum and brandy and a quantity of brown sugar.

At first the treatment appeared to work. Mrs Mum appeared on the landing at noon, very wild in the face, shouting about thieves. Nan and Mary sat on the stairs holding each other, stifling their laughter. When they had woken in the morning they had an argument because Mary's sovereign was missing from the window. Both swore they had not touched it. They began to recall other disappearances in recent months and Nellie's complaint about the spoons having legs. 'It's the jackdaw!' Nan said suddenly. They had spotted a jackdaw's nest in the garden. 'Mrs Mum's diamond! The jackdaw's taken it too!'

Her exertions on the landing appeared to have exhausted her for in the afternoon the Indian grew quite ill. She lay in her bed and moaned. She was feverish. She cried out and cursed with foreign words. 'We ought to get a doctor,' Nan said to father. 'Her cold has turned into a fever.' 'No, no,' father said. 'You must not mind. I know what I am doing. She will get worse before she gets better. I want you to leave the house. I will see to her.'

Mother was eager to go. She wanted to tell the neighbours about her outing. The children did not wish to leave because it was starting to rain but the rumbles of the woman's pain were like a thunderstorm and eventually they pulled on sou'westers and raced out into the puddles.

When they came back in the evening the house was silent. Father sat in the drawing-room drinking whiskey. 'How is she?' Nan said. He shook his head. 'She is not at all well. You must realize that foreigners do not have our resistance to the common cold. I fear she may not last the night.'

At bed-time Nan went up to look at her. The Indian was dead. Bark-coloured eyelids draped her savage eyes. Her punctured nose did not narrow and flare. Nan put out a hand. She wanted to make sure she was gone. She had to touch her and know that she had gone cold. She was startled to find that the woman's skin was soft and as warm as one's pillow in the morning. The Indian's eyes flew open. Nan covered her mouth in horror. She was being revisited by the nightmare she had before the holidays, of being in the morgue and gazing into the malevolent face of the foreigner. For seconds she stood, stiff with dread, unable to move, until the Indian very slowly raised a hand and gripped Nan strongly by the arm. 'Thieves,' she groaned. 'Thieves and poisoners.' 'No!' Nan cried. She attempted to break away but the woman's grip was like iron. 'You will all suffer for this. You will suffer always. You will not have him for I had him first.'

For weeks after this Nan had nightmares. She still awoke weak with fright when the Indian had recovered and mother had retreated more completely than ever. One night she woke shouting out so fearfully that Mary could not calm her and father had to come. 'Shut up now,' he said. She clutched at his hands. 'You're all right, now. Go back to sleep.' He disengaged his fingers but she threw her arms around him and held on. He put his arms around her and then he held her very tightly, rocking as if he had had a nightmare and was in need of comfort. 'It will be all right,' he said. 'What will you do?' she whispered. She needed useful information. He sighed. 'I'll think of something. I'll think of something one day.'

CHAPTER 25

One day the boys who were hanging over the bridge at Sullivan's Cross were rewarded with the sight of a man coming towards them on the river, lying on his back. He had a bursting look, like a fried white pudding. He glared at them as if they were an unpleasant surprise. His leather toes, pointing at the sky, were indifferent.

The boys crossed the road and dangled on the bridge at its other side to watch the corpse coming out. When it had glided away out of sight they went home. One of them then told a man on a tram.

It was a lovely day for the funeral. The weather held. People stood about the grave like picnickers. They shaded their eyes with hands and spoke of holidays and politicians. There were such a lot of people, acquaintances he had at one time or another helped, the jobless, the despairing, poor buggers down on their luck. How long they had lasted, mother thought, watching them through the black snow of a funeral veil spotted with velvet.

She stepped away from a grim little knot of neighbours and went to peer into the grave. The neighbours, fearing that her nerves might be excited and that she might attempt to fling herself on top of the coffin, lumbered forward and seized her by the elbows. She shook them off and stayed where she was. She wasn't excited. She just wanted to see the box, like a thin wardrobe, to make sure he was still there. She stayed keeping watch. 'It's all right,' she thought. 'He's safe, we're safe,' and then she had to wrestle with a little smile, struck by the perverseness of him, going into a hole under the ground on a day when everyone else turned out to enjoy the heat of its surface.

It was the custom, following burial, for people to crowd the house of the bereaved, eating sandwiches, drinking tea and whiskey. Some of father's relations turned up – a sister called little Moll, a cousin Edgar with his tall uninteresting children. Mostly it was the neighbours. They came bearing little triangular sandwiches, appetizing cakes, bowls of trifle. No one had to worry about refreshments. Father's store still beckoned hospitality. Mother was on the sofa, hidden under a black veil. Occasionally a glass of whiskey or a cigarette was poked in behind this drapery.

The women were arranged around her, on the arms of the sofa, at her feet, solicitous. They urged mouthfuls of food. They spoke of father, his good looks, his skill at festivity, his charitable attributes. She had been given a little pill and a glass of whiskey, and she was dazed. She couldn't help feeling happy. The house was full of neighbours. They were making much of her. They were talking about father.

'What became of Mrs Mumtaz?' someone said.

There was an unhappy silence. Mother looked around slowly to trace the musing and found that it was Mrs Lehane, tiddly on gin, who had lost the cowardice to keep quiet.

'I don't think, dear, that anyone is concerned, at this time . . .' Mrs Guilfoyle said. But they were.

Mother lifted up her veil and hung it on the rim of her hat. She looked amused. 'I am afraid there is no longer room for charity cases,' she said with a little laugh. 'Mr Webster was a very charitable man.' There was a photograph of father in a silver frame. It had been on the wall for years but after his death mother had taken it down to put it on a low table by the sofa where she could blow smoke at him in an intimate manner.' He was an exceptional man. It is a privilege for an ordinary person' – she cast her graceful hand around to embrace the company – 'to live with an exceptional one, but it can be trying.' She leaned back as if the effort of this summing up had exhausted her and closed her eyes. In a moment she sat up again, very alert, and spoke as if everything depended on her words. 'You know,' she confided to her neighbours, 'I was compelled to pretend that the Indian was employed in my house as a servant.' She shook her head. 'This was not the case.' The neighbours leaned forward humbly for the truth. 'In reality she was an unfortunate case from the asylum. A mission priest prevailed upon Mr Webster. He felt it was his duty . . . his Christian duty. Duty.' She looked at her lovely hands and sighed, seeing with distaste the unavoidable shift in this region. Bright, acrobatic tears windowed her eyes, suspended. One could not tell if she wept for the future or the past. 'I would receive all the black savages in the world if it would bring him back,' she whispered. 'We were head over heels in love.'

'Woman dear,' Mrs Bradish reproached. 'You must not lose faith. Your husband will not be lost to you if you have faith.'

'He has been summoned by God,' mother said stubbornly. 'That is that.'

What had happened to Mrs Mumtaz? No one knew. No one ever asked again. On the day the policeman called with news of the body in the river, mother had gone directly upstairs, where she stayed for a long time talking to the Indian. In the afternoon she had sent the children to the church to pray for their father while she rested. When they returned home, she was in the big bedroom, arranging father's things on the dressing-table. The windows were wide open. The bed was made up with the severity of a cot in a convent.

'Where is she?' Mary had said.

Mother turned from her task. 'Of whom do you speak?' She looked chilled, but from the inside, and her gaze was cold. Mary had been about to say 'Mrs Mum' but she had the sense to realize that mother would tell her to speak properly, not to use baby talk. Instead she looked all around the room in bewilderment, seeking embroidered shawls or saris, an Aran cardigan, some little brass spice pot. She sniffed. No hint of spice yellowed the air. The room was heavy only with tradition and habit. She looked at the dressing-table. Alongside father's brushes and perfumes was a tumble of paperbacks, mostly bloody murders. She crossed the room slowly and pulled out, one by one, the little drawers. There were mother's pins, father's studs; here a brown paper bag sealed with a twist. She opened it and looked inside. It was half-filled with toffee sweets. Mother came to her and touched a plait. 'There is only us chickens,' she said.

When the funeral was over and the neighbours had gone home, bringing with them the remains of the sandwiches for tea, mother went to bed. Nan brought up warm milk. 'Is there anything else I can do?' Mother lifted herself up and leaned on an elbow. She studied her daughter. 'Yes,' she said. 'Yes – but later.' She lay down in a nest of pillows that had been arranged for two heads. 'Sleep tight,' Nan said, kissing her on the forehead.

'Nan?' A sleepy whisper.

'Yes, mother.'

'Bring up the photograph in the silver frame. Put it here.' She patted the locker at her bedside. 'I shall want him beside me when I wake up.'

After she had put the photograph of father by her mother's side and waited for mother's breathing to take the renewing rhythm of unconsciousness, Nan began to cry. The roof had been taken off their lives. They were women on their own, exposed to the horror of pity; not because they had to make their own way without a man but because a man had found a way to do without them.

Mother rose up suddenly, still asleep, with a snarling desolate whimper. 'Nnn . . .' she struggled against her locked brain. Nan quickly thrust her father's photograph into mother's hands. Mother opened her eyes fractionally and dropped the picture on the bed. 'Nnn . . .' she moaned again. 'It's Nan. I'm here, mother, I'm here.' 'Nellie!' Mother wailed.

When she had drifted into sleep again Nan left the room and ran downstairs calling for Mary. The house was empty, not in an ordinary way, but as if all the furniture had been taken out and pictures removed from the walls. She went out. She ran across the road to Dandy's house. She wanted to discuss the lives they would have at the university.

'You're lucky,' Dandy said. 'You're lucky not to have a father to torment you any more. You can do anything you want. We're all still afraid to move sideways with my da. If only he'd drop dead.' Nan said nothing. Her head was full of the feel of her father's embrace. She had been surprised to find his arms warm, to discover that she had nothing wounding to say to him, that she had not wanted him to move away.

'Feeling mopey?' Dandy said.

Nan shook her head vigorously. 'No. No, I'm not. Father would never have let me go to university. He'd have married me off to some old ibex. I can do whatever I want now.'

'How do you mean?'

'I'll have money – my inheritance. Father said the factory was my inheritance. I can even pay for you too if your da won't.'

'Hey, that's gifty. I've got a great idea. Let's go and see Anastasia. Maybe she'll knit us stripy scarves and we can pretend we're at university already.'

When they got to Doll's house they were disappointed to find that the fat girl no longer occupied the front step; there was only Doll, her pink angora sweater marked with baby spills, her hand anchored to the handle of a pram.

'Where's Anastasia?'

'Gone home. Her own ma's expecting.' She turned away with an indifferent look but Nan saw tears in her eyes. She's afraid, she thought scornfully, she's afraid of Minnie Willard; and then she leaned forward on the railings and her tears splashed over the dusty spikes, leaving her face in a filthy state, and her shoulders shook and shuddered with fear.

Mary was in the Indian room. She had not answered Nan because she did not want her to know she was there. There was something she had to do and she did not want anyone to know. For a long time she sat on top of the trunk, swinging her legs, shuffling in her hands a little stack of rectangular cards, like a deck of playing cards. When she was sure the house was at rest and would not shift and squeak to betray her, she put the cards in the pockets of her dress and went to the wardrobe. She lowered her arm into the boot. She traced, in its hollowness, the foot that was beneath the earth, down as far as the toe, where she found the key. She took it out and stood with it clenched between her hands, trying to picture in her mind the things she had imagined on the inside – the silks, the spoons, the slippers made of coloured thread.

Had she dreamed them up as she dreamed up letters penned in emerald ink? On her own mediocre examination marks the only remark was: 'given to day-dreaming'. She could still see the alien fabrics. Perhaps they were presents brought back from India by father for mother, and mother, with her customary vagueness, had forgotten all about them. She pushed back the tiger-skin and unlocked the lid. She looked inside. For minutes she stood and stared, holding her breath, affirming for her memory the curved leather base skewered with studs. The trunk was empty. Nothing! There was not the smallest thing left if there had ever been anything there. She stood for so long that the stains on the leather, splotches of usage, became engraved on her brain and stayed there forever, like wine marks. When she could breathe again she took from her pocket the little slice of cards and knelt on the floor to spread them out. They were holy pictures. It was the custom of the smaller children in school to contribute a holy picture with a message of sympathy to any other child who encountered the excitement of losing a parent. The saints on these miniatures had been tamed by the artist's hand until they were neither flesh nor spirit, man nor woman. Ladies' bosoms were erased by windswept drapes. The holy men wore long hair and had pink cheeks and mild expressions. In the same way her father had been modified by the sentimental inscriptions of the little girls. She had a favourite. 'God spied a daddy worn with care and bore him to His heav'nly lair.' She squatted on the floor and examined each of the pictures in turn until the sanctity had been transmitted. Father's yellow hair lengthened and curved. The red in his cheeks paled to the rosiness of dawn. The glare of his eyes was tinged with awe. She collected the pictures one by one and arranged them on the floor of the trunk. 'Our father,' she said, 'who art in heaven.' She closed the lid and turned the key in the lock. She replaced the tiger-skin. She skipped down the stairs and out into the garden. The key was still in her hand. She walked along the path to the back of the house and on the sill of the kitchen window she laid the little gleaming key to the Indian trunk.

In the morning it was gone and they never found it again. The jackdaw came in the night and bore it to his heavenly lair.

CHAPTER 26

There was a wonderful court case. A widow, Mrs Roseberg, sued a Polish merchant because he had failed to make her the mother of God.

It was this delicate matter, saved up by the thoughtful neighbours, that finally revived mother's appetite for life and freed her, after eight or nine days, from her wretched sleep.

Nan and Mary were glad to see the grown-ups. There was no food in the house. They had forgotten to put out the china pitcher for the milkman and the eggs, the potatoes, the tins of sardines, had all been eaten up. There was no money. Whenever they worried mother about these problems she shook them off and said, 'Leave me be.'

The adults now bustled around the kitchen, filling the kettle, setting out a tray. They clicked their tongues when they saw the state of the cupboard and took money from their own purses, sending the children to the shops for milk and bread and ham and potatoes. One of them had brought a cake. The chink of china, the smell of sliced ham and sponge, were agonizingly homely. The children followed the neighbours around, sniffing back tears of self-pity.

'Poor lambs,' the women said, but one could tell by their excited tone that they were not attuned to the slow pace of pity. They bustled up the stairs under a quiver of china and pastel food. The children clambered after them. 'Now, dears, don't disturb your mother,' Mrs Bradish said irritably. They dawdled until the women had pushed open the bedroom door and then they slid into the room.

One of the women was propping up mother on her pillows. The curtains had been drawn enough to let in a little slice of light on her face. 'No,' she whispered. 'Let me sleep.'

'You must eat, dear,' said Mrs Lehane, handing her a triangle of bread with no crust and a dewy morsel of ham. 'You must keep up your strength.' Mother pushed the plate away. Mrs Bradish, who was pouring tea into cups arranged on the dressing-table, looked up and said, 'Come now, missus, you are not the first to have lost a husband. There are people worse off.'

'What do you mean?'

'I refer to a widow woman who paid a rag-man to visit her boudoir every week. She paid him money.'

'Paddy von . . .' sighed Mrs Guilfoyle. Mother was beginning to sit up properly. She pushed hair from her face and stroked her cheeks, feeling her return to life. 'Who?' she said. 'Who is this person?'

They told her how the well-off widow had importuned a strange young man, a chance caller, and invited him to assist in the coming of the Messiah. The boy had accepted an invitation to her bedroom for a different sort of intimacy. He wanted access to her husband's wardrobe to rummage and bargain for the dead man's effects. The widow outlined her plan to him. She told him that she had it on authority, the very best – Divine – that this was required of him. The boy was young. He was shocked. He had always assumed that the Messiah, when He chose, would come through the proper channels, a properly married man and wife. He expressed his mind. The widow sighed and went away. She came back with a mahogany box, bound in brass. After she had opened it, right under his nose, no revelation could seem outlandish. It was filled with notes of money in large denominations. Each note was a month's earnings. She took one out and flicked it at his face. 'If it would assist your faith . . .' He took the money and put it away. 'I have never done this before,' he said. 'I know,' she said. 'That is why you have been chosen. It is the flaw of the new testament to think that the mother of God should be a virgin. It is the father of God who must be pure.'

'I suppose,' he said, 'under the circumstances, that I should leave on my clothes.'

She turned her back. 'No. Such clothing as you wear would be an offence. You must offer your body as God made it.'

When she turned around again she had undone the front of her black mourning dress and some of her undergarments and presented him with her breasts, very white and substantial, like some luxury item that a poor family would purchase by the quarter pound. He began to undo his assorted garments. 'You have the eyes of a woodland creature,' she said. 'You have the body of a fawn. My darling. Grant, O Lord, your blessing to your servants.' She was unpinning her hair. One by one its soft, dark coils fell caressingly over her breast. He fell with fervour to his task.

That, more or less, was how the neighbours told it.

Mother ate her sandwich thoughtfully and accepted a cup of tea. 'Is this in the newspapers?'

'No, missus!' The neighbours were shocked. 'Only the *Irish Times*, being run by Protestants, would give it house room.'

'It said all that in the *Irish Times*?'

'Lord, missus, no! It said that the widow had sued the merchant for the return of money she loaned him. You have to read between the lines.'

Mother ate a piece of cake. She licked the cream from her fingers. 'I do not understand,' she said, 'how you can read such things between such narrow lines.'

The women laughed. 'The case has no need of publicity. It is famous. For the duration of the hearing the courthouse has been filled with men. Every public house seethes with its details. It has made the men blackguardly. They bring home tales to the tea table.'

Mother laughed excitedly. She looked alive again, pretty and rested. 'I am still confused,' she protested. 'If the young man kept his appointments, why did she have to drag him through the courts?'

'The issue failed to materialize.'

'She failed to bring forth.'

'Oh, dear.' Mother was looking around for her handbag. When she found it she looked inside and took out a pack of cigarettes. She lit one. 'But surely she could have accepted it as the will of God, in this more than any other instance.'

'Will of God, how are you,' said Mrs Bradish. 'The woman was past forty-five. It would have taken more than the archangel Gabriel and the Holy Ghost put together to get any shakings out of the bag. No, missus, there was no hope of that from the start. It was a rub of the relic the widow was after.'

'Well, in that case . . .' mother waved her cigarette.

'The affair suffered an intervention of a more mundane nature. The boy took a passion for a young girl. He felt that it was no longer appropriate to pay intimate visits to a middle-aged widow. He served notice of his intention to abscond. The widow was mad as a bandit. She told him that unless he remained to fulfil his contract, he must return all moneys loaned to him forthwith.'

'Perhaps,' mother suggested, 'it would have been easier in the long run to give her back her money.'

'Well, he couldn't, you see. The money was gone. He had spent it on a nice little business. He bought himself a little shop on Clanbrassil Street.'

'What became of him?' mother wondered. 'Did he have to sell his business?'

'Now there's a peculiar thing,' said Mrs Guilfoyle. 'You felt in the end that there was an angel on somebody's shoulder. After five days the defending counsel called upon the chief material witness – or spiritual witness – the party who had made the announcement to Mrs Roseberg in the first place. The judge announced a fifteen-minute recess. Some of the men removed their hats. They all kept watch on the ceiling but there was nothing – no angel, no dove, no particular ray of light. The case was dismissed.'

Mother got out of bed. She patted down the pillows and blankets in a soothing manner so that evidence of her occupation was removed. She went to the dressing-table and stood over the litter of teacups, brushing out her hair. 'I think,' she said, 'that I shall have my hair cut. Mr Webster admired long hair but a bob would be so much less trouble. Imagine' – she turned to her friends with a little smile – 'a woman, who has seen her husband safely to God, encouraging a man to do that.'

'To do what, mother?' Mary's intent voice startled the women. The children had been as quiet as spiders. They had not so much as extended a hand toward the tray of delicious food. They were fascinated by this woman who was to re-enact the birth of Jesus. They knew all about the dull little figure of the Virgin Mary but there had been no mention of a man in the boudoir. There was Joseph, the carpenter, but it had been impressed on them that he was a blithering old fool.

The women had forgotten about them. 'Run along, girls,' mother said, looking amused. 'You may take down the tray and have a little feast.'

'Why, mother?' Nan said.

'Because this is most unsuitable.'

'Why?'

'Because only rude, unmannerly girls question their mother.' She gave them a stern look. She had to put her hand over her mouth to smother her smile.

They ate the ham and the bread and most of the cake. They had two pots of tea. They thought that so much food must lull them into obedience but they could not settle. They had been pricked by curiosity. It was an actual ache at the back of the head, extending to the jaw, like neuralgia.

'The Jews believe that God will come back,' Nan said. 'They are waiting.'

'Imagine if they are right,' Mary said. 'Suppose He is waiting to come back, waiting for the rag-man to do whatever thing he was meant to do.'

'It's no good supposing,' Nan said. 'You have to know.'

'They won't tell us. No one will tell. Grown-ups never tell you anything interesting.'

'Nellie did.'

It was Nellie they missed. It was Nellie they all missed.

'If she was here, we could ask her,' Mary said.

'Or if we were there.'

They had no trouble finding the place where Nellie lived. 'Above Mulligans,' she always said and Mulligans was a well-known spot near Leonard's Corner, a little hut of a shop that sold turf and potatoes and sticks for the fire. She was on the third floor. They had to climb up a dark stairway with a smell of lavatories. 'Nellie!' They called out. 'Yes.' Nellie's response was gruff. 'Open up,' they cried. They banged on her door. 'It's us.'

It was a long time before a tiny bit of the door was opened and they could see a sliver of Nellie's face, suspicious. 'What do you want?' 'It's *us*,' Mary said in astonishment. 'Let us in. We've come to see you.' Nellie considered. 'No,' she said. 'Youse go on home. Leave us alone.'

'Father's dead,' Nan said. 'He was found in the river.' Nellie hesitated. 'We've brought you a piece of cake,' Mary said.

'Dead, is he? Well, now.' She opened the door. Now that this hurdle had been crossed, they found themselves unable to take advantage. They stood in the doorway, gawping. There was no furniture. Damp boards stretched across the floor on which there were only wooden crates, serving as seats and table top. Two greasy mattresses held half the floor and one of them was full of children who were half-dressed in shrivelled cardigans and whose boots poked out under their blanket.

'Don't stand there swallying flies,' Nellie said to the children.

'You've no furniture,' Nan said. 'Are you moving house?'

'Very possibly, unless I pay me rent,' Nellie sniggered. 'Haven't you got a job?' Mary said. 'I have an' I haven't,' Nellie snapped. 'Ah, who'd have me? Didn't your mammy fling me out with no refrins.' 'We'd have you,' Nan implored. 'We all miss you, Nellie. Mother calls for you in her sleep. Please come back to us.'

Nellie yanked one of the children from the mattress and put a kettle in her hand. 'Go down to the yard and get's a fill, Susan,' she said. 'Them's May and Josie,' she introduced her children. 'That's Susan.' She indicated the ghostly little girl who scampered out with the kettle, in her vest and knickers and cardigan. She worried the other two. 'Get up, you little layabouts. Get dressed. I'm expectin' company.'

'You mustn't mind about us,' Nan said.

'I don't,' Nellie said. She wanted to hear all about father's death, the funeral, the disappearance of Mrs Mum. She gave them tea and ate the cake that they had bought, but offered none to her children.

'So we're on our own now,' Nan finished. 'There's no one to look after us. Won't you come back?'

'I won't come back with me cap in me hand.'

'It's we who have come to you,' Mary pointed out. 'The Indian is gone, father is no longer with us, there will be no more poor buggers. Mother is determined on that. There'll be hardly any work to do. We can sit and drink tea and read stories from the newspapers. You'd like that, wouldn't you? You used to.'

Nellie shook her head. 'Them days is gone.'

She told her own children to clear out, to get a move, her business friend was due. They pulled raggy dresses from one of the crates and put them on over their cardigans. They ran out indifferently and clattered down the stairs. The children sensed that their audience was near an end. 'We wanted to ask you something,' Nan said. 'About the widow who paid a merchant to make her the mother of God,' Mary crowded her.

'Well, then,' said Nellie. 'What do you want to know?' She sat on one crate and from another she pulled an assortment of clothing – long black stockings, a satin dress, a pair of battered dance shoes.

'The man,' Mary said. 'What was he supposed to do? What did she give him the money for?'

She stretched out a broad leg and pulled on a stocking. It had a hole but she arranged it so that it would not show. She tied a garter. The small eyes focussed on the children. 'He did the most peculiar thing it's possible to imagine – and the most ordinary thing in the world.' 'What did he do?' Mary urged, but Nan had begun to be nervous. There was a strange look to Nellie. She had never seen it before. She put her hands on Mary's shoulders. 'We must be going,' she said. She steered her sister to the door. Mary pulled free and turned again to the maid. 'The man . . . ? What was he like?'

'Ah, now . . .' Nellie pulled her spotted dress off and sat in a torn slip, her hair dragged awry by the manoeuvre. 'There is the oddity of oddities. The wida was a most respectable class of a woman, well set up, but she had a serious taste for her business. Her jiggle-o was a well-known dangerous madman, a character, a rag-man.'

She vanished again as she pulled the satin dress over her head. The dress was old. It was badly crumpled and the material under the arms had lost its colour; but it was definitely a party dress. Nan could understand why Nellie did not wish to return to the drudgery of housework. In spite of the miserable appearance of her room, she was obviously having a very good time. She put on some purple lipstick and a scent so strong it caught at the pit of their stomachs, making them feel queasy. She squeezed into her dance sandals. 'His name was Schweitzer. He wheeled a creaking pram filled with old clothes and terrible noises. Children ran away from him and it was rumoured that he would capture them and sell them for the dinner table. The wida would have no one but the rag-man, the sellers of hens and used clothing, no infection . . .'

'Shyster?'

'. . . Shyster the Jew.'

Nan was astonished. 'Shyster's not like that,' she protested.

'Now you mark my words and mark them good,' Nellie said. 'There bei'nt a man in the world who has but one thing on his mind – and it isn't his prayers.'

'You're wrong,' Nan argued. 'Shyster was always saying his prayers. He and his brother, Sam . . .' she was interrupted by a knock at the door. Nellie took no notice. The door was pushed open and a drunk staggered in, a bleary, belching sort of man. The children backed against the wall but Nellie stepped forward to deal with him.

'How's my darling?' he said. She walked straight into his clutching arms. 'I'm all right.' She put her purple mouth wetly on his thistled one. 'Give us me money.' 'Get them bloody kids outa here.' He handed her a pound. 'Get out!' Nellie cried and the children ran, down the smelly stairs, out the side door of Mulligans, along half a mile of streets until they were too tired to run any more and leaned panting against a wall. 'He gave her money!' Mary said indignantly. There were tears in her eyes. 'It was business,' Nan said firmly. 'She told us it was business.' 'No, Nan!' Mary sighed. 'It's not business and you know it. Grown-ups get money for nothing. He gave her money for nothing. The widow gave Shyster money for nothing. We never get anything. It's not fair.'

Nan took the younger child's hand and they walked the rest of the way home. Their hearts continued to pound long after they had recovered from the effects of their run. 'The most peculiar thing it is possible to imagine,' Nan kept thinking. 'The most ordinary thing in the world.'

When they got home mother was at the kitchen table with printed papers, documents, receipts, spread out all about her. Her cigarette burned neglected in her fingers while she gazed at these incomprehensible male items, as absorbed as if they were a murder story. 'What are you doing?' Nan accused. She felt she could not bear any more changes. Mother raised her face but it was a while before she took them into view. Her mind was absent. 'Your father's papers,' she said. 'I have been going over them. A wilderness.'

'They are too complicated.' Nan was automatically protective. 'The lawyers will sort them out. Put them away, mother. I'll get the tea.'

'No,' mother said. 'They are not really difficult if you go slowly.

When I said wilderness, I was thinking of lost.' She spoke in her usual dreamy fashion. She was smiling faintly. 'It would appear, you see, that all is lost.'

CHAPTER 27

'I have decided,' mother said. 'To open a rooming house. Gentlemen only. Women expect too much. Business gentlemen. It is not, of course, that we need the money but one has to fill the days and they will be protection.' She made her announcement to the neighbours after the solicitor had concluded the business of father's estate. They sat around the dining-room table with the good china and an apple tart which Nan had been instructed to make. Nan poured the tea and watched with hostility each morsel of tart that vanished into heedless mouths.

There was no money. Father had left nothing but debts. The factory was bankrupt. The house had been mortgaged.

Mother had invited the solicitor to the drawing-room for the reading of a will. There was no will, nothing but the evidence of documents unfulfilled. The man was embarrassed. Mother took the news very well. She seemed animated by it. 'One would never have thought,' she said, 'to hear such news in such a *good* room. There are still full bottles of whiskey and rum in the sideboard, waiting to be opened.' She got up excitedly and opened one of these bottles and poured a drink for the visitor.

Nan kept thinking of her lost inheritance, of the tribe of fallen women stamping their sewing machines with no intimation of the catastrophe.

Only one thing really concerned mother. When the solicitor had gone she drew the children to her urgently. 'This is our secret,' she said. 'The neighbours must never know. We must all strive to keep up appearances.' She told them of her plan. She would sell the piano to buy extra beds. Advertisements would be placed in the newspapers; 'only a stone's throw from the city by motor car.'

'But, mother!' Nan was touched by her mother's bravery. 'How will you manage? A boarding house will be dreadfully hard work.' 'I am sure,' said mother, 'that I can rely on my little Nan.'

'Of course. I'll do everything I can, but school starts next week.'

Mother put down her pencil and the jotter she had been using for calculations. She drew deeply on her cigarette. 'School?' She produced the sound narrowly, as if it was a foreign word.

'I'll help in the evenings.'

'School?' She turned to look at Nan and her brown eyes seemed a mass of spinning flecks with no depth. She laughed. 'Let me tell you about school,' she offered gently. 'School is a place where children are sent to keep them from beneath their parents' feet in the daytime. It is a garden, walled off from life. Childhood, you see, for both the young and the mature, is a luxury.' Her smile faded. 'There will be no luxuries in this house from now on. No charity cases and no luxuries.'

'I'm fourteen,' Nan said.

'Fourteen?' mother marvelled. 'How the time flies.'

'I can't leave school.' Nan was frightened. 'I'm not old enough.'

'Not old enough to argue with your mother,' mother rebuked mildly. 'Old enough, I should hope, to make up a few beds and cook a light supper.'

The women on the verandah raised glasses of honey-coloured liquid and spoke of poems and affairs. The setting sun caught the fiery stripes of their college scarves.

When Nan was able to look at her again, mother appeared to be frowning. 'Too old, Nan, *much* too old for tears.'

CHAPTER 28

Mother was remarkable. She ran the house single-handed although Nan, of course, did the chores. She was always cheerful. Her courage was an example to everyone. How bravely she smiled, polishing the silver frame of father's photograph.

Nan was not cut from the same cloth. People told her this. In the two months that had passed since father's death her shape had altered and her face, as if to mould her to her task. She grew taller and thinner. Her face lengthened, its dreamy look lifted and underneath there was a frown. The house too had become amoebic, shifting its shape to accommodate the lodgers. Their home was filled with men, so many that they seemed packed into every crevice. 'Mrs Webster's gentlemen,' the neighbours called them; although they were not proper gentlemen, as mother pointed out, but the sons of farmers – schoolteachers, grocery assistants, junior clerks, police officers. They all seemed the same to Nan, faces set like cold pudding, loud boots and loud voices, tramping a strange and unwelcome world into their sealed one. When they talked among themselves it was not of things that mattered to their lives but of obscure affairs: the Free State, Mr James Douglas and his argument on the Divorce Bill with the Catholic Truth Society, the Anglo-Irish manor houses that had been burnt to the ground by patriotic blackguards during the months of the summer. Like tennis players they tossed back and forth insignificant talk – a proposal in the senate that a third of the constabulary should now be Catholics; the debate on whether the new mandatory qualification of spoken Gaelic for civil servants should be extended to municipal doctors. No one in the house had ever argued so forcefully before, except about the quality of meals or the cat's lack of gumption. The thing that surprised Nan most was the amount of work it took to keep this indifferent troop alive. She was up from her bed in the kitchen at seven to make huge urns of tea and piles of toast. She had to prepare their beds, collect laundry, haul enormous baskets of shopping. She cooked endlessly, her limited repertoire – stew, fries, tarts, Queen of Puddings. If only they had been more rewarding; if only they were handsome or amusing or rich.

In spite of the endless work the family was still poor. Mother eked out her profits to pay old bills. It was vital, she said, to protect father's name. The lodgers ate better than the family, which had to make do with bread fried in the fat of rashers enjoyed by the paying guests. Nan's stretch in height had come at an unfortunate time. She no longer fitted the little dresses she had worn during the summer, nor the previous winter's woollens. There was no money for new clothes. She had to wear women's clothes which were offered to mother on her behalf by the neighbours. She tried to alter the dresses with belts and shorter hems but when she looked in the mirror there was an indeterminate creature, neither child nor woman, scowling out of the glass. 'Why, I'm just like Doll Cotter,' she thought in despair.

But she was not. Doll Cotter was pregnant. It was the new topic among the neighbours. One of them had peeked into a pram that Doll was wheeling and admired its content. 'Lovely, isn't he?' Doll had cooed. 'You'll have babies of your own some day,' the woman said kindly, and Doll nodded happily. 'Yes. I'm having a baby next year.' 'Don't be silly, child,' the woman had laughed until she remembered that Doll was not a child. She was seventeen.

The neighbours did not mind the scandal. A birth was always interesting. It was the girl's attitude that provoked them to censure. She refused to be ashamed.

It was a well-known thing that young women, not knowing what was to follow, occasionally allowed a man to talk himself into their downfall, but they always went to England on the boat and did not show themselves until the baby was safely in the hands of the nuns.

Doll Cotter would not go away. She told everyone about her condition. One of the neighbours went so far as to suggest that her presence was a bad example to the other little girls in the neighbourhood, but Doll was stubborn. 'What would my mammy do without me?' she said. 'It's only a baby. How would a baby be a bad example?' When they had failed to acquaint her with her shame they attempted solicitude. 'Who is this man? He must be made to do right by you. Someone must speak with him.'

'I'll speak to him,' Doll promised mildly and she would not say any more. She told Nan, though, one day when they met in the village, Doll steering her pram and Nan weighted with shopping. 'I'm having a baby,' she said. 'I know,' Nan said. 'That's gifty.' She did not think so but she could tell that Doll was bursting with happiness. 'Do you think so?' Doll's face lit up with her smile. 'You're the only one who's pleased.'

'I think it's wonderful,' Nan said and she did think it wonderful that something had at last happened to make Doll happy. 'Tell us about it.' They went to the park and luxuriated in a mossy hollow, spreading out their women's overcoats, sharing a quarter pound of broken biscuits that was intended for the lodgers. 'We're getting married,' Doll said. 'In December. He's bought a shop with rooms above. His name will be painted on the front. When it's ready, we'll be married.'

'Where did you meet him?' Nan wondered. 'At the party?'

'Oh, no. I've known him all my life. We bought our clothes from him. But I did, in a way, meet him through the party.' She told Nan how she had gone to the house in search of him on the day of the party, dressed in Anastasia's pink angora jumper. She was hoping to buy a skirt, pink, silk or velvet, that would match. She was amazed when he opened the door to see him dressed in fine clothes and he was surprised by the fluffy womanliness of her jumper. For a long moment they watched each other, and then she remembered why she had come. She was disappointed to learn that he no longer dealt in old clothes but happy for him that his ship had come in. She went home and sewed a skirt from a pink satin slip.

They did not meet again for some time because he had run into a difficulty with the law but she saw him every day because she walked into the city and sat in the courtroom. With Anastasia at home, she was free to come and go as she pleased. One day, he managed to send her a note. He said that he had no right to speak to her now, but that one day, if things went in his favour, he would wish to speak to her seriously. She knew what he meant. She liked the word. Seriously. After that she did not see him at all for Anastasia went home and she lost her freedom. Much later, they met in the street, he in more subdued suiting and she once more in cast-offs. She tried to pass by but he blocked her path. 'I love you,' he said. She did not believe him and so it was necessary for him to show her that he did.

'What's it like?' Nan was compelled to whisper. No matter how one tried to ignore it, all things returned to the mystery for which the widow had paid out money, because of which Doll had found happiness.

'What's what like?'

Nan looked away. 'Being lovers.'

Doll was surprised by the question because she had not thought of it as something that could be defined, any more than laughter or crying. 'It's like . . . flowers,' she said. It was a pity that it was almost winter, that all Nan had for comparison as she went home with her bags of shopping was a grim line of shuddering chrysanthemums in the park, their webbed leaves grey and curled like the wings of bats. She could not understand about lovers. She had had romance – although that seemed a thing of the long distant past, belonging to her childhood. Lovers meant some closer thing, a sharing of all that was private. Once she had felt as close as she imagined it was possible to feel, skin and spirit, with Dandy Tallon. They had loved the scent of each other, the grains of dirt in one another's hands. She could not envisage this layering with a man. Romance was all right but she could not endure a pooling of utilities. She hated making their beds. They were a ransacked city, violated and abandoned. Women's pillows smelt of eau de Cologne. The men's beds were primitive territory. Sometimes they carried a jungle smell as if to warn off other animals.

Nan let herself into the house and began, all at once, the hazardous tasks of making tea and setting table and lighting fires. She was late and had not time to remove her overcoat but ran about from room to room, banging down stacks of plates, violently shaking the hissing pan, poking and cursing at humoursome fires. Once she caught sight of her face in a mirror, and was almost made to smile, so comically grim did she look, as flustered and furious as Nellie. How safe their lives had been when they laughed together over father's poor buggers. Mary was protected now and Nan could not escape, even if Dandy had not become a bookworm and there was somewhere to go, because Mary was too small to take her place.

It seemed to Nan that days ran into each other, merging like puddles, in a dark gutter. There was nothing to make them different. It was not only the work that dismayed her. It was the lack of prospect. Her parents had always been insubstantial figures, leaving space in their wake for the shaping of her own world. The lodgers were utterly solid. They were at the centre of her world and they blocked out its light. 'If only,' she thought, 'Nellie was here.' Nellie would make jokes about them and turn them into figures of entertainment like the men in her own past. 'If only I could have a sign that there would someday be something different.'

One day mother was standing at the drawing-room window hugging herself against the chill while Nan made up the fire, taking little sips at her cigarette, when suddenly she waved her cigarette like a conductor's baton and cried out, 'Look, Nan! Oh, look!' Nan came to the window, keeping out of sight because of her sooty appearance. 'It's a motor car.'

'It's stopping, Nan. It's coming here.'

They both watched while the shining black car growled to a halt and rattled into stillness like a big bewildered insect. Nan was thinking that perhaps it was one of father's buggers who had come up on his luck and had returned to repay the family. Perhaps he was a rich and handsome old man with a big house full of maids, who would take them to live with him, leaving the lodgers seated around the table forever, waiting for their next meal. The man who stepped out of the motor did not conform to her fantasy. He was a gingery, whiskery whale of a man. He wore a beige wool suit with a large nutmeg stripe, like a treacle tart. 'Expensive cloth, though . . .' mother mused. He had the walk of a wealthy man. He swung the gate back confidently and strode up the path.

'Answer the door, Nan,' mother said in a tone of nervous excitement, then, seeing the cut of the child, she restrained her. 'No, you have enough to do. I shall see what he wants.' She smiled at herself in the hall mirror as she went to the door.

'Yes?' She opened the door to the visitor.

'Finnucane.' He extended a bunch of little pink fingers like a litter of newborn mice and plunged them into her hand.

'How do you do?'

'Powerful, ma'am,' he said, and he looked it, 'now that I have made your acquaintance.' He wanted a room. Mother was elated. She had hoped to become the envy of the neighbours with a string of motor cars outside her front door but all she had achieved so far was a bracelet of rusting cycles lounging against the railings. He had money. Like most of the lodgers, he came from a farm but he did not choose to live on the land and had put his holding up for sale. His intention was to purchase a store in the city. He planned to buy a house with several maids' rooms and a garden and motor house. He had a thousand pounds to spend on the house alone.

Clearly he was a determined man. He had heard of mother from one of her previous tenants and had sought her out specially, wanting the comforts of a home while he set about establishing himself in the city. 'I am afraid it is not up to much,' mother apologized while she treacherously showed him the Indian Room, from which two gentlemen were later that evening to be peremptorily dismissed. 'We are not wealthy. You will be used to finer things.'

He heaved his fat leather suitcase on to a penitential little bed. 'The trappings of money may be had for the asking,' he beamed. 'But a virtuous woman is priced above rubies.'

It was natural for them to attach themselves to him; natural for the children to tail him at a close distance for he was likely at any moment to pull from his pocket pennies or toffees. 'I thought I'd fancy chocolate cake,' he'd say, twirling a box from the Teatime Express by its red waxed string, and he always made sure that half of it was left over for mother and the children. He brought little bunches of flowers for mother, concealing them behind his back until he leaned forward, almost touching her with his whiskers, and sprang them out on a plump arm. Mother did not seem to mind this closeness. The children liked being near him for he did not have the stiffness of other men. Even the lodgers came to depend on him. His presence lightened their company. He bought a new piano and asked mother if she would give it house room. One evening Nan came to clear the tea things and was astonished to find Mr Finnucane leading a sing-song, his paws belting the keys while the rest of the men crouched around him singing in taut tones.

He worshipped mother. It was clear that he had come to the house purely to make her acquaintance and was now intent on cementing their friendship. Nan was happy with this arrangement because he made mother merry. He was kind and tolerant with the girls. Once when Nan was loading a tray to take it to the kitchen he lifted it from her hands and carried it for her. 'You're a wonderful little woman,' he said. 'You're much too good for all this. One day you'll have what you deserve. I'll make it up to you. You wait and see.'

And he was rich. If he married mother they would have a house full of maids and she would not be needed around the house. She could go back to school and join Dandy at the university. She began to conspire toward this end. When she saw mother and Mr Finnucane whispering together, she would lead Mary from the room. With the house full of lodgers there was nowhere else for them to go so they waited, shivering in the shed with the hen and the hedgehog until Nan estimated that they had had enough time to talk and then they went back inside. Nan was impressed by Mr Finnucane's cunning. He knew how to please mother. Instead of attempting to court her directly, he tiptoed around the path of her marriage, admiring her courage in carrying on alone and the extraordinary handsomeness of the ghost which frowned out of the silver frame. Mother was elated. Seated at the kitchen table with her cigarettes and Mr Funnicane's gift of port or whiskey, she would talk and talk, refashioning her marriage to a more comfortable fit for her memory. She spoke of outings and presents, hinted at a union that went beyond the mind, knitting as intricately as Anastasia, a dazzling pattern of years and days. 'We were head over heels in love,' she would say, flushed with happiness and he, modest and crafty, would nod at the photograph which was between them. 'I can understand that.'

Doll Cotter got married at the beginning of December – not a proper wedding, a skulking affair for the fellow was not a Protestant like herself, nor even a Catholic, but Jewish. She was still thin. If she had not boasted of her condition no one need ever have guessed and her wedding, in spite of its other complications, might have drawn good wishes from everyone. As it was they had to turn their heads the other way and look to mother for news of a proper wedding.

The house was full of plans for Christmas. The lodgers were returning to their homes in the country, apart from Mr Finnucane, whom mother had invited to stay, and who had promised in return a turkey, a tree, boxes of presents. In spite of the tedious work that would continue until the lodgers' departure, the house had a relaxed feel. Christmas and the presence of Mr Finnucane induced a festive mood in the men. They occasionally joked with Nan or smirked at her. They helped the children sort out Christmas decorations and suspend them around the walls. Mary made paper angels and hung them in the hall. 'Poor father!' She sighed as she viewed her handiwork with satisfaction, but she was sympathizing with his personality rather than mourning his loss. He had always worked himself into a frenzy coming up to Christmas, had insisted on the puddings being boiled in a cloth to his mother's recipe, so that they came out slimy and leaden; had brought home tramps and a turkey with its feathers on. For the first time in her memory, the weeks leading up to Christmas were not like the tremors of an impending earthquake, but a period of giddiness and pleasant greed.

Mr Finnucane invited mother to a pantomime. The children waited tensely for her to make up her mind. They knew that he would make his proposal of marriage then because they had not been included in his invitation. 'Yes,' she decided. It was the first time she had agreed to go out since father's death. The children plotted toward the success of the outing. 'You must buy a new dress,' they wheedled. 'You must wear something that is in fashion.' She looked at them. Nan in particular she studied. 'Yes,' she said, surprising them. 'Perhaps, this once. I think it will be money well spent. We will buy something in the city.'

It was an exciting day. Mr Finnucane insisted on transporting them to the city in his Arroll-Johnston. The rest of the men were left to contend with a table set in advance with plates of hazlett and cold ham. The children were conscientious about the mission. They did not permit themselves to dawdle at the gloriously provocative shop windows. They pulled one another past the rowdy queue for Santa at Pims. If mother saw how badly they wanted these things she might be tempted to squander the money on them instead of spending it on herself. In fact she scarcely noticed their restraint. She was busy controlling her own desire. 'How beautiful! Oh, how lovely,' she exclaimed, as she pressed her face against the windows draped with brilliant gowns in scarlet and white and tinsel silver. 'Of course,' she reprimanded herself. 'I shall choose black . . . One must have respect.' Plain black satin dresses were in fashion. There was no shortage of them. Mother fingered them dutifully but her hands shrank back in disappointment. They wandered in and out of half a dozen dress shops until the children grew bored and poor

Mr Finnucane sweated and sighed. At last, the clever assistant in Slynes offered mother a tunic and skirt in black art silk. The back, which dipped in a graceful curve, was covered in Chinese embroideries in beautiful gaudy colours. 'Oh!' mother exclaimed, feeling it. It was so lovely that her voice trembled with shock.

'Try it on,' the children urged.

She slid a minute glance to Mr Finnucane. 'Oh, no,' she laughed nervously. 'I am not accustomed to putting on clothes in a shop. That is for the younger generation. Nan must be our model.'

'Oh, mother,' Nan scowled. Since she had grown, she hated having attention drawn to her appearance.

'We cannot buy a pig in a poke,' mother smiled.

Nan took the outfit into a little narrow tent with a slice of mirror nailed to the wall. She dropped her own clothes on the floor and stood in her petticoat watching her reflection. 'Ugly, ugly,' she said, and tears slid down her face. Her face had assumed a look of disapproval that reminded her more and more of Nellie. Her hair was long and limp with neglect. Her hands had a weathered appearance. She pulled the tunic over her head to hide the view and stepped into the skirt. She stood with her eyes clenched until she heard a little swish of curtain and mother's voice. 'Come out, Nan, and let us see you,' and then – 'why, how pretty. Nan, I'm proud of you.' She opened her eyes in surprise. Mother was right. The outfit looked lovely. Under the bulk of the neighbours' clothing she had not noticed that her body, thinned down and lengthened, had become graceful. The outfit showed off her figure. She had grown to the same height as mother and it fitted perfectly. She put her hands in the pockets and tried to look indifferent, but instead she looked aloof, sophisticated.

Mother and Mr Finnucane were smiling at her in a proud sort of way, as if they had created her. 'I think,' said mother, 'that it will do.' Her hands trembled at the extravagance as she counted out the three ten shillings notes and two half-crowns but Mr Finnucane made her put her money away and flourished a five pound note. He gave the children threepence each and told them to amuse themselves while he bought mother a cocktail at the Central. Naturally, they headed for Woolworth's. Relieved of the tedium and the need for financial restraint, they fingered everything on the stands, tried on earrings and scent and stroked the ribbons on chocolate boxes. When they had completed this preliminary spree Mary went to look at toys and Nan was compelled to the toiletries counter. It wasn't just because of the boxes of pink soap painted with sprays of lilac or the silver-wrapped cubes of powdered bath salts. It was the girl who was selling them. Nan had noticed the pretty red-haired young woman with green eye-shadow and brilliant lipstick the moment she came into the shop but she needed a closer look to make sure that it was Dandy Tallon. At first she refused to believe it. She had kept a picture in her mind of Dandy astounding the nuns with the knowledge in her head, grooming herself for a glorious future.

She stayed back until the counter was free of its swarm of shoppers. It was Dandy all right. She could tell by the haphazard way she parcelled up the useless little gifts. 'Dandy,' she said. Dandy looked up without surprise. 'What can I do for you?'

'What are you doing here? Why aren't you at school?'

Dandy rearranged the display that had been disturbed by customers. 'Don't be a daft egg. I've left school. Everyone leaves school at fourteen. You did. Everyone does.'

'You're not everyone!' Nan cried.

'It's all right. Twelve bob a week.'

'No, it's not. You were going to university.'

'Don't be foolish. That was just a game. Only the piddling rich go to university. Everyone else gets a job.' Nan scraped irritably at the glass shield of the display case. 'Look, you have to buy something or go away,' Dandy said anxiously. 'I could lose my job.'

'I wish you would. You should be at school.'

'Don't be silly.' Dandy was growing impatient. 'I can't afford to lose my job.' 'Why?' Nan's petulant demand made her sound as if she had never known need.

'It's a secret. If I tell you will you go?' Nan nodded. 'It's Primmy. She wants to be a nun. We've known for ages but we couldn't say anything because of my da. If he found out he'd kill us all. He'll have to know sooner or later but not until Primmy's got her dowry and it's too late. She needs a hundred pounds. Ma's putting a bit by and I send over my wages. I know it sounds strange but it's all Primmy wants. She has to do it.'

Nan squandered her threepence on a tin of talcum powder. She would give it to mother for Christmas. Mother did not use talcum powder, but perhaps, in her new life, she would. Of all of them, mother was the only one who was to have a new life. The rest of them were like an unsatisfactory crop, not to be harvested but to be ploughed back into the earth to sustain the unique, the prizeworthy. She could see that this was right. Mother was not like anyone else. She was the pick of the crop. She cheered up when she collected Mary to bring her back to the hotel and remembered that mother's new life must also include them. 'Aren't you dying to see mother all dressed up?' she said to Mary as they squeezed through the crowds in fairy-lit streets.

'Dying,' Mary agreed happily.

But when the day came for the pantomime mother would not relieve them. 'I've got a headache,' she said stubbornly. 'I am not ready to go out. I am not well enough. It was a mistake.' 'You must take a little nap,' Nan urged. 'I'll bring you up some tea and an aspirin.' 'No,' mother said. 'I am afraid an aspirin will not improve matters. I believe I am getting the 'flu.' She would not go to bed. She sat in the kitchen with a languid hand touching her forehead. 'What about the pantomime? What about Mr Finnucane?' the children cried in consternation. 'Mr Finnucane has already been informed and is civil enough to accept that one cannot be healthy to command. It is agreed, Nan, that you will go in my place.'

'Oh, mother, no, he must cancel the tickets and take you when you are better.' She did not want to be the first to wear the lovely outfit. She wanted the limelight for her mother.

'Don't argue, dear. I am not well. It has been agreed.'

In spite of her indisposition, mother helped Nan to get ready. She washed her hair and fluffed it out with a comb. She loaned Nan her jade earrings and applied a trace of lipstick to her cheeks to bring up her colour. 'You look very nice,' mother said at last, surveying her efforts; and she did. She could not stop her eyes from shining in such a beautiful outfit. She tried hard to be sorry that she was going instead of mother but she had no control over a little dancing heartbeat that made her smile in such a silly way and removed her from the days of drudgery. She wished that someone younger and more handsome than Mr Finnucane was taking her out but she made up her mind to be as nice as possible to him so that he would not mind being lumbered with two half-grown daughters.

Mr Finnucane had brought a box of chocolates. It must have weighed two pounds. The sweets were arranged in a single layer in a big flat box shaped like a heart. A violet bow ornamented its curves. On the bottom of the box was an artist's representation of each chocolate locked within. Mary gazed longingly at this pattern as the plump pink gentleman presented the gift to Nan. Nan was struck with generosity. 'I'm giving these to Mary and mother,' she said; 'to make up for having to stay at home.' Mother was not pleased. 'Where are your manners, Nan?' she demanded. 'When a gentleman brings you confectionery, it is for his enjoyment as well as your own.'

'At least let me open them,' Nan said. 'Let me leave some for Mary.' 'Try to behave in a grown-up manner,' mother pleaded. 'You cannot go into the theatre with a half-eaten box of chocolates.' Nan said goodbye to them. She whispered to Mary that she would bring home the best of the sweets. It made her feel grown-up and quite pleased with herself.

They did not open the box after all. Mr Finnucane had planned a little supper at the Shelbourne and did not wish their appetites to be damaged. Nan was not sure about this plan. She had already had her tea and she had not asked her mother's permission but her chivalrous escort said it was the done thing, her mother would not forgive him if he did not treat her properly.

She did not much enjoy her supper. She felt uncomfortable in the restaurant, surrounded by much older and more assured company, compelled to eat fish and chicken and a shivering sweet and to drink a very bitter wine. She was not hungry. She felt sorry for the waiters who had to stay up so late to remove her unfinished courses. She knew how hard they had to work. She felt, for the first time, ill at ease with Mr Finnucane, who was treating her as an equal, telling her, for some strange reason, about his life.

Afterwards they drove home by the canal. He stopped the car at the edge of the water and, leaning around toward her as if he had something important to say, he dropped the damp, whiskery pinkness of his mouth on to her mouth. He began to kiss her in a ponderous, munching way, like a cow eating grass. She was too astonished to do anything. She did not want to be rude. She thought perhaps he felt obliged by courtesy to do this. He grunted in a bewildered way and his hand fell wearily on her leg. It was heavy. She tried, discreetly, to shake it away, but it held on and gripped painfully, and then in a startled burst of speed, like a rat or some other little animal, it scurried up her leg, past her garter. Nan was mortified. She did not know what to do. She kicked at his legs to free herself. He looked hurt. 'Here, now, it's all right, you know,' he said in a concerned way. She shook her head, unable to find the proper thing to say. 'Take me home, please.' 'It's all right, you know,' he said. He put his hand into the neck of her tunic and reached down. His fingers were beneath her underwear. He was trying to rub away her chest. He was grunting in a queer way. 'Let me take your hand, my dear, just a touch, just a touch,' he begged softly, as if ordering the seasoning for his soup, and he pressed her hand into his lap. Her hand shot away. She sat shivering, her stomach bunched hard with shock, until, with catlike instinct, she turned and spat full in his face. 'Take me home,' she said. 'I'm going to tell my mother.' He sat glumly staring ahead for some moments and then he climbed out and started up the car. For a while he was silent, then he said, 'I should have thought, you see, that you would have understood . . .'

He was attempting to apologize. Old fool. Why did grown-ups all have to act like lunatics? 'This is not satisfactory,' he continued sulkily. She could not believe it. He was complaining.

When they got to the house he would not come in. 'I shall lodge in a hotel tonight,' he said. 'You may tell your mother that I shall not be returning. When I have an address I will make it known so that my bags may be sent on.'

'Coward,' Nan thought scornfully. 'He's afraid to face the music.' She did not care. All she wanted was to escape to the safety and sympathy of her family, but she could not simply jump out and slam the door. She had to get the chocolates. They were expected. They had been taken from her hands and placed on the back seat when Mr Finnucane stopped at the canal. She attempted to reach back in an indifferent fashion but Mr Finnucane trapped her wrist. 'If you are staying, stay and if you are going, go,' he said peevishly. She went. She could not get at the box.

They were waiting up for her. Mother's 'flu seemed much improved. Her eyes were very bright. 'How was your evening? Where is Mr Finnucane?' Nan was keenly aware of Mary's disappointed look at her empty hands. 'Mr Finnucane is gone. Gone for good. Good riddance to bad rubbish.' Mother rose from her seat. She looked dreadfully dismayed. 'Gone? What are you saying?'

'Oh, mother.' Nan began to cry. 'He's awful. He's an awful old man. He tried to kiss me. He tried to . . .' Mother shot a warning glance in Mary's direction. 'Every man will attempt that,' she said. 'It is up to the woman.'

'He's gone. He won't be coming back. He's gone to a hotel.'

'What are we supposed to do?' mother demanded. She was angry. 'You have lost me a very good rent. Mr Finnucane was going to pay for our Christmas luxuries. We may beg for bread now, let alone luxuries.'

'You don't understand.' Nan was sobbing. She needed comfort but found only criticism. 'He was touching me. He was trying to make me touch him. The dirty old madman didn't even care that I was almost his daughter.'

'His daughter?' mother looked amazed.

'We knew, mother.' Nan calmed down and wiped at her eyes. 'We knew he was going to ask you to marry him. We thought it was all right,' she added lamely.

'Me?' Mother looked outraged. 'Me marry Mr Finnucane? You must be out of your mind. Do you think I would marry another man with your father not six months in his grave? Do you imagine I would *consider* Mr Finnucane, having been married to a man like your father?'

'There were hints,' Nan mumbled.

'There were more than hints,' mother said impatiently. 'What am I to do with you? Will you always be so hopeless? I promised your father I would see you safely settled. You could have been very well married. We could all have been looked after for life.'

CHAPTER 29

❧

They reached the forest at four. The last red wintry light had died from the sky. Only a yellow smear across the grey, like ointment, and one bright bulbous cloud remained. It was deadly cold. They had to stamp their feet to feel them.

'It's starting to snow,' Mary said.

A scrap of white like a single star twirled down out of the sky and clung to the tweedy brown floor of the forest, then vanished.

'We'll have to hurry,' Doll said. She pushed her pram through dark lanes of firs which swayed and creaked with the piety of praying nuns. Nan felt unable to go on. She was tired out by the lodgers. She could not imagine what she was doing so far from home, so late, on such a day and she remembered then that home was inhabited by the sense of her failure, in the poorness and the dullness that she had helped to preserve.

Mary sniffed as she walked. She held the hen against her cheek for warmth. 'There will be no Christmas dinner now,' mother had to tell them; 'unless you wring the bird's neck and roast it.'

Since then Mary had carried Elizabeth with her everywhere.

Only Doll had a proper sense of purpose. She knew where she was going. In earlier days Doll had looked up to Nan, had turned to her for protection. It seemed now that their roles were turned around. Doll felt secure from outside and in, completely unafraid. She would not have cared any longer about the assaults of Minnie Willard although Willard, in any case, had ceased to taunt her. In the space of a summer she had become a quiet and pained-looking young woman. She had her hair cut short and called herself Minerva. These days it was Nan who looked lost and Doll, who came to visit her mother every day to help with the babies, had to ask why. Nan told her how Mary and mother had depended on her and she had failed them. She had done them out of lives of luxury, had ruined their Christmas. 'There will be nothing now,' she confessed. 'No presents – not even a Christmas tree.'

Doll said: 'Once, when we were small – when there was no money – my mother took us up to the mountains for a snow picnic. That was gifty.'

Doll was in command of this outing. 'Pick a tree,' she told the children. 'Pick out whatever tree you like best.'

They divided to move solemnly between ragged ranks of fir. Caught in the hush of the coming snowfall, they moved on tiptoe. Utter silence, even the faint grizzle of the pram wheels smothered by hush until Mary, finding herself alone beneath the giant trees, cried out: 'Here it is! Here's a whopper!' It was in fact quite a scrawny tree that she clutched but she had been afraid and wanted the others to return.

The snow came. It seemed to the children that it chose to move in the direction of Mary's tree. It clung in luminous lumps to the green tufts, making it bright against the sullen sky.

'It's like the cotton wool we used to put on our Christmas tree,' Mary said.

'It is our Christmas tree,' Nan said.

From the bottom of the pram Doll removed the mysterious bag. One by one she unwrapped the tiny tissue packages. There were glass balls, cardboard angels, ornate candles on tin pegs, streamers of glowing tinsel. They began, very seriously, to attach the decorations to the tree. No one could reach the top to secure the fairy so Nan tied her to a string and held her until a gust of wind came.

She allowed the wind to launch the fairy and she tied the string to the highest branch she could reach. The fairy hovered, lopsided, in a cleft and was tugged free by an icy breeze. She darted in the air a little distance above the tree.

'Nan! Look! The fairy's flying,' Mary breathed. 'Oh, Nan!'

Doll had matches to light the candles. Each time she lit one, it was snuffed by the wind. Nan was opening the second bag, taking out cold meat and pudding, biscuits, lollipops. 'Here,' Doll said. 'Give us one of those.' She unwrapped the lollipop and held it in her mouth until it grew sticky. She rubbed the wick of a candle against the sweet surface so that it was coated in sugary syrup. She lit another match and sheltered it with her hand while she held it to the sticky candle. It took light. Each of the candles was lit from the sugared one and they pegged them on to the branches of the tree.

'You have to make a wish,' Doll said, standing back to admire her work.

Nan pushed her hands into the pockets of her big coat and wearily cast about in her mind for some discarded desire that might be blowing about.

She was confused. The beautiful Christmas tree caught at her heart and filled her eyes with tears and her heart with faith. It was different when she was small and Christmas had filled her with greed and she wished for the death of Sister Immaculata and Minnie Willard, for wheelbarrows filled with chocolates and sacks of ginger biscuits. It was only a faith in Christmas trees. She had no desires. It wasn't just to do with there being no money. It was because she was a woman now. Women only wished for the mundane. 'I wish you children would be quiet . . . I wish father would not bring home such unappetizing types,' she heard her mother say in her head; and she was suddenly seized with desire and surprised by the strength of its pull. She wanted to be home again with her mother. It was now that quiet hour after the men's tea. She should be in the kitchen with mother, making fresh tea while mother smoked her cigarettes. She always looked forward to this time when she had mother to herself and they talked together like grown-ups. Sometimes she forgot what a privilege it was.

Mary's wish was simple and direct and was fulfilled on the spot.

'Here,' Doll said. 'Your Christmas present.' She gave them each a shilling.

'Oh, no,' Nan protested. 'We couldn't.' She knew Doll had not much money. Her husband still supported his mother and sisters and his brother who was going to be a surgeon.

'Go on,' Doll insisted. 'I know kids never have anything to spend.'

In the light from the tree the coins were a lovely silvery pink.

'We can go to the pictures now,' Mary said. 'Crowds are still queueing for *The Four Horsemen of the Apocalypse*. We could go tomorrow.'

'Is that what you'd like to do?' Nan said.

She looked away. For a long time she gazed at the tree, the long arms of the candle flames, choked by wind, reaching out like the souls in purgatory who cried out to you to pray for their release.

It was not these voices that Mary heard. It was Nan's chorus of posies from the summer concert. She had a sudden thought, a vision. Dressed in white and ornamented with the greaseproof paper wings worn by the flies in the concert, they would turn into angels.

With swift organization and stern discipline, they could be made to perform a programme of Christmas carols, here, around a real Christmas tree, deep in the forest and already so beautifully festooned. If the event was held on Christmas Eve (thirty angels with two parents each – threepence per parent, she calculated rapidly) there would be time afterwards to buy a chicken and some crackers. Perhaps Nellie could be persuaded to come . . .

Mary sighed. She had no doubt about her ability to organize such an outing and claim almost a pound in profit. It was the responsibility that wearied her. Everything was up to her. Poor mother did not understand. Nan had become a fallen woman who, time and again, would have to be lifted from fate. If there was someone. She remembered then that there had been someone who knew about the facts of life, who was responsible for women everywhere. 'Our father,' she said, 'who art in heaven . . .'

They stood beneath the tall, twinkling triangle of light. The sky behind was black, not even a star to light it. All the world was invisible except the most beautiful part of it. They watched until the heat of the candles began to melt the snow and it slid from the branches in soft thumps and splashes and then they crouched to eat the food they had brought for their picnic.

'Perhaps' – Mary chose a biscuit with a piece of sugared jelly set in its centre – 'the ladies are no longer fainting. Perhaps we should buy something nice for mother. Poor mother has been so disappointed.'

A flap of wind made the tinsel shiver like bells and blew out the candles. They were left in the blackest dark. Doll wrapped up the remains of the picnic and put them in the pram. She took the shuddering hen from Mary's arms and tucked it in at the bottom of the pram, away from the baby's feet, as her husband had shown her. They stood silently, trying to see. Their tree was hidden. Only the silver star of the fairy's wand could be seen, dancing above the Christmas tree. Nan had a sudden memory of another fairy, a magical creature shining out of the darkness; but that was long ago. 'Yes,' she said. Her voice sounded pleased. 'That's what we'll do. We'll go out tomorrow and buy something nice for mother.' She felt a layer of responsibility lifting from her shoulders. Mary was growing up. From now on they would live in the real world.

They felt for one another's hands and began to find their trail out of the forest.

HOT WATER MAN

Deborah Moggach

As East meets West, cultures clash in a most unusual and surprising way . . . Karachi 1975: from north London come Christine and Donald Manley. Christine, an emergent feminist, is resolving not to play the memsahib, Donald works for a chemical company selling the Pill (which is ironic because they can't conceive), disapproves of his wife's behaviour and recalls fondly his grandfather's tales of the Raj. From Wichita comes Duke Hanson who thinks string-pulling and adultery un-American, that is, until he meets Shamime . . .

GETTING IT RIGHT

Elizabeth Jane Howard

A hairdresser in the West End, Gavin is sensitive, shy, into the arts, prone to spots and, at thirty-one, a virgin. He's a classic late developer – and maybe it's getting too late to develop at all?

Then one night Gavin finds himself at a posh penthouse party and, caught between Joan and Minerva, suddenly he's developing very rapidly indeed . . . Comedy sparkles, touches and seduces us through the next whirlwind fortnight as Gavin begins, at last, to get it right.

'Her very best novel to date' – *Options*

GINGER, YOU'RE BARMY

David Lodge

When it isn't prison, it's hell. Or that's the heartfelt belief of conscripts Jonathan Browne and Mike 'Ginger' Brady. For this is the British Army in the days of National Service, a grimy deposit of post-war cynicism. It consists of one endless, shambling round of kit layout, square-bashing, shepherd's pie 'made from real shepherds', P.T. and drill relieved by the occasional lecture on firearms or V.D. The reckless, impulsive Mike and the more pragmatic Jonathan adopt radically different attitudes to this two-year confiscation of their freedom . . . and the consequences are dramatic.

VICTIM OF LOVE

Dyan Sheldon

Paul Sutcliffe has one wife, two children and two lovers. He is a sensitive, kind and intelligent man who has always been committed to equal rights for women. Women do not threaten him; he is one of their biggest fans. Also, he believes in love.

Linda Sutcliffe is in her thirties (though on most days she feels closer to sixty). She has a career and a family, mostly because Paul thinks she should have them. Everything Linda does, she does for love.

Why is it that, suddenly, everything is conspiring to let Paul down and Linda is filled with dreams of being the person she has never had the chance to be . . . ?